J.J. MEYER

Spades

Trouble In...

First published by ImPress Self Publishing Services 2020

The characters in this work are purely fictional; however, certain events and points of interest did take place. This is a work of fiction. All of the other places, incidents, organizations, and dialogue in this novel either are the products of the author's imagination or are used fictitiously.

First edition

ISBN: 978-1-945493-35-5

Cover art by Daniel Traynor
Editing by Linda Thomas

This book was professionally typeset on Reedsy.
Find out more at reedsy.com

Other Books You Might Enjoy

The Cooper Family Series
Volume 1 – 7
(Shoshone Pass, Separate Trails, South Creek, Double Edged,
Legacy Trail, Courage Trail and Sherando)

All the above-mentioned titles are available (autographed for
you) by emailing me at jacobsgrampy@msn.com <u>or</u> your
favorite independent bookstore or online bookstore. You can
also follow me on Facebook – Jim Meyer Western Author

Author
Page-https://www.amazon.com/Jim-Meyer/e/B0182S590W

Characters

Todd Morgan - Civil War Survivor, owner of Stony Creek Ranch, Wyoming Territory.

Jonathan "Crusty" Harrison – banker turned ranch hand, Elizabeth "Liz" Connolly's lover and co-owner of Sweetwater Ranch, Wyoming Territory.

Elizabeth "Liz" Connolly – Co-owner of Sweetwater Ranch, Wyoming Territory, Crusty's lover.

Priscilla Parker – owner of Parker's Boarding House, Lander, Wyoming Territory.

Megan Parker, daughter of Priscilla Parker.

McGruder – livery owner, North Fork, Wyoming Territory.

August McDavitt – Union Officer, West Point Graduate; lawyer, brother of Farleigh McDavitt, partner in McDavitt & McIntosh, Assayers & Gold Buyers, Lander & South Pass City, Wyoming Territory.

Flaherty McDavitt – brother of August, partner in McDavitt

& McIntosh, Assayers & Gold Buyers, Lander & South Pass City, Wyoming Territory.

Jonas McIntosh – partner in McDavitt & McIntosh.

Shoshone Joe – half-breed and a friend of Todd, who raises dogs and horses.

Hanson – Sutler of the trading post at Ft. Washakie, On the Wind River, Wyoming Territory.

Walking Many Places – friend of Todd, brother of Feather In Air and Bright Star, son of Sioux Chief Standing Tall.

Josh Hackenfield – ranch hand at Timber Creek Ranch and Sweetwater.

Hiram Bender – wagon maker, horse trainer, owner of Bender's Farm, Lander, Wyoming Territory.

Colonel John Wilder – Commander, 1st Cavalry, Wyoming Territory.

Colonel Johnson – Commander, Ft. Washakie, Wyoming Territory.

Pat Hendrickson – U.S. Marshal, Sweetwater, Wyoming Territory.

Tom Murphy – U.S. Marshal, Lander, Wyoming Territory.

Gus & Turk Langstrom – brothers, friends of Todd, miners, owners of homestead sections next to Todd.

Pete Boyd – friend of Todd and the Langstrom's, miner, owner of a homestead section next to Todd.

-1-

"Y ou awake amigo?"

"Why, am I supposed to be?" Todd replied to his friend Crusty.

"You're the one who wanted to ride into the sunset like the mighty hunter. We did what you wanted and only found this dry gulch with little water, a scattered limb here and there, and sagebrush."

"So you're saying that we should have stopped sooner, found water and grass for the horses, enough firewood to cook our food and keep us somewhat warm during the night?"

"Yeah, that about sums it up nicely."

"Back to your original question, I could use another couple of hours of sleep before we start out again."

"We should be leaving right now, not later," he said, but Todd had already fallen back to sleep. Crusty mumbled under his breath, "While you are sleeping, I'll get the horses rubbed down and saddled. Afterwards I'll have some coffee and a couple of biscuits. I have got to get you on a more regular schedule; otherwise we won't make it to the Yellowstone." He led the horses over to the trickle of water that had pooled ever so briefly before it disappeared into the rocky soil.

An hour later, Todd, who could have used much more sleep

and Crusty, who was wide awake, were making good time on the trail toward North Fork. Todd just happened to glance up toward the mountains, yawned and said, "We best get ourselves to our destination before those thunderclouds turn into one nasty storm."

"Well, amigo, what are we waiting," Crusty replied.

Upon their arrival the wind had started to pick up as the first drops of rain began to fall. "Let's see if we can put up our mounts at the livery and sleep in the hayloft until this storm passes," Todd suggested.

Off in the distance they could hear the crackle of thunder as he spoke to a young man who was standing in the livery doorway. "We need to put up our horses and find ourselves a place to sleep, like maybe up in your hayloft?"

"I'd let you, but the owner, Mister McGruder, is a stubborn cuss and he'd have fits if he found you up there come morning. The Hotel Fancy is just down the street a block or so and they have rooms at reasonable prices. I'll unsaddle your horses, packhorses, rub 'em down, and feed them. That'll be two bits for each horse." Todd thought it was a mite high, but given the circumstances he didn't have much choice in the matter. He and Crusty grabbed there rifles, saddlebags, supply satchels, bedrolls, and headed for the hotel.

Beyond the batwing doors, there was a sign on the wall just inside the entrance <—**Hotel – Saloon**—>. "I'll get us a room, Crusty, while you get us a table and a couple of beers." "I'll get us a room, Crusty, while you get us a table and a couple of beers."

Todd signed the guest register, asked for a two-bed room and paid the hotel clerk for two nights, just in case they had to stay an extra day because of the lousy weather. After he found their room, he deposited their things on top of one of the beds. Locking the door, he tucked the key in his watch pocket before heading back down to the saloon. After having eaten hard biscuits or corndodgers and beef jerky on the trail for the last week they both ordered a T-bone steak, baked potato, string beans and sweet potato pie.

While they ate, Crusty said, "This'd be a good place to get those additional supplies we talked about on our way up here. We certainly have no idea if there are any towns or trading posts between here and the Yellowstone. We might as well make a list, and put down what we both want on it."

Todd replied, "We'll need those large traps like the ones they use for beaver and some stringing wire for snares. I plan to pan for gold if the opportunity presents itself, so I better get a couple of pans. I'll use one for panning and the other to eat my food out of. I'm thinking that a couple extra pairs of blue jeans, wool shirts, and heavy socks would do me well once the weather turns cold."

"Twelve dollars ought to cover everything and we'll have about $650 left. That should last us a couple of years at least, unless of course we strike it rich," Crusty said with a little laugh.

"If it comes down to having or not having any food in order to survive, the money will pay for what we need. I'm hoping we are successful at whatever we do. Only time will tell."

They decide to divide up what they needed. Todd made out the list of non-perishables: seven steel traps, twenty feet of stringing wire, four woolen blankets, four pairs of leather work gloves, four woolen shirts, four pairs of blue jeans, two boxes each of rifle and handgun shells, and an extra pair of work boots. Crusty's list included ten pounds each of flour, coffee, dried kidney beans, sugar, dried apples and yeast.

When they were through with dinner, they had a couple of beers and decided it was time to turn in and get some much-deserved rest. They passed by a poker table where a few bystanders were watching the proceedings. Todd whispered to Crusty, "I wish I could get in a high-stakes game like this and come out the winner."

"Wishful thinking!" Crusty replied.

The card game continued into the wee hours of the morning, but there was no clear-cut winner. The dealer, who was also the owner of the saloon, said to the card players, "Two more hands, then we'll call it quits until later this evening. We'll start back up around 8 pm. is everyone in agreement on that?" Two of the card players grumbled, but it was agreed that they would continue this game later. All the players gathered what chips they had in front of them and retired to their respective rooms; the dealer took the 'pot' and put it in an unused pitcher before taking it to his office and put it in his safe.

-2-

As the storm raged, the rain turned to hail and beat against the tin roof in perfect rhythm lulling both Todd and Crusty to sleep. They soon were dreaming about events that had occurred in their past.

Todd got himself situated in the crotch of a first growth Oak tree of massive proportions while his fellow soldiers were doing the same thing in the other trees that lined both sides of the roadway. The sergeant major was walking from tree to tree checking on his men, when Todd spoke up saying, "I wish the commander would make up his mind, Sarge. First, he has us dig a trench 'bout 50 feet from the road. I thought it would put us on equal footing so to speak with them Yankee soldiers as they walked in front of us. Now you're telling us that he has decided that his plan won't work well enough so he wants us to conceal ourselves in these old growth trees and blend in so that when the Yankees are abreast of us we can open fire. The next thing you know, he'll have us up in the trees and tell us to jump down on top of the Yankee Calvary when they ride underneath us."

The sergeant replied, "Private, you gotta mouth on you, I will say that. The commander knows what he's doing, and I hope for God's sake, you do yours when the time comes. Every time we've tried to outsmart them damn blue shirts, they've been one-step ahead of us. I want a victory for a change, rather than having our asses handed to us. Get some sleep, you'll need your wits about you come morning."

"You don't have to get upset, sergeant."

"I'll do more than get upset, especially if you don't do as I expect when the time comes, or my boot will be up your ass!"

The following morning found the 7[1] Tennessee Regiment[1] up against heavy resistance. The 1st battalion, of which Todd was a member, managed to repel their attackers. He was wounded in the left shoulder and retreated to a rear echelon where he was treated in a field hospital. Later he was reassigned to the Division of the West under General P. G. T. Beauregard[2], where he was a runner for the general. During one campaign, he was caught in crossfire. When the skirmish ended, he and several other solders were surrounded and taken prisoner. They marched north for several days to an abandoned warehouse that was being used to house the prisoners and stayed there for several months under terrible living conditions. The building's windows were all blown out, the roof was half gone, and when it rained, the other half sagged further and further down. The biggest fear was that it could come crashing down at any moment crushing them.

As the war dragged on, they were transferred to another prison camp in Illinois. He and the others were all told by the Sergeant of the Guard, "Sign the loyalty oath boys, and if you

---

[1] 7th Tennessee Regiment – https://civilwarintheeast.com/confederate-regiments/tennessee/7th-tennessee-infantry-regiment/

[2] General P.G.T. Beauregard – https://www.historynet.com/pgt-beauregard

promise not to take up arms against the Union, we will release you and you can go home to yo' mommas." In the hopes that he would be released, he signed the papers when in fact, there was no formal agreement to release anybody.

The weeks dragged on, and Todd, like the others who had signed the oath, became more and more disillusioned as the prospect of ever being released was like a mirage in the desert. In February 1863, he was part of a prisoner exchange for an equal number of Union soldiers. After the exchange was completed, he and two other prisoners made their way to the Mississippi River and once there, they turned south. Their goal was to reach St. Louis. They met several other men along the way. Some were deserters, while others were too badly wounded to continue the fight against a superior Yankee force. He bid his compatriots goodbye as they took their own road back to their farms and homes.

He barely made enough money after working at several odd jobs to clothe and feed him. Upon his arrival in St. Louis he had to find steady work regardless of what he had to do. It was a matter of survival. He found day work unloading cargo ships. One day when he was walking to work, he found an old pair of boots and a torn coat in some trash left by the side of the road. On another day when he was down by the river, he found a floppy hat with three bullet holes in the crown; wearing it was better than no hat at all. He took to sleeping under the buildings that were close enough to where he could find steady work.

On another occasion, he found an unused shanty along the river and decided to call it home. He figured it was about two miles from the wharf. There was enough scrap lumber to build a bed off the floor and it sure beat sleeping on the ground under buildings. He stashed his foodstuffs up in the rafters so the river rats wouldn't eat it. Once a week, he'd strip his clothes, wash them using a bar of lye soap and lay them on top of the reeds to dry. He made sure there were no barges or steam boats coming up or going down the river as he swam in the swirling water using the same bar of lye soap to wash his privates, under his arms and his hair before he'd get out of the water and lay on the tall grass lining the shore letting the sun dry him. It didn't take long before he realized that he needed something more than working for next to nothing, fourteen hours a day, six and sometimes seven days a week.

One day when he was walking among the many saloons and whore houses along the waterfront, he saw a banner on the side of one of the waterfront bars **MEN WANTED TO HELP TAME THE WEST** in big bold letters. He memorized where to go and the following day he went to the courthouse. He followed the directions posted on the side of the building to a downstairs office. Once there, he waited in line for his turn to find out what it was all about. He wasted no time in signing up with the 1st Cavalry, Lightning Brigade, under Colonel John Thomas Wilder[3]. The country was in the final stages of the Civil War, but now instead of gray, he wore blue. He was a crack shot and when asked how he became so good he simply said, "Been huntin' all my life." Once the armistice was signed at Appomattox Courthouse[4], he, like many of the soldiers he had met, traveled further west. He found himself

---

[3] 1st Cavalry, Lightning Brigade, Colonel John Thomas Wilder – https://en.wikipedia.org/wiki/Lightning_Brigade_(US_Army_of_the_Cumberland_1863)

[4] Appomattox Courthouse - www.softschools.com/facts/civil_war/appomattox_court_house_facts/3611/

in Green Springs, Wyoming.

That same spring day Emmett Cooper was looking for ranch hands; Todd signed on and went to work. No one ever asked him if he'd been in the war and he never talked about his experiences either.

A bright flash and loud crack of lightning brought him fully awake. He sat up, rubbed his hands over the stubble on his face and stared at the blackness that was interrupted periodically by more lightning. As he lay back down, he laced his fingers behind his head and slowly drifted back to sleep.

Meanwhile, Crusty, who was on the other side of the room was hugging his pillow and dreaming about Molly O'Bannon, an Irish lass that he had met at the emporium in Green Springs. She clerked there and had told him more than once that she wasn't interested in the likes of the drunken cowboys that came to town every month. She wanted someone who was stable and could provide for her in the long run. He tried to convince her that he wasn't like the others, but she'd heard that line before. He'd kept trying every time he came to town until she finally relented and agreed to go out to lunch the following day.

During lunch they made small talk and afterward, he walked her to a shanty that she rented near enough to the jail so that if she was bothered, all she had to do was yell for help and the sheriff or one of his deputies came running to see what the trouble was. He turned to walk away when she said, "What's your hurry?"

"No hurry. Since today is your only day off, I just figured you needed time for things you couldn't normally get done during the week."

"Thought maybe you'd like to stay awhile and we could talk

some," Molly said.

"I'd like that very much," he replied. He wiped off his boots on the bristle mat outside her doorstep before he entered her abode. It was a tiny place, only one window in the large room set up as living space with the back part curtained off for dressing and sleeping and a back door leading to the outhouse, he presumed. Off in one corner was a small but adequate cast iron stove with a teakettle sitting on it and a wicker chair next to it.

Molly seated herself on her bed and said, "Tell me about yourself."

Crusty removed his hat and set it on the end of her bed, got comfortable in the wicker chair and said, "I might as well start at the beginning.

I was born Jonathan Harrison in Omaha, Nebraska. My father is the president of The First Mutual Bank of Omaha and he expected me to follow in his footsteps. I became disillusioned after a few short years while working at one of his banks. Unlike my father, I enjoyed being outdoors and spent as much time as I could down by the river with my friends whose families were either farmers or ranchers. I certainly had the educational smarts to be an extremely rich man by any standard, but to me financial wealth wasn't what a man should be measured by. I felt that wealth came from knowing the difference between good and evil, right and wrong, with some common sense thrown in.

My friends taught me how to use a rifle and there were occasions when I would bring home a deer or turkey, much to the chagrin of my parents. I preferred working with horses and cattle and making a difference with little successes to the 'beat of my own drum', so to speak. On the eve of my 20th birthday, I told my father that I was moving further west to which he replied, "Over my dead body you are."

I told him to stop being so dramatic and there was nothing he could do to stop me. I would be leaving in the morning and bid him goodnight. The following morning during breakfast my parents tried in vain to talk me out of what I intended to do, but finally gave in and wished me well. They gave me enough money to support myself until I could find a job. My friends all thought that the name Jonathan was too long and began calling me Crusty. They all said I had 'crust' because of some of the jobs that I took on that no one else dared. I found myself in Green Springs and hired on as a cowpuncher where I developed this uncanny ability of being able to handle cantankerous bulls, I even tried riding a few of them. I must admit though that roping and dragging a cow or a bull out of the brush was a mite easier than riding them. I met Chet Henderson when I was working at the Bar W. Mister Henderson usually got what he wanted and after seeing me handle those ornery bulls for the Bar W, he knew I was the man he was looking for. He hired me away as a cattle hunter for $45 a month. He wanted me to go up into the hills that surrounded his ranch and hunt for strays and herd them back down to the valley. He told me it was a rough job and if I was as good as what he had seen then I should do just fine. It was lonely work, but satisfying, plus I was getting an education far beyond what any book could teach me.

Over the years that I worked for Mister Henderson, I became quite adept at finding ornery bulls and cows in places that the other ranch hands wouldn't have thought to look or cared not to. I remember one particular bull that was blind in one eye and had half a horn on one side of his massive head.

I called him 'Butt Ugly'. To top it off, he was just downright mean! That bull managed more than once to find his way up into the timberline but in turn, I was always able to find him and herd him back down to the valley.

The last time was during a blinding snowstorm that swept down off the east face of the Tetons. 'Butt Ugly' was caught between a downed tree and a frozen creek bed. I brought two lariats with me, and it was a good thing that I did. I managed to get one around the bull's massive head and tie it off around a large boulder. I got the second lariat around his head also, but I tied it around the saddle horn and over the course of an hour or so and in spite of the slippery conditions, my horse and I managed to pull that cantankerous bull out of the spot he was in. You'd think that bull would be grateful, but that was not the case. Once freed he charged my horse, but the first lariat that was tied around the boulder held firm and jerked him right off its feet. As he lay there dazed, I quickly dismounted and tied the rear legs together and the front ones with piggin'string. That bull tried in earnest to break the ropes that were holding its feet together. I dragged that cussed bull all the way back down to the ranch before I undid the ropes and let it go. Butt Ugly didn't like me any more than he did before, but he never tried to break out again either.

He fathered several hundred calves over all those years before Mister Henderson decided that he was getting too old and put him down. Rather than eat him we just buried him up near the timberline. It only seemed right. That's my story!"

"I had you pegged all wrong, Crusty. Had I not been so stubborn about letting you take me out, maybe you wouldn't be going with your friend up to the Yellowstone wilderness.

Would you write me and let me know how you are doing?"

"I'd be happy to write you, but I have no idea how long a letter could take to get to you."

"It doesn't matter just so long as I know that you are alright. If you decide to come back this way I will be happy to go out with you again."

"Molly, if'n you don't hear from me in a couple of years, you'd do well to find yourself a nice man and marry him. I will always think of you as a close friend."

"Please don't think of me as being forward, but may I kiss you?"

-4-

Todd woke early and peered out the window. He noticed the rain was still coming down at a steady pace. Not wanting to wake his friend, he quietly got up, went out the door of their room and down the hall to the communal bathroom and relieved himself. When he came back, he sat in the only chair in the room with his feet propped up on the windowsill and began cleaning his pistol. If Crusty still hadn't woken by the time he finished, he decided he'd go downstairs and have breakfast. Crusty woke just as he was going out the door and Todd said, "I am going to get some breakfast."

"Give me a few minutes to get the cobwebs out of my brain and the sleepers out of my eyes and I'll come join you."

"Meet me in the lobby and bring your rain slicker with you. You'll need it if we decide to go outside." A few minutes passed before Crusty sat down next to Todd on the circular, tufted, red velvet divan in the middle of the lobby and said, "I wonder if that poker game is still going on?"

"There was no clear-cut winner when they all decided to stop as it was getting late. I wish I could get in on that game, but I think it is too late to join them. Someday, when I have enough money, I'd like to sit in on a high stakes game like that."

Crusty thought playing cards was a waste of hard-earned money; he saved what he didn't spend on drink and a good home-cooked meal. This morning he was interested in getting a good breakfast, getting their supplies and leaving North Fork before Todd lost any of his money in a poker game or on a wheel of chance[5].

After finding a café, both of them ordered coffee, pancakes, eggs, ham, and biscuits with huckleberry jam. During breakfast Todd remarked, "I think it's going to rain all day. We should go over to the general store after breakfast and get the supplies that we talked about last night. Hopefully after the rain stops we can get back on the trail. We'll need to make up the time we lost due to this lousy weather. We must get to the Yellowstone wilderness and build us a cabin and a shelter for the horses before winter sets in."

The shopkeeper told them that he would bundle their supplies and have it ready for them when they were leaving town. After they paid for what they purchased, they decided to take a walk around town and see what stores there were. There were six saloons, the general store, two hotels, a livery, doctor, sheriff's office, lawyer's offices, and an assortment of other small shops. Down the side streets were personal homes. They crossed the sodden, muddy street, scraped their boots that were caked with mud on the edge of the boardwalk before walking up the other side toward their hotel. They stopped at the livery to make sure the horses were being well taken care of. As they entered the livery, no one appeared to be there yet. Given what they were told yesterday that the owner always came in early, this seemed a bit strange.. They didn't

---

[5]   Wheel of Chance – similar to roulette.

see their horses in the stalls either. They thought that perhaps the horses had been put out in the paddock adjacent to the livery despite the rain Looking out there, they only found a couple of sway backs and a pair of mules, but certainly not their horses. They heard groaning coming from the back part of the barn. They both drew their pistols as a precaution and made their way toward the sound. They found a man slumped over a feed bucket on the floor. Crusty slowly turned him over; he had been pistol-whipped and had an open gash above his left eye. The old man looked up at the two of them and said, "Who are you?"

"My name is Crusty Harrison and this is my partner, Todd Morgan. Likewise, who are you?"

"Name's McGruder and this is my livery. I come in early to check on the stock, water and feed them before I start a fire in the forge where I do my work and get my tools ready for another day. As soon as I opened the side door, I knew something was wrong, but with my failing eyesight I just figured that worthless snot I have working for me forgot to close a door when he left last night. Two men came out of the shadows leading several horses and before I could say anything, one of them used the butt end of a rifle and knocked me out."

"You will make good on replacing our horses, saddles, and pack frames won't you?" Todd asked quizzically.

McGruder gave a blank stare as if he had been gut shot. Todd said, "We boarded our horses here in good faith, paid for their keep, and now they are gone. If you are going to say no, we can all go down to the sheriff's office and he can settle it. What's it going to be, Mister McGruder?"

"We don't have to bring the sheriff into this. I don't get

along with him as it is. If one of you will stay here, the other can come with me out to my place, and you can pick out four horses from my stock. When we come back here, we'll go to the general store and get the other things that you need to replace. Will that do ya?"

"That'll suit us just fine, and we also want a bill of sale on the horses, saddles, bridles and pack frames, so that you don't try to have us arrested for stealing before we leave town," Todd replied.

"Don't trust people?"

"We only trust people we know and we hardly know you."

"I like a man who stands up for his convictions," McGruder said. "Let me get cleaned up and then we will leave. The one who stays here can tell anyone who comes looking for me to fix something that I had to go back to my ranch and I'll be back in about an hour or so." Crusty replied, "I'll stay." He knew that Todd would pick the best horses he could for their trip. The rain was now a constant drizzle, with a light fog that had rolled in as well.

An hour later, Todd rode down the muddy street leading three horses tied behind him. They took the horses to the livery, put them in four stalls near the front of the barn. He said to Crusty, "I'll be back in a few minutes. Mister McGruder and I are going to the general store to pick out two saddles and two pack frames to carry our supplies." As they walked across and down the street he said to Mister McGruder, "I hope you can find out who took the horses. As much as you don't like the sheriff, you'd be wise to make him aware of the theft just in case he finds them."

"I know you mean well, but that son-of-a-bitch probably stole them himself," McGruder said.

"Suit yourself and when you get back to the livery would you please tell my partner to bring the horses over here."

When Crusty arrived, Todd said, "We might as well get the supplies we bought earlier. When we get back to the hotel we can see if we can put the horses in the barn behind it."

Once back at the hotel, he asked the clerk, "Can we put our horses in your barn out back?"

"Why don't you leave them down at the livery?"

"No thanks! We've lost four from there already." Puzzled, the clerk replied, "Let me check with the boss, and if he says it's okay, I'll show you where you can put them. I'll be right back." He came around from behind the counter and went through the door connecting the hotel to the saloon. He came back a few minutes later, "Boss says its okay with him. Let me put up a sign telling folks I'll be back in a few minutes." About the same time Crusty strolled in, the clerk was about to say something when Todd said, "He's with me." The two of them and the clerk went out the side door of the hotel and Todd grabbed the lead ropes of two of the horses; Crusty did likewise with the other two as they walked into the dimly lit barn. The clerk said, "Pick any empty stalls." Crusty moved one horse out of a stall so that all of their horses were in the last four stalls. He put the horse in a stall with one empty one on each side of it from two other horses that were already in the barn. "Can we use your feed?" Todd asked.

The clerk replied, "Two bits should cover what you'll use."

-5-

For safety's sake, they decided that they would put everything up in their room, especially the new saddles, bridles, pack frames, horse blankets, and all the supplies they had just purchased.

"You know, Crusty, between doing all this extra work and the weather, I am getting sleepy. So I think that I'll just go back to bed and get some extra shuteye. I don't know what's worse, shopping for supplies or riding the trail looking for a stopover for the night."

Crusty replied, "I'll go for a walk while you get some sleep. While I'm out do you want me to pick up a sandwich for you?"

"Sure. Ham with a touch of mustard on rye bread would suit me just fine."

After they parted, Crusty walked back over to the general store and bought two additional quart canteens, a double-bladed ax with a sharpening stone, a hatchet, two extra wool blankets, and a sewing kit. He walked down to the café and had two sandwiches made, one for each of them, before walking back to the hotel. He decided that he'd clean his gun much like Todd had done earlier that morning. Afterward, he stretched out in the chair, laced his fingers behind his head and drifted off to sleep.

The rain stopped during the late afternoon, but the air turned humid despite the drying sunshine. Early evening found both of them fully awake and they decided to go down to the saloon. They both ordered beer and ate their sandwiches. Crusty remarked, "We've been off the trail for two days. We'll have to make up that time. I'd like to leave just before sunrise tomorrow and head northwest toward Fort Washakie. Once we get to the fort, we'll stay the night and leave early. We'll follow the Wind River into the Absaroka Range, crossing over the mountains toward Gros Ventre Wilderness and eventually we should reach the southern tip of the Yellowstone Wilderness."

Todd was still tired and replied, "I'm guessing that it will take us twenty days or more to get to the Yellowstone. We can only hope that Indians won't bother us along the way. We both know that the Shoshone is at peace with the white man. I think most of the trails that we will be taking are in their territory, so we shouldn't have a problem. It's the other tribes who roam the mountains that we don't know much about like the Sioux[6], Arapahoe[7], and Cheyenne[8] that worry me."

"We are as prepared as we can be; we can only hope and pray for the best. We'll pack in the morning after we get a good night's sleep. We should get a dozen extra biscuits at the café after we have breakfast there in the morning."

Around 7:30 pm, the owner of the saloon called all the card players together who had drifted into the saloon over the last

---

[6] Sioux Indians - http://native-american-Indian-facts.com/Great-Plains-American-Indian-Facts/Sioux-Indian-Tribe-Facts.shtml

[7] Arapahoe Indians – https://en.wikipedia.org/wiki/Arapaho

[8] Cheyenne Indians – https://en.wikipedia.org/wiki/Cheyenne

hour or so and said to them, "We have put the poker table next to the staircase. I expect all of you to check your guns, including derringers and boot knives with the bartender. I'd like you to take the same seats you had last night. We have set up a bar table along the back wall, pointing to the left of the poker table, with soda crackers, bread, cheese, sliced ham on a bed of lettuce, black olives, mustard and water. If you want something stronger, just raise your hand and one of my bartenders will see to your needs. We'll resume playing at 8 pm. If you run out of money, I will not take IOU's, pocket watches, or your horse as collateral on a note and you are out of the game. If everyone is in agreement, lets get started."

The players removed their frock coats, jackets and hats and hung them on the coat rack. The bartender collected their side arms and pocket pistols and knives if they had any and put them under the counter. A few of them went over to the bar table and made sandwiches, and each person poured a glass of water before they sat down. The owner of the saloon called the first game, "Five-card draw. The person with the most chips at the end of the night takes the pot. Are there any questions?" There were none.

The card game had been going on for a couple of hours when the fifth seated player folded. He was out of money except for enough to keep him fed and housed for a few days. At the end of the next hour, the fourth player said, "This is getting too rich for my blood. I need what money I have left to make it through the winter." The dealer yawned and said to the remaining three players, "This would be a good time for all of us to take a break before we resume the game." None of the players objected, they all needed some fresh air and to stretch their legs. The saloon owner spoke to one of his bartenders, "Take the shotgun from under the counter and sit at the poker table; keep everyone away."

Twenty minutes later play resumed, the players went back and forth as one or the other won another hand. After about an hour, the third player dropped out almost flat broke. The owner of the bar said to his bartender, "Give him a beer, shot of whiskey if he wants one and a couple of sandwiches to go. He deserves it! The remaining two players asked the dealer for a new deck and one said to the other "One last hand, winner takes all, no limit." Each player had just about an equal number of coin and bills in front of them and at this point it was going to get interesting. The older of the two decided to have a shot of whiskey with a beer chaser; the dealer shuffled the deck, cut the cards, and asked, "You got a preference for the last game?"

"Both players said, "Five-card stud.[9]" The first two cards, one down and one up, were dealt and each player bid $100; rounds two and three were met with each round being more expensive than the previous one and now a tidy sum of $1,500 sat between them. The younger player ordered a glass of water, while the older player ordered another whiskey with a beer chaser feeling fairly confident that he had the winning hand. During the next round, which both of them knew was the last time they could bet, the older player decided it was time to see if the younger player who had been extremely lucky throughout the evening, said, "Time to see who has sand," and pushed his entire remaining pile of money in the center of the table and confidently said, "452 dollars!"

The other player gulped, asked for another glass of water,

---

9   Five Card Stud - https://en.wikipedia.org/wiki/Five-card_stud

but counted out exactly the same amount and pushed that into the middle as well. The dealer gave a seven of spades to the older player, who tried to hide his excitement, and to the other player a jack of spades. The younger player spoke after nearly three hours of being silent, "Sure hope you don't get too upset if I beat you."

"Sonny, with what I have, there is only one hand that can beat me."

"Show me what you got."

The older player turned over his down card revealing four of a kind and began to pull the pot toward him. The younger player said, "Does this beat you?" Much to everyone's' surprise, there, lying on the table, was a Spade Royal Flush[10] the dealer said, "If I didn't see it, I wouldn't have believed it. You surely did beat his hand." The older player was stunned. The final jackpot winnings amounted to $1,804. The player who won said to the dealer, "Here's fifty dollars for your services. Can I have a couple of dry pitchers so I can put my winnings in them? I'll bring them back in the morning." The dealer motioned for two empty pitchers to be brought over; the money was stuffed into them. The player stood and said, "Nice playing with you folks," strode out through the batwing doors and disappeared into the night.

---

[10] Royal Flush - n. A straight **flush** consisting of the five highest cards of one suit, ranked as the highest hand in certain games of poker.

-6-

A s Todd sat up in bed he whispered loudly, "You awake, Crusty?".

"Yeah."

"We might as well get up and leave since we are both awake. After we get the horses saddled, I'll come back up here and get the pack frames for the other two."

A chilled, September air, greeted them as they walked from the back of the hotel over to the barn. Upon entering, they found someone sleeping in one of the stalls, who woke and said, "I have a gun pointed at you. I don't mean you any harm, but you startled me."

"We're just here to saddle up and leave. We won't bother you, just give us a few minutes and you can go back to sleep."

"Sure; okay," a sleepy voice said hesitantly.

They saddled the Sorrel and the Piebald before putting halters on the other two. They took all four horses over to the hitching rail behind the hotel. Todd said, "I'll be right back with the pack frames; you can go up to our room and get our bundles of supplies while I get these pack frames on." After they tied everything down, Crusty remarked, "Let's stop by the café before we head out and have breakfast, especially since we don't know when or where we'll stop for the night."

After breakfast and before they mounted up, Todd checked the ropes on the pack horses to make sure everything was tied down securely. As they're riding along, both of them noticed Canadian geese flying south for the winter. Todd remarked, "They always know when it's time to leave the North Country and we're headed in the opposite direction. Seems strange, doesn't it?"

"They are doing what they do year after year. We, on the other hand, are trying to forge a new life for ourselves. I suppose we both will end up where we are supposed to be when the time comes," Crusty replied. They were riding a trail on the leeward side of the Absorka Range[11] when Todd remarked, "I'm getting a feeling that we're being followed. I'll fall back and circle around while you keep heading north. It might be a good idea if you take your rifle out just in case I need you to back me up in a hurry." He reined his horse to the left and headed up one of the numerous draws and side canyons along the trail they were on and over a ridge to where he could look down on the trail. He saw a rider about a mile back riding at a slow but steady pace.

The sun was now directly overhead and Crusty thought *Next stream I'll rein up and let the horses drink and crop grass for a while.* Once there, he went into the bushes along the side of the trail to relieve himself. As the rider approached, Crusty came out of the bushes startling the horse. It reared and threw the rider off. Crusty grabbed the reins before the horse galloped away and walked back to where the rider fell as Todd rode up. The person rose slowly and brushed the dirt off and said to the two of them, "I was in the barn this

---

[11] Absorka Range – https://en.wikipedia.org/wiki/Absaroka_Range

morning and thought that after you left I would just follow you. If I got into any trouble, I could yell out and either one or both of you would ride back to see what all the commotion was about."

"You took a big chance on that." Crusty responded.

"First off, My name is Elizabeth Connolly, Liz for short and until last year my father and I ran a small spread up near the Ramparts[12] that's a series of canyons about ten miles from here. My father died of injuries he received from a beating. I have been working our farm ever since his passing. I needed supplies so I went to North Fork and cashed in some gold nuggets I had. I got more in cash than I expected, so I hid some away in the barn behind the hotel and kept enough to try my hand playing poker. I got into that high-stakes game back at The Fancy and won the last hand. I felt that if I hid out in the barn after the game no one would find me there and try to rob me of my winnings. After you left, I decided to saddle up and follow you. I'm on my way back to my place."

"You are certainly brave to be riding all by yourself with all that money, hoping that you'd make it home safe. We are trying to get to the Yellowstone wilderness and do some hunting and trapping," Todd replied.

"You should go to Fort Washakie which is another forty miles or so from this point before you head into the wilderness. It's the last place where you can buy supplies. Why don't you accompany me to my home and stay the night. I'll get you on a trail that will save you some time getting to the fort which is northeast from where my farm is."

"That sounds right nice, but we don't want to impose on

---

12 Ramparts - https://en.wikipedia.org/wiki/Rampart_Peak

your hospitality," Crusty replied.

"You're not. It gets a mite lonely up where I live. Just follow along behind me."

As they neared her farmstead around mid-afternoon, a large black dog growled at them. She spoke to the dog and the dog wagged her tail and walked back toward the rear of the cabin. "That's Maddy, she guards the place when I'm gone. She's friendly enough, but don't make any sudden moves or raise a hand towards me, even as a gesture of friendship. She'd tear your arm off. Dad taught her to be watchful over his children as we were growing up."

Todd said he would take care of the horses, while Crusty tended to the pack horses. They stored their supplies, saddles, bridles and horse blankets in a small barn next to the corral. Liz took her saddlebags with her into the cabin and when she came back outside, said, "Could one of you, chop some firewood?"

"I will," Crusty replied, "just after I finish unpacking the horses." He picked up the ax next to the wood pile opposite the corral and next to a large garden and started splitting the wood. Meanwhile, Liz used a bucket of water left on the ground next to the pump, poured some down the inside of the pump casing to prime it and filled two of several buckets sitting on the ground. She set one on the porch and the second one inside the cabin.

Todd took an empty bucket and filled it several times and poured it into the horse trough just inside the corral fence. He dragged three bales of hay from where they were stacked next to the barn over to the corral, broke them apart before tossing them into the corral for the horses.

Liz returned to the cabin where the dog was resting in the

shade. Bending down, she stroked her head and said, "I see you've been a good girl protecting the house and my chickens while I've been away." Maddy just sighed and rested her head on her paws once again. Liz went into the chicken coop and gathered six eggs, putting them in a small wicker basket and set it on the ground outside the fence before she grabbed a fat hen, brought it over to where Crusty was chopping wood and said, "I need to use that ax for a minute."

"You want me to do that for you?" He asked.

"I am used to it, but thanks for asking." She deftly handled the ax and set it next to the stump before she put the chicken down on the stump and steadied it with her left hand and with one swift motion picked up the ax, chopped off its head and said to him, "Would you mind throwing the neck and head over in the trees?"

"No problem."

When he returned, Liz handed the ax back to him, picked up the basket of eggs and walked with the chicken to the porch on the back side of the cabin. She put the hen on the porch before opening the cabin door and set the basket of eggs on a dry sink. She sat in a rocker and began plucking the feathers off of the chicken. When she finished, she immersed the hen in the bucket of water and washed it both inside and out. Once inside the cabin, she placed the chicken in a roasting pan on top of the dry sink, smeared butter over the entire chicken, added a pinch of salt, pepper and set it on a grate in the fireplace to cook. Before she did anything else she needed to put away the money from the gold and her winnings from the poker game. She went over to the corner near the fireplace, pulled up a woven rug, opened a trap door in the floor and went down into her root cellar taking her saddle bags with her. In a corner was a large cedar-lined box on the bottom shelf. She took a canvas bag from each side of the saddlebags, and stuffed them down in the box, closed the door and latched it. On her way up the ladder, she grabbed a couple of onions, several potatoes, and a glass jar of green beans that she had put up at the end of June from her garden. She put everything she brought up on the dry sink and went back to close the trap door, pulled the rug back over the top of it and moved a rocker on top of the rug. She hung an oil lamp on a peg near the chair before setting an open book on it, upside down. She took the empty saddle bags and tossed them on her bed on the opposite side of the large room and went about preparing the rest of the supper.

Crusty brought in an armload of firewood and laid it on the hearth, went out and returned with a second armful and set it on next to the other one. When he went back outside he said to Todd, "I think we have her squared away. Are the animals all taken care of?"

"I just fed and rubbed down all the horses. I made sure that the gate is secure for the night. I tied an extra length of rope around the fence and the gate post with a double hitch knot. I did that all the time I was at Timber Creek."

"Whatever you say, *amigo.* I think dinner will be ready shortly from the smells drifting out this way. You know this place is like what I am hoping we can build, it has a nice comfortable feel about it."

-7-

They put their bedrolls next to the fireplace while Liz set the table for dinner. Todd went over to the cook stove and brought the coffee pot over to the table while Liz brought over a serving platter of roasted chicken with vegetables and boiled potatoes. Todd held a chair out for Liz while she sat; Todd and Crusty took their seats. She served while Todd poured each of them a cup of coffee. After a prayer, a friendly conversation ensued among them. Liz mentioned that she had a brother that she hadn't seen in years.

"Why did he leave?" Todd wanted to know.

"When my father, mother, my brothers, and I moved here it was a thick forest all the way down to the river. My father knew that we were about a day's ride from North Fork and thought that this would make a good place to raise his family. He staked out an area, marked it on a map given to him by the government and filed it the next time he went to town. It is about the same size as a quarter section, give or take an acre. We lived in our covered wagon and a couple of tents until he and my brothers erected the barn first, then this cabin after clearing the land and cutting the timber. After a few years, we were doing pretty well with farming and raising a few cows for milk. My mother would turn some of the milk into butter

31

and cheese. When we knew we were going to town, she would make extra and take it to the general store to sell or trade for the goods she thought we needed.

On one occasion my older brother Frank went hunting. When he didn't return, my father and younger brother Henry went looking for him and found him next to a bear that he apparently was skining. They found another set of bear tracks leading away from his body. He mustn't have seen the second bear that mauled him to death, They buried what was left of him.

My dad was beside himself with grief, and my younger brother got a good dose of reality. My mother took the news terribly hard and all but ignored my brother and me while she grieved. Dad relied on Henry more and more to get things done around the farm. He was at best twelve years old at the time. After a while the responsibilities began to wear on him and one day he told Daddy that he couldn't do it anymore. They had a terrible fight both verbally and physically. Henry decided to stay in the barn after that. He felt detached from the family and he didn't want to be in the same house with either of my parents. One day he just walked away and as much as my pa looked for him, he finally resigned himself to the fact that Henry, too, was gone.

The chores fell on my shoulders, but after a while my dad decided that he'd cut back on the farming, only kept a couple of cows for milk and started to go off into the hills to look for gold. My mother and I did the best we could until her health deteriorated and she died in her sleep one night. Dad wrapped her in one of her quilts, placed her on a travois and we took her up to where my brother was and buried her next to him. Pa thought it was fitting that they be together.

One day when he was up in the mountains, he found a stream about a mile or so from this cabin and started to mine it using the placer method[13]. The gold dust and nuggets that he found, he'd put in satchels that he made from deerskin and put them away. When he thought he had enough, he would take them to town to have them assayed, weighed, and turned into cash. He took me to his diggings so that I'd know where it was, just in case something happened to him. On one of his trips to North Fork to get the nuggets assayed and turned into cash, he was waylaid on his way back here. Whoever did it, beat him senseless and took all the money he had. When he woke several hours later, he managed to get back on his horse and the horse brought him home. I took care of him, but he was busted up something terrible and died in my arms. The following day, I wrapped him in a quilt and took him to be buried up on the hill next to my mother. I vowed to find out who did it and bring them to justice. To this day, I haven't found that person, but someday I hope to. Now you know my story, sad but true."

"We are glad you told us your story. Does it bother you being all alone?" Crusty asked concerned for her wellfare.

"I haven't had any trouble so far. Please excuse me for a few minutes." She left and went outside. Todd added a log to the fire and rolled out his bedroll, Crusty rolled out his saying, "The mountains can wait a few days."

"She must remind you of Molly O'Banion," Todd said with a smirk.

"Oh, shut up!"

---

[13] Placer Method - www.definitions.net/definition/placer mining

-8-

Todd was getting itchy to leave after a couple days of resting and enjoying Liz's cooking. He knew that if they didn't get close to the Yellowstone before the snow came, they'd have to wait until spring, something he hadn't planned on. Whatever Crusty was thinking about, Todd was unawares. He just hoped that Crusty would come to his senses and they could be on their way. Liz was as smitten as Crusty was and one day he said to Todd, "Well partner, I hate to do this, but I have decided to stay on here with Liz. I know you and I have been planning this trip to the Yellowstone wilderness to start a new life, but you'll just have to do it by yourself."

"If that's what you want, I'll be leaving in the morning and taking half of what we brought with us and $400 of the money that was mine to begin with. If you ever change your mind, look me up," Todd replied.

"You'll always be welcome back here if you don't find what you're looking for up in the mountains."

Liz was making breakfast and said, "Breakfast will be ready shortly; Todd if you'll go saddle my horse after you have yours all ready, I'll take you to that trail I told you about. The weather looks good for riding today. You should get to Fort Washakie by tomorrow afternoon."

Todd went out to the small barn, put a rope halter, thick blanket and pack frame on his mare, and loaded the supplies that he and Crusty decided he needed for his trip; next he saddled his horse and Liz's. He gathered the reins of the two horses and the tether hanging from the pack horse and brought them all to the rail in front of the porch. He went inside for breakfast and once finished, goodbyes were said before Todd and Liz mounted up. She took the lead and Maddy ran alongside of her as they traveled up the trail. She pointed out various markings off in the distance for Todd to go by. She took him past where her mother, father and brother were buried, twenty yards north of that point a well-defined trail had been cut through the lodgepole[14] pine forest. "I wish you God's speed on your journey. Would you do one favor for me," she asked.

"I'd be glad to."

"If you ever run across my brother Henry "Hank" Connolly, would you tell him what I've told you about our parents. If he ever gets down this way again to stop in and see me. I do miss him."

"I surely will. Thanks for everything Liz, especially your hospitality. Keep Crusty in line for me. He's a good man and you'd do well by him." As Todd started down the trail, he turned in his saddle one last time to wave goodbye, but Liz and Maddy had already started back down the trail toward her cabin.

"Oh well," he said under his breath before continuing down

---

14 Lodgepole Pine tree - https://homeguides.sfgate.com/lodgepole-pine-tree-42985.html

the trail. He estimated that he had ridden about four hours and had crossed two swift flowing streams with fish swimming in both of them, thinking, *I can only hope where I settle that fish will be as plentiful as they are right here. At least I won't starve for lack of food.* He noticed that there wasn't much in the way of any game the lower he got. He hadn't seen any deer or bear tracks and thought that perhaps the game simply didn't travel after a certain point on the mountain. He'd make sure that wherever he did settle there was plenty of bear, elk and deer sign.

He made mental notes on what he needed to buy at the fort: a compass, spyglass, extra bullets for his rifle and pistol, skinning knife, two more lariats, sharpening stones and oil for both the knives and axes. He followed the course of the trail until just before dusk and settled in a draw with a trickle of water and sufficient grass for the two horses and hobbled them. He gathered just enough deadwood to have a decent cooking fire, warmth and once again in the morning for coffee and biscuits.

Once he settled in for the evening, he let the fire die down to a bright blue flame, found the horses and undid their hobbles, tied a tether to each and brought them close to the camp and tied them to a tree. He rolled himself in his blankets and went to sleep. He woke just as the sun was breaking through the clouds, got the fire going again from the embers for coffee, and heated the biscuits that Liz had given him. When he finished with his meager breakfast, he poured the remainder of the coffee on the coals and scraped some dirt with his boot to cover the ashes.

He surveyed the desolate landscape of sagebrush, pine, and scrub oak, before he mounted and took to the trail once again and hoped by early afternoon to finally reach the fort. Just as Liz had said, Ft. Washakie appeared off in the distance. He rode to the gate and asked permission to enter. He was asked to state his business, "I am traveling to the Yellowstone, but I'd like to stay the night." To which a corporal shouted instructions to the men down below, "Open the gate." As Todd rode in, he noticed that all four walls were manned by soldiers as if they were ready for a battle. After he dismounted, he said to a private standing near the gate, "What's going on?"

"Four days ago one of our scouting parties returned with two of our men dead and several more wounded. The post commander, Colonel Matthew Johnson, has ordered all civilians and friendly Indians assemble inside the fort for their own safety until he can determine what all that was about and why the other Indians are raising hell. We have been at peace with the Shoshone for years, but there are other tribes, the Sioux and Cheyenne, who frequent the area and stir up trouble every now and then. I guess you could say that now and then is now."

"I guess I got here at the right time. Where should I picket my horses and do I need to see the post commander?"

"Take your outfit over between the barracks and the trading post and tie them to a hitching rail; then report to the post commander's office," as he pointed to the second building down from the barracks. Todd walked the horses to where he was told and tied them off, and from there he walked down to the building. Upon entering he found three sergeants, a couple of corporals and a private who was sitting behind a desk. The private said, "State your business!" Todd told him the same information that he told the corporal.

The private said, "Have a seat and I'll see when the post

commander can see you." Todd took his seat next to one of the sergeants. He smiled and sat still until the private came back into the room and said, "Mr. Morgan, the commander will see you now." Todd got up and followed the private and was told to have a seat in front of the large oak desk. Colonel Johnson looked familiar to him, but he couldn't place where he had seen him before. Colonel Johnson said, "Morgan is it? Were you in the 1st Calvary, Lightning Brigade under Colonel Wilder during the war?"

"Yes, sir, I served as the colonel's aide before I mustered out."

"Good to have you amongst us, Mr. Morgan. Can I assume you would lend a hand if we needed you?"

"I will."

"Splendid, splendid. Did you come through the forest to the west and if so, did you see any Indian sign?"

"I came from the area known as the Ramparts. I didn't see any indians, nor did I see any game either. It was unusually still in the forest, almost too quiet if you ask me."

"Well, in a way that is good news. If you weren't bothered, then we only have to find out where the hostiles are besides that direction. On another note, you can stay in the barracks if you'd like or you can bunk in the hayloft above the stable, your choice of course. I'd recommend the barracks where it's warm and dry. A little camaraderie would do you well, also, Sergeant Morgan."

"Colonel, I haven't been called sergeant anything in over fifteen years, couldn't we just call me 'Mr. Morgan' while I am here at the fort? I wouldn't want to have to pull rank on any of your men." They both laughed and the colonel said, "Mr. Morgan it is." The colonel walked Todd to the outer room, shook his hand, and said to one of the men, "Sergeant Muldoon, please see that Sergeant, I mean Mr. Morgan, has a bed in the barracks, is shown where he can wash up, and where the chow hall is. Also have one of the privates show him where he can put his horses."

Saluting, Sergeant Muldoon replied, "Yes, Sir."

Sergeant Muldoon was a gregarious Irishman and welcomed Todd to the fort saying, "It isn't much, but it's home to me. I have been here through three post commanders and I plan on retiring at the end of this month. Then I can be like you, free to do what I want, when I want."

"I know what you mean, sergeant, but being free has many different meanings to each person. I don't have to answer to anyone but myself and I am free to come and go as I please. Freedom, however, shouldn't be taken lightly. It took me several years after I mustered out to feel like I was my own man once again. You will adjust like I did, but it takes some time."

"Good analogy, Mr. Morgan. Do you know the Colonel personally?"

"No, I don't. He must have been in the same command as my former commander was during the war."

"What did you do during the war, if you don't mind me asking?"

"I was an infantryman and an aide for a brief period of time to Colonel John Wilder, 1st Cavalry, Lightning Brigade."

"You fellows saw plenty of action, especially in Tennessee. Colonel Wilder was a prisoner of war if I remember correctly."

"Yes he was and he saw plenty of action; we were both prisoners, but I was a gray belly. After I was in one of your prisons for a couple of years, your army gave me a choice and I took it. I signed a loyalty oath, and eventually I was part of a prisoner exchange. Once I was mustered out of the Confederate Army, I decided to make my way to St. Louis. After a while it became apparent that working fourteen hour days, six and frequently seven days a week wasn't to my liking. I saw a poster on the outside wall of a saloon and decided to join up and put on the blue. I became enchanted with Colonel Wilder's war stories and felt it would be an honor to serve under him. He was an honest man, had high morals, and he treated all of his men fairly. Once the war was over, most of us decided to get out and start our lives over again as we knew it before the war. I had a hankering to travel west and after several ranch jobs, ended up working for Timber Creek Ranch down in Green Springs, where up until a few weeks ago I was a horse wrangler for the most part. A friend of mine and I decided we wanted to travel to the Yellowstone wilderness and do some trapping and hunting before we settled down for good. My friend took to liking a girl we had met so we divided up our supplies and I am headed there after I leave the fort."

"I had thought about doing that myself when I got out at the end of the month. You wouldn't be interested in a partner would you?"

"I'd consider that. Let me mull it over and I'll give you an answer in a couple of days. From the looks of things, it appears that I'll be staying here at the fort longer than I had anticipated because of this Indian uprising."

The colonel had sent scouts out to find what the Indians

were up to while life inside the fort for soldiers, peaceful Indians, and civilians alike continued unabated. The guards in the parapets had been reduced by half during both day and night guard duty. After staying a couple nights in the barracks, he rose every morning at the first sound of the bugle. Todd and several of the soldiers made their way to the chow hall for breakfast.

When he finished eating on the third day, Todd went to the trading post to see if he could get some additional supplies that he might need. The sutler[15], a man by the name of Hanson, thought he could charge more for the goods he sold than what they were actually worth, given the current situation. The prices the man was charging were outrageous and Todd said so along the lines of, "Your prices are double what I paid for similar items in North Fork just a few days ago. I think I will let the post commander know that you are robbing people blind. I need the goods, but not at your prices. I think I'll just sit out on your front porch and let other folks know you're overcharging for supplies."

Sputtering, Hanson said, "You can't do that. I'll have you arrested for interfering with my business."

"Go right ahead and we'll see who does what to whom." Hanson stormed out his front door on his way over to see the post commander.

Todd sat on the store's front porch and casually mentioned to people walking up the stairs, "Prices seem a bit higher than what they were a couple of days ago. I guess with all the commotion outside the fort the sutler feels he can charge more. But don't take my word for it, go inside and have a look

---

[15] Sutler - https://en.wikipedia.org/wiki/Sutler

for yourselves."

The Command Sergeant accompanied Hanson back to where Todd was sitting and said, "Seems you're causing quite a stir, Mister Morgan."

"A stir is it? Well, hell, I was just informing folks that the sutler here is taking advantage of the current situation. I don't suppose he happened to mention that when he went to see the colonel, now did he?"

The sergeant looked at Hanson. "Is that true?"

"Well, you can't blame me. After all, there is no telling when I'll be able to get new supplies, now is there, sergeant?"

"You do have a point there, but the colonel told you to be fair about what you charged, didn't he?"

"Yes, he did."

"Then I suggest that you raise your prices about ten cents and be satisfied with that," the sergeant replied.

Grumbling, Hanson replied, "Oh, alright," and went back inside the trading post.

"Now Mr. Morgan, does that solution satisfy you?"

"Yes, he has a point about resupplying. I'd be in the same frame of mind, but since you made it more reasonable, I'll trade with him and keep my mouth shut. If he tries any more shenanigans, I'll just remind him what the colonel told him."

-10-

In passing, Todd said to one of the privates in the barracks, "I haven't seen Sergeant Muldoon around, do you know where he is?"

"Sergeant Muldoon and Corporal Harris are out on patrol to see if they can locate any Indians. They should be back, either later today or tomorrow, if things go right for them."

"Thanks. I hope everything does go right for both of them. The sergeant seems like a good man."

"He is one of the fairest men on this post; when he retires at the end of this month, not only the Army but this post, will lose a good soldier. He'll be hard to replace and sorely missed."

Todd had been thinking that having a new partner wouldn't be such a bad idea. He'd have to get used to the way, Muldoon did things, unlike Crusty whom he had known for a few years.

Because he had been delayed by the indian problem, Todd figured it would take him at least eleven days to get to the Yellowstone and once there he would have to pick out a site, build a shelter for himself and the horses. He knew that Muldoon would take a while getting used to his new-found freedom, but having military discipline in his blood, he more than likely would be a hard worker rather than not.

Three days hence, Muldoon and Harris and a squad of four

troopers arrived back at the fort looking bedraggled, hungry and everyone was in need of a shave and bath. Todd said in passing to Corporal Harris, "When Muldoon is rested and has the time; I would like to talk with him."

"We both have to be checked out by the post doctor. I'll mention it to him that you want to see him." Todd was unaware that Sergeant Muldoon had been confined to bed in the post hospital. He sought out Harris who said, "The sergeant is in the hospital; he has malaria[16], severe dehydration and is very weak."

"Can I at least see him?" He asked.

"I'll check with the doctor and let you know." A few hours later he found Todd and said, "The doctor told me that no one can see him for a couple more days, maybe even a week and then only for short periods of time." Todd wanted to tell Muldoon of his decision to have him join him on his journey to the Yellowstone. The days were slipping by, but with Muldoon in the hospital, he'd have to make other plans.

The sutler had apologized in earnest to Todd just a few days before. Being a devious son-of-a-bitch by nature, he was hoping that he could convince Todd to take two extra pack horses along with him up to miner's camps on the same trail that he would be taking. Given what had transpired before he apologized, he didn't quite know how to ask him. He decided to wait until just before Todd was going to leave the fort.

Now that Muldoon wouldn't be going with him after all, Todd decided that having a dog might be a good idea. He asked around and was told that if he followed the Wind River north about three miles and took the first branch to the east

---

[16] Malaria - http://www.webmd.com/a-to-z-guides/malaria-symptoms

for a mile or so he would come to Shoshone Joe's camp. He raised dogs and maybe he'd sell him one. He rode out that afternoon and followed the directions given to him. Arriving at Joe's camp, he was welcomed and shown several older dogs and a new litter of puppies, who had just been weaned. Joe had just started to train them and said they would be ready in a few days. He decided to buy a yellow lab, paid Joe for her and said, "I'll be back to pick her up." Once he got back at the fort, he decided he would join the soldiers, have a good meal and go to bed early. The following morning he'd stop in and see Muldoon before he made his final preparations.

He learned that the Indian hostilities were between two tribes, the Sioux and Cheyenne. It seems that a Cheyenne hunting party had come across a small Sioux camp in their territory. One thing led to another and the Cheyenne killed several of the Sioux. Upon finding the dead Indians, the Sioux chief, Johns' Come Quickly ordered his braves against all who entered the trails surrounding their main camp. That initial scout troop was out riding and not looking for anything in particular when they were attacked. When Muldoon, Harris and the troopers went out, they came upon Johns' camp. After several days of negotiating convinced the Sioux chief to call a council and resolve the issue without damaging the relationship that they had with the military and the white settlers in the area. Muldoon would let the commander at the fort know that there would be peace in the region once again; the attacks would stop. Whatever the war council decided, it would put an end to the conflict as far as the military and the settlers were concerned.

Todd stopped by the fort hospital to see Muldoon and said, "Given your condition and as much as I would welcome you to join me on my journey to the Yellowstone wilderness, you're in no condition to travel for several weeks. I have to be there as soon as I can or else the snow will close the passes and prevent me from setting up a camp. I would have to wait until spring. Perhaps if you feel better and want to join me in the spring, you can."

Muldoon replied, "If I hadn't gotten sick, I would have enjoyed going with you. I'll see you next year." Todd left the hospital knowing fair well that Muldoon might not be joining him in the spring or at any other time. On his way back to the barracks, Hanson stopped him and asked, "Since you're going up the trail would you take two extra packhorses with you and drop them off at two miners' camps along the way?"

"You're kidding, right?"

"Actually, I'm not," he replied. "The supplies have all been paid for, but with the Indian trouble I wasn't able to deliver the goods. I just thought that—"

But before he could finish, Todd said, "First, we have a disagreement, you bring the military into it, then you apologize and now you want me to do your work for you. You have balls mister, I'll grant you that. Do your own work."

"Why if I left the trading post to deliver those goods I would have no one to watch my store for me."

"I guess you should have thought of that when you started trading with the miners. If you want to pay me, I might consider it as a business proposition."

"I'll pay you $50 to take the pack horses to their camps."

"I was thinking more along the lines of a $100."

Sputtering, Hanson replied, "That's highway robbery. You will wipe out what profit I had on those two orders. It'll cost me more than what they are worth. I won't pay what you're asking."

"Suit yourself, but that's what it'll cost you to get the goods to the miners." Once said, Todd walked away and went over to the stable; he had to get his horse saddled and get the pack frame on the mare before he loaded his supplies and get to Joe's before sundown to pick up the dog. He went to the post commander's office to say goodbye and then over to the post hospital to say goodbye to Muldoon. He found him asleep, so he said to the orderly, "Please tell Sergeant Muldoon that I stopped in to say goodbye and thanks for his friendship. I hope he gets well very soon."

The orderly replied, "I'll tell him, Mr. Morgan. You have a safe journey." Todd walked back to the stable to find Hanson waiting for him and he said to Todd, sarcastically, "Here's your damn money and the pack mules are ready to go."

"Hanson, we are not friends. This is strictly a business deal. I will make sure the goods get to their rightful owners." He took the money, gathered the tether to each mule and tied them one behind the other. He took one of his lariats and looped it around his pack horse's neck before tying the other end around his saddle horn and led the horse and the mules along behind him toward Joe's.

When he got there, Joe said, "I see you're working for Hanson now, eh?"

"Not really, the miners paid for the supplies and since I was going their way, I agreed on a business deal with him. He paid me what I asked for and I figure to give each of the camps where the supplies are going $30 a piece. Hanson had to have charged them more than necessary and probably charged them for getting the supplies to them as well. I could have kept all the money, but why be greedy. I'll make friends with the miners by giving them something back from what he charged them."

"Do you know a Shoshone named Two Shoes?"

"Yes, I rode with him many times while we were trying to capture mustangs. Why do you ask?"

"He is my uncle and he had talked about a man named Morgan who was very good with horses. Would that be you?"

"That's me!"

"If you can stay a couple of days and break a few of my new horses, I'll repay you the cost of the dog and give you a new horse besides. You can also get used to the dog before you go. Do we have a deal?"

"We do." Todd unsaddled his horse, took the packs off the mare and the two mules and turned them out in a pasture that Joe had next to his cabin. Joe had made provisions for him to sleep inside with him and his woman. Todd would start breaking the horses in the morning.

-11-

After staying three days and breaking six horses for Joe, Todd and the dog became accustomed to each other. They set off for the first miner's camp some fifteen miles from Joe's along the Wind River. The weather had turned much colder over the last several days and he figured he still had a good two weeks before he'd get into snow. He made good time and arrived at the first miner's camp later that afternoon. The lead miner was a man named John Carson and he was ever so grateful to finally get the supplies and the $30. The miners, who were relying on that supply order, had run out of nearly everything. They all invited him to stay the evening; tomorrow he had a twenty mile ride to the next camp. While sharing their food Todd asked, "How much did you pay Hanson for the supplies?"

Carson replied, "We gave him $85 to cover the cost of the supplies and to get them back to us. Why do you ask?"

"Hanson was overcharging for supplies because of an Indian scare recently. I am guessing that what you received is about half of what you should have gotten. He doubled your price thinking you'd never know. He gave me a list and what he charged you for the supplies. I suggest that when you go to the fort again that you go see the command sergeant and complain that Hanson overcharged you, and that you'd like some help in getting what he didn't give you for the money you gave him originally."

Carson and the other miners were very appreciative, saying, "If there's ever a time we can do anything for you, just get word to us and we will be there for you."

He slept peacefully knowing that he had set the stage for a wrong to be righted. After breakfast, he said his goodbyes in the early morning light and headed for the next miner's camp. He had gone about twelve miles or so when it became overcast and the temperature began to drop dramatically. He said to the dog, "We best find us a place to hole up for the night. I feel snow is coming a bit sooner than anyone expected it to." The dog looked up at him, barked once, and then they continued down the trail looking for a place that offered shelter, water, and grass for the horses and mule. He could see a flicker of light off in the distance and wondered to himself if, by chance, it was the next miner's camp. He rode another couple of miles or so when he came upon three Indians huddled around a roaring campfire. He was wearing an amulet[17] that Joe had given him, which prompted one of the Indians to say, "Friend, come sit by our fire, share meal, sleep here while storm come."

"First, I must get my horses and the mule some protection from the snowstorm." The Indians showed him where their horses were; he tethered and hobbled his horses and the mule. He gave each some feed and threw a blanket over the top of his supplies and that of the mule. He took his rifle, canteen, and bedroll with him. They had killed a turkey and were roasting

____

[17] Amulet   -   http://www.religionandnature.com/ern/sample/
Walker—Shoshone.pdf

it over the fire; he talked with them using sign language and in Shoshone.

They were not Shoshone, but Sioux, a hunting party looking for elk and deer to take the meat back to their main camp some forty miles north of where they were. Todd told them he was headed for the Yellowstone to hunt and trap. They told him, "Watch out for Arapaho, Cheyenne and other bands of Indians along the way. Keep to the main trail through the Tetons and look for the river that flows away from the big lake. Go a few miles to a smaller river that is Northeast from the valley, the mountains will protect you from harsh winds, plenty game, good for trapping." They had built a lean-to out of spruce to block the snow and wind; after they had eaten, they turned in.

He fed the dog scraps that were left over, and then took two blankets and his bedroll to the leeward side of the lean-to. He laid one blanket on the ground; put his bedroll on top of it. He had the dog behind him and took the other blanket and threw it over both of them and went to sleep. During the night, the dog made a throaty growl that woke Todd. The horses were agitated. Todd and one of the Indians got up to see what the problem was. After finding nothing they returned to the campsite. In sign Todd said, "Must be the wind."

The brave, who knew some english, said, "Cougar, make horse skittish. They ok now that we check and no find anything. We go back to sleep, your dog will know if he is close again and will tell us; we will be ready for it." There were no more incidents the rest of the night.

-12-

In the morning, the Indians headed north while Todd took a more westerly track. The snow wasn't as deep as it could have been and must have stopped during the night. He guessed that he was traveling in the right direction to reach the other miner's camp. He'd gone about ten miles when he smelled smoke and he changed his course slightly. Up ahead, he could see a wisp of smoke curling out of a chimney. He reined up and hollered out, "Are you the Langstrom mining camp?"

In halting English, a voice replied, "No, they are farther up the trail. They don't take kindly to strangers. Be careful!"

"Thanks," he said to the voice. He continued up the trail and slowly made his way toward the cabins in the distance. As he neared them, he shouted out again, "In the cabins, are you the Langstrom Mining Camp?"

"Who's asking?"

"My name is Todd Morgan and I have come from the fort with the supplies you ordered a while back at the trading post." A door opened and three scraggly men pushed against each other as they spilled out of the cabin and said in unison, "Thought Hanson plumb forgot about us. Welcome, stranger!" Todd dismounted, untied their pack mule and led it over to them. The oldest looking of the three men said, "You're welcome to stay the night. The best we can offer you is a meal and coffee now that you have brought those supplies to us. You have no idea how grateful we are."

"I think I know. I last went to the Carson mining camp and they were in the same dire situation as you are. I need to get over the pass so I can get to the Yellowstone before the snow gets any worse."

"My name is Gus," one of the men said, "Come with me!" Todd went willingly and as they climbed a small hill the man said, "As you look west those are the Tetons and to the north is the Absorka Range. All the passes are closed until spring and you'd be a damn fool to try and get over them."

Dejectedly, Todd replied, "I guess I'll have to go back to the fort at first light and wait until spring comes."

"From the looks of things, I guess you had a mind to do some trapping and hunting?"

"I did."

"Not too far from here up the next canyon 'bout four miles is an old miner's cabin with a swift running stream and plenty of game. Stay the night with us and we'll take you there in the morning. If you like what you see, we'll help you fix it up. It'll give us a chance to repay you for getting our supplies to us and if you stay, we'll be your neighbors."

"Seems fair enough to me," Todd replied. Once he was back at the cabin he took his horses over to their barn. He led the horses inside and tethered them to the posts holding up the hayloft. He unsaddled his horse, unpacked the mare, and led the new horse that Shoshone Joe had given him around the corner from the other two. Then he rubbed them all down with straw, grained, and watered them. He had the dog stay with the horses. He took a couple of biscuits and some jerky from his saddlebags, put the food in a tin pan he found leaning against a wall. He took his fry pan and went outside to scoop up some snow so that she'd have water as it slowly began to melt. She looked up at him soulfully but he knew it would be best if she stayed there and reluctantly, closed the barn door behind him.

He walked over to the larger of two cabins, wiped his feet on a well-worn rug and knocked before entering. Inside, there were two sets of bunk beds off to one side, a table with two benches, and another table off to one side of the fireplace where one of the men was preparing a supper of ham and beans. It was comfortable and orderly with bear and elk skins on the walls, a couple of bearskin rugs on the floor, and two rocking chairs near the front wall with a small table and an oil lamp on it. They had put a small book rack on the other side of the wall with several tomes in it. A coffee pot sat off to one side of the fire with vapors coming out of the spout. One of the men was putting away their supplies and the third man was coming into the cabin with an armload of firewood. Thinking, he said to himself, *If I can make that miners' cabin as nice as this, I won't mind not making it up to the Yellowstone after all.*

Back at Sweetwater Ranch, both Crusty and Liz decided they liked each other well enough, but still they had reservations about getting married. Each had been single for so long and they didn't know if they were compatible enough as a couple. He built a room behind the barn that could be expanded in the future if they hired anyone to work for them. He would sleep there and eat his meals with her in the cabin.

They had decided to buy some yearling cows and a young

bull so that over time they'd have a right size herd for the size of spread that Liz owned. He talked with her one evening, "I plan to ride back to the Henderson Ranch and see if Mr. Henderson will sell me twenty or so calves and a bull. I'll be gone about three weeks."

"Can I go with you?" she asked.

"Well, sure, if you want to."

"I do. I don't want to be all alone while you are gone."

"I can understand that, and besides, I'll enjoy your company getting there and back."

She could visit with Mrs. Cooper while he was discussing business with his old boss. They had decided to leave on Thursday morning after they secured everything on the farm. Liz said to the dog, "Stay." "Guard." The dog looked up with sad eyes, and then slowly walked back toward the porch, curled up on her favorite rug and looked mournfully while the two of them rode away.

Liz led out as she had done so many times before going toward North Fork, but took a different way that she knew. It would save them two hours at the very least on a trail that was south of North Fork on their way to Green Springs. Three inches of light snow had fallen overnight, much the same as Todd was experiencing. Crusty was wondering how his friend was doing and silently wished he had followed through with the promises he had made, but female companionship, especially out here, was much more appealing than traipsing around the wilderness. They decided to follow the Wind River south and from there, along one of its tributaries that ran east of Green Springs.

Once there, they would follow the road that led to the Henderson Ranch and just down the road from the Cooper

Ranch. If Mr. Henderson wouldn't sell them some cattle, then maybe Mr. Cooper would. They camped about three miles southwest of North Fork along a meandering creek with ice formations along the edges.

Crusty said to Liz as they huddled in front of the fire, "I am hoping that we make good time. I'd sure hate to be stuck down in Green Springs because of bad weather. If we can get there in three or four days and conclude our business in two days, we should be in good shape to get back to your farm before any serious weather develops. I am hoping that if we can get a bull calf and nine to twelve yearling cows, you and I should be able to handle them. If we only do thirteen to fifteen miles a day, we should get back here by the end of the month."

"Well, if we come back the way we are going to get there, we will have good graze and water. I brought enough supplies to keep us on the trail for three weeks or so, more than enough time to get us back to the farm," Liz replied.

"Why don't you sleep on this side of the fire and I'll be on the other side where I can keep an eye on you and the horses."

"You'll get cold. Why don't we both sleep on the side opposite from where we are and that way, I can help you if you get tired."

"Because, I don't want you to have to do my job and you won't be as warm."

"You with your high morals, Crusty, are enough to drive a sane man, or woman in my case, nuts that's why. I am fully clothed and with you next to me we will both be warm. It isn't like we were going to make love on this cold night."

"Someday, I will make love to you," Crusty replied, grinning like a Cheshire cat.

"And someday, I'll let you." Liz said with a twinkle in her eye.

-13-

T odd and the miners went to the cabin the following morning. He looked inside and other than a broken window and dirt on the inside there was nothing amiss. He liked what he saw and between him and the three miners the fixed up the abandoned cabin. He thanked them and said, "I'll see you in a few days."

After they left, he sat down on a hastily made stool and figured out how to build an attachment onto the cabin for the horses. In order to save time and timber, he set out to cut some lodgepole pine that he found not far from the cabin. He rode his horse and brought the new horse along with him and several ropes to pull the logs after he trimmed them to where he'd build the shelter for the horses.

The weather had turned much colder, but no more snow had fallen since that first storm that he had encountered with the Indians. In the meantime over the next few days, he went about the task of cutting down thirty-five trees. All the while, he had an eerie feeling that someone or something was watching him. His Colt 45 was in his holster looped over the pommel. It was adequate firepower if the presence was a man, but if it was a bear, wolf or mountain lion, he would be out of luck. He planned to rectify that by retrieving his rifle the next time he went back to the cabin. He continued to work and occasionally looked over his shoulder. After a few minutes, the presence was gone.

After he trimmed each tree, he tied one end of the rope around two of the logs and tied that rope off on his pommel; he put the second rope around two other logs and around the second horse's neck. He grabbed the halter on the second horse and the reins of his as he stood between the horses and walked at a steady pace dragging four logs at a time back to the cabin.

He continued to ferry the logs that he had cut back to the east side of the cabin. Once they were in a pile, he took a break, had something to eat and drink. When he finished, he took the small sleigh that he had built to carry firewood in and rode back along the trail to pick up any deadfall that he had seen along the way. Once back at the cabin, he pulled up to the end of the back porch and piled the deadfall there. The rest, he put near the chopping block for when he had time to split them into fireplace size logs. Next he put the horses out in the corral that he had built and walked around the cabin. His gut feeling was to keep a watchful eye.

On the far side of the creek, he noticed a horse with rider staring at him. He was about to raise his hand when a shot rang out just inches from the top of his head. Todd scrambled to the far corner of the cabin and as he raised his rifle to return fire, the rider was gone. He went back to the corral, got one of the horses to ride bareback and said to the dog, "Guard," before he grabbed a canteen and walked the horse down to the creek.

He filled the canteen before walking across to the other side and observed hoof prints of one horse in the soft earth and found it strange that only two of the four hoof prints were shod. He mounted and followed the trail from a distance, just in case of an ambush. He guessed that he followed the horse prints about four miles up into the timberline before they disappeared. He traveled in circles, going wider and wider each time, but found nothing. He decided to stop at the Langstrom's camp on his way back to the cabin. He reined up just outside the main cabin, knocked on the door, but there was no answer. He walked over to the other cabin and found no one home there either; he went over to the barn and saw that all the horses and mule were gone. He rode south to the stand-alone cabin, dismounted, knocked on the door frame and heard only a feeble answer from within, "Come." As he opened the door it fell inward. Once inside, he found an old man slumped over next to the fireplace. He went over, helped him up, and got him to his bed. He noticed a gash over his left eye, still bleeding. He covered him with a blanket and said to him, "I will get my canteen so that I can clean your wound and you can have something to drink."

In a weakened voice the man said, "On the far side of the hearth is a bucket with a ladle." Todd found a clean cloth and using some of the water in the bucket wiped off the blood from his face and asked, "Who did this to you?"

"Rider come, kick in door and beat me before he left. He asked if I knew anyone named Morgan. I told him no, but I don't think he believed me and he began to pummel me until I passed out. I have never seen him before; he had 'white hair, white skin'. You are tenderfoot at the old cabin in the woods. I see you many times, working hard, good to have you as a neighbor who cares," he whispered as he drifted off to sleep.

Todd fixed the door, and closed it behind him before he

left. He was more curious than ever about who would have done such a thing to an old man who meant no harm to anyone. He also wondered where the miners had gone to, but he knew they had a claim up in the foothills northwest of where their cabins were. He'd check back in a few days. This rider troubled him, but there was nothing he could do about that now. He rode back to his cabin and the dog greeted him. He rubbed the horse down, gave it some feed and put it out in the corral with the other horses. It was getting dark and before he went into the cabin, he walked around it looking in several directions, but saw and heard nothing other than night sounds of birds and small animals. He walked over to the mare, rubbed her forehead and behind her ears, then took the dog and himself into the cabin for the night. The dog always slept by the fireplace, but tonight she lay by the door. He thought it odd, but maybe the dog knew something he didn't. He prepared a supper of roasted potatoes, venison strips heated in the frying pan, and coffee. He took to reading a book after supper that he picked up at the general store in North Fork. After reading a few pages, he yawned before saying to the dog, "Time for sleep."

During the night, Todd woke to a throaty growl and said, "What is it girl?" He knew if he let the dog out to investigate she might get hurt. He put on his boots, grabbed his coat and rifle, and opened the door ever so slightly. She slipped silently past him into the clear, cold night, while his eyes adjusted to the darkness. Turning ever so slightly, he saw several pairs of eyes circling the corral where the horses were. He assumed they were wolves and fired in their direction, hitting one as it ran away. The others scattered. He quickly gathered up the horses, put lariats around their necks and led them to the hitch rail. He took a chair off the porch and set it up in the corner next to the south wall where the horses were tied. It was going to be a long, cold night. The dog came back, still growling, and layed down next to him looking out into the darkness. He decided that come daylight, he'd set a few traps around the perimeter as a precaution against any more intruders. He worked feverishly over the next several days to finish building the barn so that his horses would have some protection against the weather and wolves. How naïve he had been thinking that he wouldn't encounter other wild animals so close to the cabin.

-14-

It had been several days since the last incident with the wolves and he knew it was only a matter of time before they would be back. While he was driving in the last ten inch spike in the supporting log against the cabin, he thought he heard the snap of one of his traps. He set the hammer next to the spikes on top of the log and climbed down his makeshift ladder to the ground. He put a tether around the dog and tied her to a fence post. He grabbed his rifle, bowie knife, and a lariat just on the off chance that he'd have to drag in a dead wolf. As he went around an Aspen he saw one of the wolves had been caught in the trap. He raised his rifle and shot it in the head; next he heard another trap snap shut on yet another yelping wolf. Could he be so lucky? He made his way in the direction of that sound and found a second wolf in that trap, he fired and killed it. After he removed the wolf from the trap he reset it. He quickly tied one end of the lariat around the wolf's neck and dragged it over to the first one. He removed that one and reset that trap, put the other end of the rope around that wolf and dragged them both behind the cabin. He set about skinning both wolves. He would use their meat for traps, and the skins would be sold in the spring along with any other animals he caught over the winter months.

When the miners returned to their cabin, they found their furniture overturned and their supplies strewn about, but to their relief, whoever it was never found their gold stash.

When Todd visited the old man a week later, he invited him inside and said, "My name is Moon. I am from a tribe not seen in these here parts for many moons. I live a simple life and I only ask for friendship from those who live near me. I thank you for caring about me and if I can do anything for you, all you have to do is ask."

"I must go trapping and if you have the time I would like you to stay in my cabin and take care of my horses while I am gone."

"Just let me know when you are leaving."

"The end of this week; I will bring you back some bear meat, the liver and claws." Todd had learned that most Indians regarded the claws and liver as strong medicine. Moon was grateful for Todd's friendship and help after the attacker had beaten him. Todd decided it would be a good time to break in the new horse on his first trapping trip to the Valley of Steam. Moon told him it was northwest of where they were. He was taking eight traps, wire for snares, his Sharps and Winchester with long-grain 22 cartridges. His intentions were to get as many beaver, bear, or other game that would keep him fed through the coming months, along with preparing the hides for trading come springtime. He had packed everything the night before he left and brought an extra sack of grain and a half-bale of hay for his horse and the pack horse just in case there wasn't enough graze where he was going.

The miners had drawn Todd a crude map with trail markers to help him find good hunting/trapping country. They said, "Rein right at the stone outcropping that looks like a horse's head, continue until you see the three weathered pines clumped together at the top of a knoll, then go around Bull Lake for two or three miles until the trail through the pines turns into the area where a huge dead tree is lying next to the steaming water. You will find plenty of game, including beaver, wolf and fox for trapping; elk, deer, and on rare occasions, moose and grizzly might also be found for hunting with the Sharps."

While he was riding toward the area he wanted to trap, Todd passed several ponds where beaver lodges were plentiful and he could work those if he had a mind to as he made his way back toward home. He found several areas where he could make a base camp for a week or so, but chose an arroyo that had steep sides, with aspen and pine for shelter, some deadfall for firewood, a creek for water and graze for his horses.

He set about cutting a few small trees to build a temporary lean-to and a pole fence corral further back where the pine trees would offer some protection for the two horses. He had been gathering deadfall along the way as he had been picking out a spot where he would set up his camp. He had packed a shovel, as the miners had suggested. Once he had the camp set up like he wanted it, he dug a trench around it to drain off any water if the snow melted; next he dug a fire pit and lined it with rocks from the creek bed.

The dog continued to sniff around through the underbrush and snow patches scaring up a rabbit or two, but never caught them. Todd guessed it to be about two o'clock in the afternoon when he decided to leave the dog in the camp with the horses. He didn't have to say, "Stay: Guard." He just pointed to a spot next to the corral, and the dog walked around in a circle, lay down, and put her head on her paws.

He wanted to scout out the area on foot before he started to put down his traps and snares. He grabbed a pair of snowshoes, his Sharps, a canteen, two lariats and a compass and started walking, keeping the hillside over his left shoulder as he set out. Guessing he had walked about an hour or so, he found both fox and elk tracks, but no wolf or grizzly. He counted at least four beaver lodges along a meandering stream and several ponds that dotted the area; he also saw numerous rabbit, squirrel, and marten tracks.

On the way back, he kept the hillside on his right, he crossed over another creek and caught sight of a magnificent bull elk feeding in a meadow that was ringed with the sagebrush. He quietly put a cartridge in the breech, pulled back the hammer on the Sharps, sighted and fired. The bull ran several yards before dropping down on his front legs, panting; Todd ran as fast as he could to the spot where the bull elk lay and pulled out his Colt 45 and put another shot just behind the right ear.

He had to work fast before sunset overcame him so that he could get most of the skin and meat back to camp. What he couldn't carry, he tied a lariat around a rear hind quarter and threw the other end over a branch high up in a birch tree, then hoisted it up about a dozen feet off the ground and tied the rest of the lariat around the tree trunk. He took the other lariat and tied it around the remaining hide and began dragging it across the ground toward camp. He rested several times along the way and just as the sun was setting, he came within 100 yards of the camp; he called the dog who trotted over and told her, "Guard." He walked into camp and put the pack frame on the mare, led it to the elk carcass, strung the lariat through the pack frame and had the horse drag the carcass the rest of the way back to camp. Todd was going to have an elk steak for supper, but first he'd have to finish skinning the carcass, salvage what meat he could, put it in several burlap sacks that he brought with him, tie them high up in several trees near the campsite, and then roll up the skin. He would work on it tomorrow after he set some traps in the ponds and along the trails he had walked.

He fed the two horses and gave each of them a scratch behind their ears. He used his frying pan that he had bought to cook the steak and placed it the edge of the fire, set the coffee pot on the opposite edge of the stones; he guessed everything would be ready in about a half hour or so. He sliced off a thick piece of elk meat and cut it into chunks to feed to the dog and waited for his elk steak to finish cooking.

$$-15-$$

He had been staking his traps for about a week and a half and had met with mild success taking ten beaver and five red foxes. His snares placed at various locations yielded twelve rabbits, six marten and eight squirrels. All of the furs so far were of good quality. He hadn't bothered to check on the hind quarter that he had strung up in the tree, partly because he wasn't all that sure where it was, but when he did find the tree, the hind quarter was gone. The rope was still tied around the tree and the other end dangled loosely swaying back and forth in the breeze.

He untied the rope, pulled it down off the tree limb, coiled it and put it around his left shoulder. He remembered that Joe and the Sioux Indians had said there were other tribes in the mountains. Perhaps one of them had cut it down. As much as he could have used it, he didn't begrudge anyone who could use the meat that was on the hind quarter.

He had decided that once he checked all of the traps one more time, he'd pull them and take down the snares before moving further down the valley to a new area. Perhaps to the arroyo he saw on his way up here, tomorrow would be soon enough. As he was skinning the squirrels he tossed some of the meat to the dog, which he affectionately had named

Molly, after his sister. She was his best friend while growing up in the Tennessee hill country; however, war and time had separated them.

Someday, I will have to try and find her, he thought. When the dog started a throaty growl, he looked up from what he was doing, but saw nothing. The dog started a half crawl forward still growling and began to bark. Just beyond the clearing, about 100 yards from the campsite, a grizzly stood erect with berry juice dripping from its jaws. Todd was ten feet or so from the Sharps and not wanting to make any sudden moves, he slowly backed up towards it as Molly continued to advance toward the bear.

Todd yelled at her, "Stop, girl, stop," but she didn't listen and went after the grizzly. One swipe of its paw knocked the dog aside giving Todd just enough time to get the Sharps, put a shell into the breech, cock the hammer and fire. He added a second cartridge quicker than grease lightning and fired again, but the bear kept charging through the underbrush toward him. A third round brought it to its final end only fifteen feet in front of him. He had brought the rifle up to use it as a club, but when the bear gave his last breath and its eyes fixated, he knew it was finally dead. He waited for what seemed like forever, trembling, and went over to where it lay on the ground. Just to be sure it was dead; he thrust his Bowie knife downward into its skull and stumbled backward. He collapsed out of breath and just sat there for several minutes trying to figure out what to do next. Getting up, he ran to where the two horses were and using a soothing voice calmed them down.

Next he went to find what happened to Molly. She lay in a heap near the creek and as he dropped to his knees, tears ran down his face as he gently gathered up the one friend that had never let him down since coming to this area he was now calling home.

To his surprise, he found a weak pulse and a bad wound that the bear had inflicted on her left shoulder practically tearing off her leg which was still bleeding. He gathered her up in his arms as gently, but firmly, as he could and walked slowly back to his campsite so as not to drop the dog along the way. He just laid her inside the edge of the lean-to, took an old shirt from his saddle bag and used the hot water from the coffee pot to wash out her wound. In the back of his mind, he remembered what Moon had taught him about gathering moss and mixing light sand from a creek bed to form a paste to draw out the poison from a deep cut or an abrasion.

He quickly went to the creek bed and using his frying pan scooped up some of the light colored sand near the edge of the creek. He went from tree to tree looking for moss, but only found some on the rocks in the creek. Moss was moss after all. He carefully made a paste of the sand and the moss to put it on the wound before he tore off both sleeves of his shirt, tied them together and made a bandage to wrap around the dog to cover the wound. He could only hope and pray that he had done enough to save her. He set about building up the fire for warmth but was too keyed up to think about eating.

After he settled down, he'd have something to keep his strength up. He wouldn't be any good for the dog or himself if he didn't eat. He removed the Bowie from the skull of the grizzly and began to skin the bear out. He set the bear meat aside, especially the liver. He washed out some of the sacks he had used for the elk meat and put the bear meat in them. He made a plan on what he'd do starting the following morning. He left the dog laying next to the fire and he went off to gather up his traps and what animals that had been caught; next he'd have to skin them and roll up the skins. That would take all of one day and well into the night. The following day he would build two travoises out of the poles from the lean-to and the pole fence, one for all the skins, meat and his supplies, the other to transport the dog back to the cabin. It wasn't supposed to be this way, but he kept saying to himself, *I can do this, I can do this.*

He stared up at the gray clouds in the sky and said a silent prayer. *God, if you can hear me, please save her. She, like my sister, only wanted to protect me like she did when we were children back in the hills of Tennessee.* He went over to the horses and as both came up to the fence, he scratched both of them behind their ears and poured the last of the feed on the ground for them to eat.

He went over to the creek, bent down, splashed the cold water on his face, and noticed that where he had scooped the sand there was some glitter on the edge of the stream. He hadn't even thought about panning for gold after he had set his mind on trapping. Maybe in the early morning he'd try to sift some of the sand a little to satisfy his curiosity before he left this place. He rinsed out the coffee pot before refilling it and added two fistfuls of coffee grounds before setting it on the edge of the fire to boil. He washed out the frying pan before laying strips of rabbit meat in it and set it on the hot coals to cook slowly. He gathered brush to add to the fire later. Using his bowie knife,he stripped several branches from a pine tree to lie on the ground before he put down a doubled blanket on top of them.

He checked on the dog, her pulse seemed a bit stronger, but it might only have been wishful thinking. Her breathing was very shallow, but she was alive. He made sure the dog was well covered against the chill of the night and then he pulled the doubled blanket over close to the far side of her body, so that when he finally went to sleep, his body heat would keep her warm. He ate supper with the night sounds surrounding them, took his coffee pot and cup and sat on the doubled blanket with his Winchester lying across his legs; he'd pull first watch, while God took the second. As a full moon flooded the mountain range with light, he slumped over, fast asleep.

-16-

The following morning he woke early, rubbed the stubble on his face before picking the sand out of the corners of his eyes. He took a lantern, coffee cup and his frying pan with him and went to the creek. He used the cup to scoop some of the sand from along the edge of the creek into his frying pan and swirled it around and around to see if any of that sand glittered like the sand from last night. After twenty-five minutes, he found four very small specs of gold and set them on one of the rabbit skins that he'd brought with him so he knew where they were. After two hours, he stopped. He had gold dust maybe as much as the tip of his little finger and two flakes the size of a common nail head. He carefully wrapped the skin and put it in his left coat pocket for safe keeping.

In the back of his mind, he decided to mark this arroyo on a crude map he had drawn so that when he came back, perhaps later in the winter or next spring, he would know where it was by notching two trees. He rekindled the fire and as the vapors appeared from the coffee pot, he poured himself a cup. He set one of his last biscuits to warm on a flat rock near enough to the fire before eating it.

While he was just drifting off to sleep during the night,

he thought he heard Molly whimper, but dismissed it. He checked the dog's pulse and found that it was indeed stronger; her eyes opened slightly and her tongue was hanging out, dry. Todd took water from his canteen and poured some on the tongue, rubbing it gently. He lifted her head and tried to get some of the water into her mouth. It was slow going, but he managed to get a some down her throat. He took another biscuit and warmed it by the fire before crumpling it into the cup, then added a small amount of coffee before he hand-fed the mixture to the dog. She sighed, put her head back down on the blanket and fell fast asleep.

In the morning, Todd whispered to her, "I have to go, but I will be back in a few hours. Misty will watch over you." Todd led the other horse out of the corral and said to Misty, "You watch over Molly for me." The horse whinnied, and pawed the ground. She stood by the fence as Todd put the rails back in place as if understanding what Todd had said. He put the pack frame on the mare, an old empty sack for the traps and snares, grabbed his two rifles the canteen, Bowie knife plus three ropes and set off to gather his traps, snares and whatever had been caught in them. He promised himself he'd be back by noon.

He pulled the snares first. The snares only yielded one each of rabbit and marten. *They must be getting wise to my snares*, he thought. He circled wide around the two ponds from right to left and found one red fox near the edge of the first pond; in the ponds themselves, only one yielded a beaver. He put the last two traps in the burlap bag and put the beaver and fox up on the pack frame along with the other animals he had caught.

The mare had become accustomed to the smell of dead

animals on its back and just plodded along as he pulled on the rope lead. He guessed from the position of the sun that he would get back to camp before noon. Upon entering the clearing where he had set up camp, he felt a strange presence. The burlap sacks hanging in the trees had a hole in the bottom of them as if made by a knife, blood dripping on the snow. The coffee pot had been turned over, but his skins were all there and some of his supplies were scattered around the campsite. The dog was now facing outward; he checked on her, finding that her bandages and the moss pack had been changed. Someone had definitely been in the camp, but who?

He picked up the supplies, took the coffee pot down to the stream for some water and noticed unshod hoof prints in the soft mud on the opposite side of the creek. *Indians, definitely indians,* he said to himself. After he got the fire going again and set the pot on the stones, he dumped one fistful of coffee grounds in it; he took the dead animals off the pack frame and then led the mare over to the fenced area.

Next he took the rope halter and pack frame off the mare before setting her free; Misty was in the back of the arroyo minding her own business. He took the dead animals and laid them out one by one. He'd start on the beaver, then the fox and finally the rabbits and martens.

In the two weeks that he had been in this area, he had one grizzly, one elk, thirteen beaver, six red fox, twenty-two rabbits, twenty marten skins, and a few squirrels.

Not too bad for a first time out, he thought. He took stock of everything and on one of the travois that was going to be pulled by the gelding he would put the dog, the Sharps, and basic supplies on it; the second travois that the mare would pull would have the skins, the burlap sacks and the rest of the supplies.

Later that afternoon he decided to do a little more panning up in the arroyo where the horses were. He made sure that the dog was alright before he grabbed his Winchester, the frying pan and coffee cup, and climbed into the makeshift corral. He walked about 100 feet and went to the opposite side of the creek where he had a good view of the campsite. The high side of the arroyo was at his back, giving him protection from the wind. He wanted to see if this side of the creek yielded any gold like what he found on the opposite side of the creek in the morning.

He set down the same rabbit skin on his left side like he had earlier, laid the rifle next to his right just in case he needed it, and started to pan for gold. After forty minutes or so, he had slightly more than what he had found earlier. He continued for the next hour or so before the sun's rays were throwing shadows of the mountains. Soon it would be too dark to see.

When he finished, he had a small child's fist amount of gold dust and flakes. He tied up the rabbit skin with a small piece of rawhide and put the pouch back in his jacket pocket for safekeeping. He stretched before walking down to where he could cross the creek and set everything behind Molly. He took the oat and rye mix, the remainder of old shirt and a brush from his saddlebags. He called to the horses and they came up to the fence where he had poured the oat and rye mix on the ground in two piles, before he climbed in with them to rub each one down with the remainder of the old shirt and then curried both horses. He climbed out and made sure the rails were in place and set the empty sack, old shirt and brush in the lean-to. Once he finished doing that, he took some of the fresh rabbit meat, skewered it on several small branches, placed them over the fire, took one of the two cans of beans he had left and, after using his knife around the edge, he bent back the top of the can and set it on the coals to heat.

While his food was cooking, he cleaned up the area around the campsite and stacked all the hides on one side of the lean-to. When supper was ready, he found a comfortable place to sit and using the frying pan as his plate, he ate the skewered meat and the beans he had poured into the pan. He drank his coffee, staring into the campfire. Molly was certainly better than she was in the morning. Todd made the same mush that he had made for her that morning. She ate it, licked her lips and looked at Todd as if to say, *That's it! What else is there to eat? I'm starving.*

Todd cut up two squirrels and set it before her, she gobbled it up in no time; again she looked at him and he said, "So you're going to eat me out of house and home are you? That's okay this time, but the next serving is your last until tomorrow morning." She let out a sigh as he placed the new meat in front of her and she ate all but one small slice of the squirrel meat. She drank more water than he had ever seen her drink at any time previously. When she was done, he scratched behind her ears before she drifted off to sleep. He looked at her guessing that she was dreaming about her nice soft bed back at the cabin. As a matter of fact Todd could hardly wait until he got back to his bed. It had been a very long day and he decided to turn in.

In the morning, he walked out of the Valley of the Three Pines leading the two horses. After a few hours he knelt by a stream to give the horses a chance to graze and drink for a few minutes. He took a cup and poured water from his canteen into it to give to Molly and a couple pieces of jerky he took from his saddlebag for him and her; he refilled the canteen in the stream.

He removed his bandanna and put it in the clear running water to wash his face off before starting on their journey once again. As he kneeled down, he noticed unshod hoof prints on the other side of the creek bed not more than a couple of hours old. He also noticed gold dust flakes along the edge of the creek.

Maybe we should hole up here for the night, they had been walking/riding almost non-stop since early morning and it would put some distance between him and whatever Indians were out ahead of him. For a diversion,he could do a little panning after he made camp and settled in for the night. He led the horses to a stand of pine just up a draw from where they were. He unhitched the travois of each horse, gently lowering the one with the dog on it first; next he hobbled both horses so they could graze and drink from the stream. He went about gathering deadfall to make a campfire, dug a firepit and ringed it with stones; he got his bedroll and three blankets, one each for the horses and one for himself. Being out in the open like they were, it was going to get cold during the night.

He used the pan for frying his meat like he did at his last campsite and after eating, he cleaned it before he started to pan for gold. After a couple of hours or so, he had about a half thimbleful of gold dust, just enough to buy things he really needed, not relying so much on the fur trade for his livelihood.

He marked this area on the map the best he could so that when he came back this way he could do some more panning, maybe even a little trapping, especially with the signs he was seeing. He wrapped the gold dust in another rabbit skin, took the one from his jacket pocket and put them both in his saddlebag for safekeeping. By the time he had settled in for the night he was tired, but not exhausted. Molly was showing signs of improvement, no more labored breathing and was eating well; before they set out in the morning, he'd change the moss patch and her bandage. As with every night since the incident, Todd looked up into the clouds passing through on an otherwise crystal clear sky and thanked the *Lord* for making her well. He took the first watch, while Molly and the Lord had the second.

-17-

Having been back for three weeks, Todd was already making plans for his next trip up toward the lake he found on the high plateau. Molly, though walking stiffly, was trying her best to chase the squirrels that scurried between the trees that were prevalent on the west side of the cabin. They teased the dog as she stumbled in the snow trying to catch them. They jumped from tree to tree; she tried her best to catch the quick-footed squirrels.

Todd took to sitting on the back porch almost daily whittling on a stick and staring out over the land that surrounded the cabin and up towards the snow-crested Tetons. He finally had come to the realization that he had made the right decision to stay in this area. Someday he'd make his way to the Yellowstone wilderness, but for the time being he was content to have what he had. In eight days, it would be Christmas and he was looking forward to having dinner with the miners and with Moon. They would swap stories, drink corn whiskey, and enjoy a meal and the camaraderie.

He remembered when he finally got back after his first trip; he found Moon sitting on the porch waiting for his return and upon seeing Todd said, "Good that you come back, storm come soon and cover everything in a mantle of white so that

Mother Earth can sleep." He stayed to have supper and as Todd was cooking, Moon said, "My Christian name is John; my full Indian name is Moon on Sky. You can call me by either name."

"Moon, I appreciate all that you have taught me and I thank you for taking care of my horse and cabin while I was away." Moon nodded in agreement. They ate bear steak with sliced potatoes, wild mushrooms, and drank black coffee. After supper, Todd gave him a burlap sack full of bear meat and bear claws from the skinned carcass saying, "I promised you that if I shot one I would give you meat and claws."

"And I thank you for remembering about the bear claws." Before leaving Moon checked on the wounded dog and said, "You did good, dog heal well."

During the week that followed, Todd built a storage cache between four pines near the rear of the cabin. Crude as it was, it would hold the skins and meat of any animal that he shot or caught; he had put the skins on one side and the meat on the other. When he had finished moving the skins around, he descended to the ground and carried the crude ladder over to the side of the barn and hung it on the spikes he had driven into the barn wall that faced the corral.

He had thought about constructing a small shed next to the cabin where he could work on preparing the skins before he eventually traded them at the fort. For the time being, he would use the table that he built next to the porch before taking them up to the cache for safe keeping. In the cabin, he worked on putting in a trap door to cover the hole he was digging underneath the floor. He dug a four foot by six foot hole and lined it with thin logs from a locust tree he had cut down earlier. He wanted to use it as a root cellar for the garden he planned on having come spring and as a place to hide the gold that he had found. Playing it safe, he didn't mention the gold to Moon or the miners.

The day he was to have dinner with them it began to snow. He put Molly in the barn with the horses and promised to bring her back some food scraps left over from the dinner and closed the barn door. He put just a saddle blanket on the back of the mare and used a rope halter as he rode down to the miner's cabin. Remembering that he forgot his rifle, he returned to his cabin and retrieved it, shut the door behind him and started back the way he had come. He put the mare in the Langstrom's barn before walking over to the cabin, knocked on their door and wiped his feet before entering. He had brought wild mushrooms and onions to the dinner, Moon brought potatoes and corn from his root cellar and the miners contributed an elk roast, sourdough biscuits, coffee, and corn whiskey. He put the mushrooms and onions in a large skillet, put in some lard and turned them over three or four times until they developed a light brown coating over them, then poured them into a bowl before setting it on the table. The others put out the foods that they had contributed and took their seats at the table. Grace was said and they began to pass around the bowls and plates of food amongst themselves. They talked while they ate.

The miners said that they were all friends growing up in the coal fields of Southwest Pennsylvania. The only way to make a living was to go into the coal mines like their grandfather's, fathers, uncles, and older brothers had. They all made a pact that one day they would leave and travel as far away as possible and make a new life for themselves. They traveled by train as far as they could to the border of Wyoming and

Nebraska. They bought two mules to carry their supplies and three horses to get them to the California gold fields. It was late September by the time they came to the foothills of the Tetons and found that the passes they needed to go over were already closed because of snow similar to what Todd had recently encountered.

They came upon this flat land where they met Moon. He told them they would not make it over the mountains given the time of the year. They staked a claim on about 100 acres, had it recorded and built a barn where their horses and mules would be out of the elements; they slept in the loft until they built a cabin. But soon found that it was too small for the three of them, so they built a larger one next to the first one. They used the first cabin for the supplies they had brought with them and for the things they traded for at the fort.

When spring came, they started going into the foothills of the Tetons to look for gold and noticed a small cavern off to one side of the trail. It was getting late in the day so they decided to stay in the cavern for the night. It would offer them some protection from the biting cold wind that blew down off the mountain tops. Inside the cavern there was a little creek with gold along its edges. Using a rock hammer, they chipped away at the wall where the water was coming out of and after several days found a gold seam. The more they chipped away, the more they found. So far it has yielded around 200 pounds of gold.

When they were exhausted, they boarded up the entrance and piled rocks on the outside of the boards to make it look as natural as they could. They'd come back to the cabins to rest and stash their gold ore. Once every three months they took the ore to Lander because that was the closest assayer's office. Their goal is to go on to California some day, but for the time being they are content to stay right where they are.

Two of the miners, Gus and Turk, were brothers, and the third one was Pete Boyd, a friend of theirs. They have searched other areas not too far from the cabins, but none of them has been as plentiful as the first one they found. One time when they went to Lander they took the time to file on the mining claims on the land that surrounded the areas they had mined so far. When they first arrived here, Moon had a small one-room cabin back in the woods. He kept to himself, but if they needed information or help, he was always available. They didn't realize he was an Indian until one time when they were being bothered by a small band of Cheyenne.

Early in the fall a few braves came to call, so to speak. Moon On Sky was talking with the three of them and told the braves, "Leave this place and leave these men alone. If you return, I will kill all of you in your sleep."

"Ever since then we've not been bothered by the Cheyenne, Sioux or the Shoshone," Gus remarked; Moon only nodded.

Turk added, "On a supply trip to the fort we found out that Moon, was a shaman or holy man from a tribe that left these mountains long ago. It's good that Moon has now taken you under his tutelage; he is a good teacher."

Todd told his stories of working for the Cooper Brothers at Timber Creek Ranch east of Green Springs.

Pete asked him, "Did you ever find any gold there?"

"To be quite honest with you, I never had an inclination to look for it and even if I did, I probably would have turned it over to my boss who owned 2800 acres."

As the afternoon wore on, the stories got longer and the men all got sleepier. Before it got too late, Todd decided he'd better get back to his cabin, take care of his animals and wait out the storm. The brothers wanted him to stay, but he begged off. He took some table scraps with him to give to Molly. After handshakes all around, he bundled up and went out into the cold and snow which had gotten much deeper. He went to the barn and got the mare ready for their trip back to the cabin.

It was slow going as snow drifts were beginning to form along the trail. Eventually, he saw his cabin in sight and made it to the barn door which was open as the snow was piling around it. He found Molly had been knocked out and his roan horse was missing. He put the mare in her stall, gathered up Molly and carried her to the porch, where he found his cabin door wide open with snow blowing inside of it. He put Molly by the fireplace and used the small shovel to get the snow out of the cabin before shutting the door. The storm blew itself out after two days and as Moon had predicted, the land looked like the winter coat on a rabbit, soft and full.

Mother Earth would have plenty of time to sleep and rejuvenate herself. He tended to Molly much the same way he did after she was mauled. It was as if someone wanted him to suffer and not have anything that he loved around, it made no sense at all. After a week or so, he went down to see the miners and Moon to let them know what had happened. Moon thought that perhaps a curse had been put on him, but if that was true, then why were the miners missing tools and odds and ends from the barn. No, someone had a reason to harass everyone who lived in this part of the valley. *Who is doing this and and why?* Todd thought to himself.

-18-

He went to Bear Creek Valley and had much success; finding gold at nearly every stream or creek that he came across, not a large amount, but enough to keep him wanting to find more every time he picked a new place to trap. He was becoming fairly adept at using snares for the rabbit and marten, as well as the steel traps for the beaver or red fox, even an occasional wolf, though they were elusive. He particularly liked this new area and even went so far as building a small lean-to in one of the draws facing south for warmth during the day.

If anyone was riding through the area and looked up they'd never notice the lean-to and that was just the way he wanted it. The draw went higher into the timberline than most and it had good protection from the harsh northwest winds or the crosswinds that occurred every now and then. There was good grass for the horses, a constant flow of water trickled down the stone face next to a cave where he could take the horses and Molly for shelter from the summer thunderstorms that blew up occassionally out of nowhere. The four of them were a team, each playing an important role in making each trip a success. Once spring arrived, he would go to the land office in Lander and file a land claim on the abandoned cabin and fifty acres that surrounded it that he had taken over and fixed up to be his own.

No one had come to claim it in all the time he'd been there. Next, he'd file a mining claim on as many places that he could, especially on the arroyo and on this draw here in Bear Creek Valley. His chances of getting all the streams were slim, but none the less, he would try. He thought about the last incident with the dog and the way his cabin had been ransacked. Once trapping was finished, figuring that two more trips should do it, he would take the time to find out who was doing it and why, but for the time being it would just have to be a sore point left unresolved.

He was cleaning his weapons one night after a successful day of trapping when he heard a horse nicker and his horses nickering back. He blew out the candle on the crude table he had built and grabbed his coat and carbine before slipping out of the lean-to into the blackness of the night of the surrounding forest. He followed the sounds and hoped he could see whoever it was that came calling so late at night. Peering through the trees he counted eight… no make that ten mounted riders wearing buckskin or a serape[18] riding single file down through the trees on the leeward side of the mountain in the moonlight toward the valley below. Each had a bow with a full quiver of arrows and each horse had a brand on it, two with TC on their flanks. He was very familiar with that brand; after all, he put it on nearly all the horses at Timber Creek Ranch at one time or another. He guessed he was at least ninety miles or more from there.

Who are they? he thought to himself. Just to make sure, He

---

[18] Serape - https://en.wikipedia.org/wiki/Serape

stayed in the thick forest cover out of sight until the riders had passed into the night. As the cold seeped into his bones, he began to shiver before going back to the lean-to once they were gone. Either they didn't hear the horses nickering or passed it off as one of their own, or there was no need for them to investigate if anyone else was up in the draw. He could only hope that none of them accidentally stepped on one of his traps or there'd be hell to pay.

He lit the candle on the table and found Molly laying in the corner, all curled up looking at him as if to say *you woke me, let me go back to sleep* and with that suggestion, he shucked off his boots, blew out the candle and got into his makeshift sleeping bag. He pulled the bear skin that he brought with him up to where only his head was showing and soon fell asleep.

Molly woke early and pushed the door with her muzzle and went outside to do her business. When she came back in, she nudged his hand that was hanging over the edge of the bed, but he didn't move so she went back to her corner to wait for him to wake up. Feeling a queasiness in his stomach, he rose quickly and managed to get past the doorway before vomiting his dinner and breakfast from the day before. He broke out in a cold sweat and had the dry heaves. He grabbed some snow to wipe his face and stumbled back into the lean-to where he grabbed his canteen to take some water to wash out his mouth of the foul taste and spit it on the dirt floor. With his last breath, he said to Molly, "You're on your own girl" before passing out on top of the bearskin.

She came over and nudged his hand again; it was limp. She lay next to him and he stirred a couple of times, took some water from the canteen and fell back to sleep. The fever in his body raged on until his fever finally broke around mid-afternoon two days later. He started in with the chills again and his stomach churned but he had no desire to eat or drink anything other than a few sips of water. If he could teach Molly how to fill the canteen, stoke a fire and make some coffee then everything would be just fine. He was using an outside fire pit to cook his food and keep the coffee hot, but until he felt well enough, cold biscuits, jerky and water would have to be the staples he'd live off of. He thought about his traps, but they too would have to wait, as well. His only concern was to get well enough to get back to the traps, pack up and head back home. This trip was turning into a long ordeal, much longer that he had anticipated.

I t took Todd the better part of a week to accomplish what normally would've taken him two days at most. He was still weak and even though he had a fire to keep him warm, heat his biscuits and coffee, he could barely move around. His joints ached, stomach still felt queasy, he just wasn't his usual self. He walked slowly in his snowshoes to each place he could remember where he put his snares and found only four martens; the other snared animals had been eaten by larger animals or birds of prey. The next day he tended to his steel traps which yielded only four beaver, no red fox, but at least he was able to retrieve them. Once he got back to the lean-to he sat on a blanket against the leanto as the sun filtered through the trees and he went about skining the martens, but barely had enough strength to do that. The beaver would just have to wait until he got back home. It was all he could do given how he felt.

It took him four days to get back to the cabin and even after he got there, it took him almost a full day to get everything off the pack horse. He managed to put the horses in their stalls, fill their feed buckets, and put fresh water in their troughs, then close and latch the barn door. He brought the beavers that needed skinning and the skins from the red foxes, wolf, rabbit and marten into the cabin with him. He would just have to work on them inside or on the table that was outside next to the porch and eventually he'd get them up into the cache. The cache was getting full of skins, so many in fact, that he would have to store any more inside the cabin. He desperately needed a better place where he could work on his skins so that he would get the highest price for them when he went to the trading post. As much as he needed to go out at least one, possibly two more times, he decided to stay at the cabin until he felt much better.

He went to see Moon several days after he got back. He asked what herbs he could use so if he got sick again, he could feel better. Moon told him to use a mixture of garlic, goldenseal, catnip, and thyme for fever; chew on ginger root to control any vomiting and he promised to give Todd enough for his next trip. In the spring, Moon would show him where to find them in the forest so that he could pick his own. Over the next several days he skinned the beavers and buried the meat and bones as far from the cabin that he could to keep any predators away from the homestead. He was sure the smell of the hides would attract animals like the wolf, but he had no choice. When he felt stronger, he climbed the ladder to the cache and moved the skins around, packed the nooks with the rabbit and marten, always the skinned side out to protect the fine soft white fur of the rabbit and the light tan or russet fur of the marten. He bundled the other skins and made room for his new skins. He took a few days to do homestead chores; he mucked out the stalls and spread the mixture of manure and straw on the plot of land that he intended to plant vegetables in during the spring and early summer. Next he staked out a twenty acre plot for a hayfield; he was going to seed half of the field in timothy and rye; the other half in rye and buckwheat just like the Coopers did. They always swore the combination of grains gave the horses a finer coat and they were healthier. He hadn't planned on raising horses, but he wanted his livestock to have every advantage they could. This was rough country up here in the foothills of the Tetons and the land provided good grass, but there never seemed to be enough of it.

He sat on the porch everyday to absorb the heat from the sun. As he got stronger he played tag with Molly, but wondered if he'd ever get his full strength back.

Three weeks later, though not fully recovered, he had to leave on his next trip. He packed snowshoes, and he was taking the mare and the dog. He would leave the other horse with Moon. He made sure he had enough provisions to last four weeks, hoping this would be the last time he'd have to go out. He made a saddle pack with food in it for Molly that he could strap on her back. His own backpack would be full of herbs, extra clothes, and ammunition for both the rifle and the Sharps, three blankets, two for him and the other one to put over the mare on the coldest of nights. In addtion, he brought a camp ax, and a small bundle of kindling that he had cut just for this trip. The backpack would weigh close to sixty pounds after he got everything in it. He had no choice in the matter, he needed to make sure he had enough food.

He made two dozen sourdough biscuits from the sourdough starter that the miners had given him. He also packed four pounds of coffee, a small tin of salt, enough jerky to last a month, especially when he had a cold camp, a dozen cans of beans, a half-dozen cans of peaches, two quart size canteens, a frying pan, Dutch oven and his small coffee pot. There wasn't much left in the cabin by the time he got done. He also made sure that he brought a pointed shovel and tied it on top of the frame after tying on the sack of snares he had made. He also took four each of the small and large steel traps, a bag of oats for the mare, and lastly, he would cover everything with a tarp that he had cut from a bigger one that he would drape over the supplies.

He planned on going east this time to a new valley; it would take him three days to walk there and a like amount of time to return home. That left about three weeks to get all his trapping done. He made his evening meal and fed Molly. When he was done, he cleaned up after himself and was soon asleep as the fire dwindled in the fireplace to a rich gold and blue flame. As he snuggled deeper under his elk blanket, he dreamt of being in a field full of wild flowers, having a picnic with a woman who came into his life. She had brown hair and her smile and laugh were infectious as they sat and talked with each other.

$$-20-$$

The weather did not cooperate. It took Todd an extra day to get to the valley. He had been hoping to bag an elk, their hides would be full, heavy, and enriched with color and their meat would be tasty with lots of protein. Also, the miners and Moon would appreciate any extra meat that he brought back with him. He found a draw up near the ridgeline with good cover and a small stream still running under a thin icy coating. He cut numerous spruce trees and assembled them into an adequate, but small leanto on the south facing side of the hill. When it was done he began cutting out blocks of snow and built a snow wall around the campsite that kept out most of the wind and blowing snow.

The deadfall that he found was enough to sustain him for a week; but he would have to find more. He built a fire for warmth, his supper and to keep his coffee hot. He had snared a rabbit and after skinning it, cut off the head and cleaned out the guts, then set it in the Dutch oven along with three carrots, one potato and a fist full of string beans and heaped snow into the pot, replaced the lid and set it in the middle of the fire. Using his shovel, he put the hot coals on top of the cover to help in the cooking of his dinner. There were no stones to encircle his campfire as they were under the stream's icy mantel, so he set aside thick branches that he could use behind the campfire to deflect the heat toward him and away from the snow.

He packed the coffee pot with snow and added a fistful of coffee grounds on top of it before setting it next to the Dutch oven. He waited for it to boil and poured himself a cup to keep his insides warm, if only for a short time. It was getting colder and the snow continued to pile up. He shouldn't have waited so long to get back out once again to do his trapping, but what choice did he have? Trapping was new to him and if he had bothered to ask, he would have found that the weather up here in the mountains was as unpredictable as a sudden rain squall down on the valley floor during the summer months.

He would still have to break the stream ice in several places from time to time so that the mare could drink and he could fill his canteens. He hoisted the grain bag and the bag with his food supplies up in a forty foot lodgepole pine near the campsite out of the way of hungry critters while the rest of the supplies he put in the lean-to and would tell Molly to guard when he left the campsite. He set a biscuit on the cover of the coffee pot to heat. After he finished eating his dinner, he opened a can of peaches for a treat. He brought a blanket for Molly and folded it and set it on the outer edge of the lean-to. She in turn would get what heat there was from a dying campfire and he could put his feet next to her so she'd keep them warm while he was sleeping. While he was lying there he laced his fingers behind his head and admired a beautiful sunset of purple and gold with thin, wispy clouds that blew from west to east before falling asleep.

It had been six days now and he had trapped four wolves and six red foxes. He had seen many elk tracks, but they were being elusive like the wolf was at his last campsite. One morning he decided that he would hunt for elk as he was getting low on meat for himself and Molly, and to set traps for larger game animals. He wanted to be in the area where he had seen all the elk tracks before the elk started moving during the day.

As his eyes became adjusted to the early morning light, he fanned the kindling using his hat and before long there was a blaze where he could heat up a couple of biscuits and the coffee pot. He needed some substance that would keep the adrenaline rushing through his body until at least midday. He took two biscuits, three strips of jerky, a full canteen, hunting knife, two ropes and the Sharps with extra cartridges with him.

He picked a likely site where two pines had fallen crosswise on each other. The one in the front for resting his rifle and the one on his right to block the wind blowing down over the hill. Just before daybreak his plans paid off. A bull elk, three cows and two calves were eating the first tender shoots of the aspen and white birch. To his advantage, the snow had ringed the clearing enough to thwart their escape other than a well-worn trail deep into the forest off to their left. He hoped that they wouldn't panic after the first shot, and he'd get his opportunity to shoot more than one, otherwise he would have to make a choice between a cow or the bull and hope for the best shot.

Taking his time, he aimed at the cow farthest from the bull and fired, dropping her where she stood as if frozen in time; he quickly reloaded, but to his surprise the bull turned and charged in his direction. He'd have to make a frontal shot, something he hadn't done since the war. After the first shot, the bull just kept coming, he chambered a second cartridge and fired; the bull was still charging toward him as he thought to himself *It just can't be, I know I hit him just at ear level, he should be dead.* He chambered another cartridge and waited for what seemed like an eternity for the bull to get closer; he adjusted his sight only slightly before squeezing the trigger. The bull fell less than twenty feet in front of him, still snorting, blowing air and blood out of his nostrils onto the snow. The remaining elk scattered except one of the calves. The one shot that Todd thought was the kill shot only grazed the bull's shoulder and killed the calf. If he had his druthers, he certainly wouldn't have wanted the calf killed. He quickly skinned out the bull, then the cow. He used the ropes he had brought and hung their carcasses in the trees; he half carried, half dragged the calf back to camp hanging it up in one of the trees. He walked back to the kill site and cut limbs from an aspen and made a travois out of the bull's hide and put the cow on it along with the bull's head, slung the Sharps over his head so that it lay across his shoulder blades and pulled the travois back to the camp. After nearly five hours of trudging back and forth, he had everything back in camp. He'd rest a bit before he took to skinning and cutting the meat up guessing that it would take him the rest of the day and well into the night. He made quick work with the boning knife and the Bowie as he cut the meat into steaks and roasts, separating them into different burlap sacks and hoisting them up into the trees. He took some of the neck meat and fed it to Molly. Too bad the mare wasn't carnivorous so she could also share in the spoils. As much as he hated it, he would cut up the calf and use the meat from it to keep him and Molly fed for the next several days.

He had to do something with what remained. Some of it he would use as bait for trapping the wolves and foxes; the rest he would have to take up into the timberline near the mountain ridges and bury it in deep snow hoping it would be springtime before a mountain lion or grizzly found the remains.

After several more days of successful trapping, Todd decided he would leave the day after next for his trip back home. He hadn't done any panning for gold because the stream was frozen over. He decided one morning to go up into the hills behind the camp and see what he could find, maybe an old mine or a cave that for many decades, lay hidden from most everyone except the Indians and the old time mountain men. Since he never expected any trouble, he had the misfortune of having left behind his rifle and only carried his pistol with him. He slung a canteen over one shoulder and put a small miner's chisel into his belt that held up his holster. He strapped on his snowshoes for the trek up the hill. About midway, a shadow passed over the space in front of him, but by the time he looked up it was gone. He walked slowly from west to east, down a small slope into a bowl shaped area about 100 feet across.

He spied what he thought was a cave or at least an opening between two huge boulders. He walked straight ahead, stumbled and came face to face with what looked like a man, old, scraggly, lots of unkempt hair, more beast than human. *A bear, perhaps* he thought. He neither spoke nor used sign; he just kept staring straight ahead and grunted something unintelligible. He had a look on his face of worry or at the very least, afeared.

The man-bear reached out to grab Todd, but he pulled back, afeared, gasping for air, back against the opening in the rocks from which he came, only to stumble again, trying to get away, when he stopped abruptly. He looked up to see a mountain lion staring down at both of them. He drew his pistol, but the man-bear might think he was going to kill him, so he just pointed. The man-bear turned about the same time the mountain lion leapt off the boulders straight for both of them. In a split second, he fired his weapon; after that, it was all a blur.

He eventually woke though his brain must have thought hours. It had turned colder and no sunlight shone where it had been just a few minutes before. He found himself in a cavern and looked up in a daze where he saw spires upside down dripping water. He turned his head sideways and through a fine veil of mist he saw a flame and became instantly afraid. He heard the sound of rushing water as it cascaded down the wall of granite opposite of where he was lying. The man-bear was sitting near the entrance to the cave with a threadbare blanket around his shoulders holding Todd's pistol.

Todd tried to sit up, but just couldn't seem to get his bearings, better to lie on the ground until his body caught up with his brain or vice versa. After an hour or so, he sat up and a hand offered him a cup of hot, steamy liquid which he cradled in his hands for warmth and slowly sipped it. The liquid tasted sweet, almost like warm milk and honey, but there was no cow, goat or beehive around to afford such a luxury.

The man spokefirst. "Name Henry, I smelt your meat hanging in my trees. What you want in my home?"

Todd though still a bit groggy, but he had the presence of mind to say, "I, I mean you no harm, Henry," before he lay back down and fell into a deep asleep.

-21-

While Todd was dreaming vapors and smells were wafting through the air. His senses were telling him to wake up. He looked around the room he was in and it became clear that he indeed was finally home. His traps were in one corner next to his skins, a fireplace with a low burning fire with a whiff of coffee in the air, a fur-like object lying in front of it. He slowly sat up to find Moon On Sky sitting in the chair nearest the fireplace whittling on a stick, while Molly raised her head from napping in front of the fireplace to look at him. Todd was thirsty and found his canteen hanging on the bedpost. He pulled the cork out and drank heartily for what seemed like forever. Afterward, he asked Moon, "How did I get here?"

"I found the door open three days ago, you were lying on top of your cot, your supplies were placed inside the cabin in neat order; the mare was in its stall and Molly was patiently waiting for you to wake up."

"The last thing I remember I was in a cave in the mountains. I guess the old man must have brought me here after…"

Moon replied, "After what?"

"I don't exactly know what to say, it is like everything was surreal."

"Perhaps you had a vision and the Indian spirits brought you back here."

"Perhaps. I remember falling back to sleep after having drunk sweet milk and honey next to a fire pit. Maybe I did have a vision, but I really don't remember anything after drinking that liquid."

He steadied himself as he got up and walked over to where Moon and Molly were, bent down and patted the dog's head. He went to the fireplace, took a cup from the mantle and poured himself a cup of hot, steamy coffee. He wanted to tell Moon everything that happened, but he was still too groggy and decided to wait until he had his thoughts together. Perhaps Moon could sort it all out for him.

Moon said he would stay one more day just to make sure Todd was alright and then he would go home and enjoy an elk steak. Todd wondered how Moon had gotten elk meat, but for the time being he would leave that question alone. After he had the coffee, he needed to relieve himself in the worst way and excused himself, saying, "I'll be right back," and ran like he was on fire to the outhouse. His insides were burning and as he releived himself it burned on the way out of his body. He sat there thinking, *I don't want whatever bothered me the last time, nor do I want to vomit again, but these episodes have got to stop.*

He slowly made his way back to the cabin, sat on the edge of his bed for a few moments before he said, "Moon, I think I will lie down for a while, I don't feel so good."

"You don't look so good. I will take care of the animals while you sleep."

Moon took Molly outside to run and play in the snow. He had already put the horses in the pasture. He went to the creek, filled the canteens, got two buckets of fresh water for the water troughs in the barn, then refilled one and brought it inside the cabin.

Moon lowered one of the burlap sacks hanging from a tree, took out two elk steaks and brought them inside to cook later. Next he got the horses back in their stalls, gave them feed and fresh hay after having already filled their water troughs, scratched each behind their ears, walked out of the barn, and latched the door behind him.

He found Molly sniffing a pile of snow near a tree; up popped a rabbit and sent the dog chasing it all over creation, but as usual she didn't catch it and came dejectedly back and looked up at him as if to say, *That rabbit is just too fast for me.* Moon just looked down at the dog and said, "Try harder next time." He threw a stick for her to fetch, and after several times she came back panting, dropped the stick at his feet. Moon laughed as he walked over to the steps. In the meantime, Molly ran over to the bushes, did her business, returned, and raced up the steps into the cabin where she took her spot in front of the fireplace once again.

Before long, Moon had two potatoes roasting on the coals of the fire; next he took one of the frying pans and scooped out some fat that was kept in a crock on the dry sink and put the two steaks in the pan along with some spring onions and a pinch of salt and cooked them slowly on the edge of the fire; he had cut off the ends on both steaks and cut it into chunks to feed to the dog along with a bowl of fresh water.

The aroma of the sizzling steak and onions woke Todd. He sat up slowly, rubbed his eyes, scratched his armpits under his deerskin shirt before shuffling his way over to the table and sat down. Moon had set the frying pan in the middle of the table before putting a baked potato on each plate and put the coffee pot next to the frying pan. They both ate hungrily, while Molly finished the last of her elk meat. Todd got up and went to sit by the edge of the fireplace while Moon cleared everything from the table, then took his seat in the rocker. They just sat for a while, sipping their coffee before Todd said, "Thank you for fixing dinner."

"You're welcome."

"I need to tell you a story and perhaps you can figure it out for me." He told Moon everything that had happened from the time he got to the valley in the east until he passed out in the cave.

Moon just stared into the flames, but didn't say anything for a long time. Finally he spoke. "Many moons ago, I was on a spiritual journey that took me to the mountains. I was looking for a place to find the vision of what I would do with my life once the Sioux had killed my wife, sons, and many friends. I came upon a small cave in which I could talk with the spirits. In the cave was a man-bear who was afeared. We eventually became friends. The bear and Mother Earth are partners when one must travel on such a long journey. I feel that you also met man-bear and he gave you his Christian name so that you could understand what he was telling you. It was he who brought you here and in your dreams he gave you a vision on what to do. The mountain lion was a challenge for you. Your conscious self told you to make a choice, while your vision told you how to handle danger when confronted. The man-bear guarded you from the lion, you did not see whether he had killed the lion or if the lion just ran away once the man-bear became your protector. The liquid you drank helped you from choking and stopped fluids from going into your lungs. You were probably sick when you came to that place and he made the liquid for you. It does not matter where he got it or how he made it. You will remember eventually what vision he gave you on what you are to do with the rest of your life."

"I just knew you could show me the meaning of my story."

Moon just nodded. It was getting late and both of them were tired. Todd offered Moon the cot on which he had been sleeping, but Moon declined, saying, "I sleep on the fine bear rug, the dog will keep my feet warm."

-22-

With the advent of spring, Todd could feel the warmth from the sun, and the lengthening of the days. He observed the birds singing in the trees and building nests for their new families. He too was waiting in great anticipation, so that he could finally travel to the fort and trade-in his furs. Afterwards he would travel to Lander to file a land claim on the cabin and the other properties he wanted and have the gold assayed that he had found.

He kept wondering who the 'man-bear' really was and vaguely remembered his name, was it Harry or Henry? That part he couldn't remember. If he traveled back to that same valley again, he would have to try and find him once again to thank him for his kindness.

He had taken to walking great distances with and without Molly. Ever since his experience, he wanted to be more attuned with nature and the more he learned, the better he became at it. He learned how the wood thrush made a flute-like sound and when other thrushes joined in, it sounded like only one was singing. He also observed the red fox hiding and marking its food; his bushy tail helped to keep him balanced, much like Todd did when he spread his legs apart for greater stability.

106

He also saw small herds of buffalo, the mainstay for many of the tribes, but the buffalo were disappearing because of over hunting. He vowed to be more conscious of his trapping and not take more than he actually needed to make a living. Looking for gold, however, would become a passion, something he would have to do more of in the late spring, and during the summer months, leaving the trapping for the rest of the year. He also thought about the possibility of raising horses or mules, particularly with the advent of homesteaders moving further west.

On one of his many walks he felt a presence. Upon turning around he saw and heard nothing, just an ever-present feeling. He continued to walk up into the timberline about three miles from his cabin and came upon a swift flowing stream. He bent down to take a drink and saw a reflection in the water. Looking up, high on a butte was an Indian brave sitting atop a beautiful Appaloosa stallion. He had a shield and a lance, but Todd couldn't see his face that clearly and just in the blink of an eye, he was gone. Todd checked his rifle to make sure it was loaded just in case he needed to use it. He was unsure if he should continue up into the forest or make a hasty retreat. Pondering an answer, the horseman who vanished was no more than seventy-five feet in front of him coming down the trail at a slow, but steady gait. Todd tensed, but showed no signs of aggression or fear; instead, he got off the trail and scurried behind some boulders to his left, climbing to the top of one of them to get a better look.

The Indian was well aware of his presence, stopped and turned his horse in the direction where Todd was standing on top of the boulder. The magnificent horse raised and lowered his head several times and pranced from one side to the other, waiting. What seemed like hours actually were only a few minutes, a standoff between the two men. Todd however, didn't feel threatened in any way and raised his hand using the sign of peace and the brave followed suit. The brave swung his leg over the horse's head and laid his shield and lance on the ground next to the horse. Todd clamored down the rock face and set his rifle next to a boulder, before walking over to the brave and extended his hand in friendship. The brave had an amulet similar to one that Shoshone Joe had given Todd, and said, "You are a friend of Joe?"

"Yes, I am his friend."

"I am Walking Many Places, grandson of the great Sioux Chief Sitting Bull.[19] Joe friend to many, both white and Indian. He great warrior once, before the Cheyenne killed his woman and newborn son leaving him for dead. We find him and help him back to health. He repays our tribe with kindness and vows to find those responsible. Did you help him?"

He didn't know exactly what to say so decided to try and change the subject saying, "I bought a dog from him. We have talked about where I came from, who I have seen or who I talk with; he liked me and gave me this amulet to protect me from bad spirits."

"I like you, white man; come to my village with me."

"First I must go to my cabin, feed my horses. I will meet you here when the moon is full and go with you to your village."

"I will meet you near the waterfall of the lonely river in three days."

---

[19] http://www.biography.com/people/sitting-bull-9485326

-23-

When Todd arrived back at his cabin, he put a rope halter on the mare and rode down to Moon's cabin to speak with him about his encounter with Walking Many Places and his invitation to visit the Sioux village.

Moon thought it was a good idea and said, "This is part of your vision, you will learn many things from the Sioux. Be wary, however. In some ways, you are enemy and until they get to know you, they will be suspicious. I will not speak ill of them as they were not the ones who killed my family."

"I will be careful and I will only stay a few days before I return. I will have to leave the horses and Molly, can you stay with them?"

"I like your cabin. Do you still have canned peaches?"

"Yes, I have some peaches, but I need some for myself, don't eat all of them." They both laughed.

"I will be at the cabin the day you leave," Moon replied.

Several days later, Todd rode toward the high ridge just above the Lonely River and was met by two braves. One of them said, "Walking Many Places told us to meet you and bring you to our village; follow us."

While riding along, Todd checked his gun belt to make sure

he had enough ammunition, just in case he had to shoot his way out, but dismissed that thought quickly. They traveled several miles and rode through several fast flowing streams, went through a rocky gorge, and came out into a beautiful valley. In the valley there were at least 100 elk hide and deer skin covered teepees. Off to the left of the village was a large herd of horses. As they made their way down the trail, several women and children stopped what they were doing to see this white man traveling with the two braves, most smiled; some didn't.

He was led to a large teepee where he dismounted and tied his horse to a pole that had been driven into the ground. He was escorted inside and told to sit on the bearskin rug near the fire. One of the braves said, "Walking will be here shortly."

After what seemed like only a few minutes, Walking came in covered with rabbit, marten, and fox skins, some of them dripping with blood, and said to Todd, "You look surprised. I also do some trapping, from time to time and carry the animals back to camp myself, where I skin them. It saves time, and there is no need for a horse. I can move freely, you should try sometime."

"Next time I go trapping I will give it a try. I was surprised to see so many teepees when I arrived here in this beautiful valley. I never noticed this place when I travelled around looking for places to trap."

"This is our summer camp. Our valley was discovered by my forefathers and if you didn't know how to get here, you would not find it. The gorge you came through offers many twists and turns. If you follow the right trail you will come out here, if you don't you will come out to a flat plain with view of mountains and you will not see this valley. Mother

Earth protects her children from unwanted visitors, perhaps at time she did not know you and kept you from finding us. I will speak with my father, Standing Tall, to see if you can come to this valley next winter to do your trapping."

Todd would now have to remember how he got here if permission was granted. Over the next several days he met a great number of people and some of them showed him how to tan hides, scrape hide so it was smooth as silk, and how to make clothing out of deer and elk skins. He was introduced to Walking's sisters, Feather in Air and Bright Star, his mother Dancing Waters, and his father. His father was the chief and was also curious about what he had seen before coming to this area and what he had done during his life so far.

Todd chose his words carefully so that he left a good impression. It seemed like an interview. Walking's father had not yet given permission for this white man to trap in their valley when they were not here. If he didn't give permission and Todd tried to do any trapping in this valley, Indian spirits would make sure he never saw the light of day or he would never leave this valley. If he did grant permission, Todd could only guess how rich he would be from the all the game that lived here. The spirits would protect him as well.

While they were walking along Todd asked him why he had no wife. "My wife died shortly after giving birth to my son and our medicine man could not save her."

"I am sorry to hear and saddened for your loss. Does your son live with you?"

"My mother and sisters take care of him. I see him every day and when he gets older I will show him what he needs to know to be strong, to survive and to prosper, as I have. It saddens me to talk about it and my son will never know his mother, only words will tell him how much she loved him."

Todd pondered what to say next, but decided not to say anything. He changed the subject and started talking about one of Walking's sisters. "Your sister Feather seems happy; Bright Star looks sad."

"My sister Feather is in love, she is to marry my best friend very soon. Bright Star has not yet found anyone and she has become discouraged. Time is on her side; she is young and will eventually find someone to take her for his bride."

Todd knew the loneliness and could understand how she felt. Many a mountain man had taken a squaw, but Todd had never thought of doing so. His was a hard life; taking an Indian wife would make it harder for both. Having Walking and his family as friends was probably the best he could hope for anyway.

Todd spoke and said, "Tomorrow I must return to my home. I have much to do and I hope someday to be able to return the kindness you and your family has shown me."

"Tonight we celebrate your time with us. It is good that you took time to come and be here with us. I hope you learned new things that you can use.

"I did and I appreciate what was taught to me."

The Sioux chief still had not given him permission to hunt or trap in the valley.

Until his furs could be sold at the trading post, Todd would have to borrow a plow from the miner's to till the soil where he wanted to plant a garden and put in a hayfield. He hoped that early spring rains and the summer heat would be enough for an abundant crop. After he tilled the soil, Moon showed him how to plant corn, potatoes, onion sets and other vegetables so that the rabbits and deer wouldn't eat his crops once they started to bloom. He was feeling pretty proud of himself, something that hadn't occurred in a long, long time.

He finally got around to sorting the furs and kept out one of the elk hides to make some clothes and moccasins; he kept the black bear's hide for a rug. All together his total came to one grizzly, eight wolves, two elk, seventeen beaver, twelve red foxes, thirty-five rabbits and twenty-four marten skins. He was guessing that the total dollar amount would come to around $4000. He would take some in trade, some in cash and the remainder he would put in a bank. He would take the gold he found to Lander and have it assayed and would put most of it in a bank. The miners told him that gold sold for around $21.00 an ounce should he ever find any.

He told no one that he did. His main objective was to get

the land title to the property he currently lived on and to make mining claims for the places he marked on his map. Todd remembered the story that Liz had told him about her father when he went to Lander to have his gold turned into money. He would have to hide it well to avoid being robbed, especially after he traded his furs at the trading post. He still didn't trust the sutler. There was something about the man that bothered him. Perhaps it would be wise to have Hanson give him some store credit and get what supplies he really needed before returning to his homestead at the end of the month. Todd's plan was to visit with his friend Crusty after he went to Lander and take the route that Liz showed him so that he could swing by the fort before heading back to the cabin by early summer.

He had also promised the miners that he would get their supplies and in turn, they would let him take one of their horses for a pack animal to get all the furs to the post. He also promised Moon that he would get him some things that he had asked for, especially a case of canned peaches as he had grown fond of them. He would leave the two mares and the miners' gelding at the fort with a list of supplies for himself and the miners.

Now that he had some idea what he wanted to do, he needed to make it that much more urgent to take no more than three weeks to get everything accomplished. He was going to leave the day after tomorrow and asked Moon to stay at the cabin while he was gone, just as a precaution; he would also leave Molly with Moon.

Arriving at the fort early Friday afternoon, he first went to the trading post and was told to bring his furs around to the rear of the building where Hanson would meet him on his back porch and he would look them over. Hanson was impressed with the skins that Todd had brought in and asked, "Where abouts did you say you trapped these here critters?"

"I didn't say nor do I intend to."

"Well, you don't have to get huffy about it. I was just curious."

Todd knew his game, he'd run up against men like him before. Tell him what he wanted to know and the next thing you knew there'd be trappers working for Hanson, taking it all and not leaving an animal in sight to repopulate Mother Earth.

"I'll pay you $3330 for everything." Hanson said with a quirky smile.

Todd replied, "On second thought, I think I will take them to Lander where I know I can get a better price."

He started to put the bundles back on the pack frames when Hanson said, "Maybe I was a bit low on my estimate, let me look them over again. He scratched his beard and separated them into different piles. He wrote down some other figures and said, "$3850, it's the best I can do. Beaver prices are down and the bounty on the wolves is now $25 a piece."

"$3850 and a barrel of dried apples are what I'll take and not a penny less. I want half in cash and the balance in trade."

"You drive a hard bargain, Morgan. But shake on it and it's a done deal."

Todd walked to the end of the porch and grabbed ahold of the post supporting the roof, staring off into space. *Not too bad of a trade, but I have got to make him sweat just a little more before I accept his offer. It's payback for all the bullshit he gave me when I first came to the fort last year.* After several more minutes Todd turned around and looked downcast before he replied, "Deal."

"For a minute there, I thought you were going to turn down that offer, too," Hanson replied.

"Naw, but now I wonder if'n I should'nt have."

"Morgan you are my toughest customer to deal with. I have to make some profit too when I trade them to the furrier. You can certainly understand that, can't you?"

"I am learning that you can't always get what you want, when you want it. I also have a list of supplies from the Langstrom mining camp and from a friend of mine up where I have been living. Would I be able to get them by tomorrow at noon when I plan on leaving?"

"That gives me little time to get it all done by then, how about the day after?"

"Sorry, but I have an appointment that I have to keep. If you can't get it done, I'll just take everything in cash."

"Just leave the pack horses and I'll have everything ready for you by noon tomorrow."

"And you'll get them rubbed down and fed too?" Todd stepped off the porch without waiting for an answer and walked down between the buildings. He could feel the dagger in his back from the look he was sure Hanson was giving him. He grabbed the reins of his horse, walked over to the post commander's office, and tied the horse to a rail. He dusted himself off before he entered the building. Sitting at the desk was the same private who had been promoted to corporal. Looking up he said, "Mr. Morgan, how are you?"

"I'm fine. I see you made corporal since I saw you last."

"Yes, sir, how can I help you?"

"I would like to see the colonel if he is in."

"Sorry, but he's out conducting field maneuvers and he

won't be back for another week or so. Is there any message I can give him."

"No, it isn't all that important. Just tell him I stopped in to see him and I'll stop by another time. Is Sergeant Muldoon still around or did he finally retire?"

"I am sorry to have to tell you this, but he died about two months after you left last year. The malaria and pneumonia got the best of him. We buried him down by the river where he always liked to go when he had time off. We thought it was a fitting place for him."

"Thanks for telling me. Do you think I could stay in the barracks for tonight? I'll be leaving in the morning."

"That won't be a problem. I'll give you a note to take to the sergeant. He'll find an empty bunk for you."

After Todd left the office, he walked over to the stable, put his horse in one of the empty stalls, took off the saddle and blanket. He rubbed the horse down, curried it, gave it some grain from a bin near the wall and got a bucket of water for it to drink from. He picked up his bedroll, saddle bags, and his rifle before going over to the barracks. He gave the sergeant the note and in turn, the sergeant directed him to a cot on the back wall. He stowed his gear under the cot before walking over to the chow hall and paid for a meal. He sat down with some of the other troopers he had met the last time he was here.

After dinner, he took a walk around the inside of the fort. He noticed that some of the buildings had been rebuilt in stone and the old logs were stacked in neat rows by the back wall of the fort; it also appeared that they had started to dig a new foundation for another building, perhaps a new bunkhouse or a hospital, which were both in need of replacing. He decided to stop in and see the post doctor, but he too was on field maneuvers with the commander. He finished his walk and went back to the barracks.

In the barracks there was a friendly poker game going on and he was asked if he wanted to join in. "Don't mind if I do." He sat down and took out some money and started to play. After he yawned several times he said to the men, "Next hand will be my last, I guess I am more tired than I thought I was. I need to get some sleep."

-25-

He rose early on Saturday morning, went to the chow hall and had a hearty breakfast of fried potatoes, ham slices, three eggs, corn bread and coffee. While he was eating, he engaged in small talk with the men at the table. Once he finished with breakfast, he went over to the trading post to see Hanson. "I've had to change my plans and I will be leaving my horses here for a couple of weeks until I return. I will send a telegram to the orderly at the post commander's office to let you know when I will be back to pick up the pack animals. Sorry to make you work so hard on gathering the supplies together."

Hanson just stared at him for a couple of minutes and said, "You have got to be kidding me. I stayed up nearly half the night getting those supplies ready for you and all you can say is I'm sorry. I ought to charge you extra for the time I had to put in getting that order ready for you."

"I said I was sorry, but my plans changed. Haven't you ever had to change your plans after you have thought it out more clearly? Do what you think is fair, even if you have to charge me to restock the items on your shelves. I will see you in about two weeks or so. I still need my money before I leave."

"I don't keep that kind of cash readily available. I can give you a Letter of Credit and you can draw it at the Bank of Lander when you get there."

"I'll need some cash, a couple of hundred ought to do it, then I'll take a notarized letter signed by you and the acting post commander for the balance before I leave around noon."

"I'll have your letter for you." Todd could again feel the daggers in his back as he walked out of the trading post and back to the barracks. Sooner or later he'd have to stop pissing the man off, though for the time being, he was enjoying himself, but those 'daggers' were beginning to dig deeper and itch, as well.

He left after noon chow from the fort as if he was headed toward Lander and as soon as he was out of sight of the fort he reined his horse toward the Wind River. He had decided to go visit Crusty first before travelling to Lander. He hoped that would throw off any would-be robbers that Hanson may have alerted. He was hoping that he would make it to Liz's farm in two days.

Todd made good time the first day, camping near Salt Spring[20] and just to be safe, he decided to have a cold camp. He hobbled the horse and then removed the saddle, blanket and rifle, placing them well up under the overhang. He took two biscuits and some jerky from the saddlebags, grabbed his canteen and sat down underneath a rock overhang. He had just started to doze off when he heard hoof beats on the stone face near the trail about 100 feet or so south of where he was..Quickly he rose and got to Misty before she could whinny and held her head down. He remained as still as possible not

____

[20] Salt Spring – flows into part of the Salt River. https://en.wikipedia.org/ wiki/Salt_River_(Wyoming)

wanting to give away his position. The rider continued on a northwest track passing within a few yards of where Todd was and he caught a slight glimpse of the rider and the horse.

The horse looked familiar, but he couldn't remember where he had seen it before; perhaps if he thought about it for a while it would come to him. After twenty minutes or so everything got quiet again; Todd decided to put a rope around the horse's neck and bring her closer to the outcropping for the night; he would put the hobbles back on just to make sure the horse didn't have other ideas once he fell asleep.

Fortunately, he was headed in the opposite direction of the mysterious rider, but he'd keep his eyes and ears open for any sudden noise or movement. The rider could go in circles hoping to pick up a trail. Waking early, he saddled the horse and decided to travel directly south along the shore of the Wind River to where he thought Liz's place would be. After travelling about five hours, he reined up and dismounted to stretch and to let the horse graze and drink.

He rode another couple of hours and thought he saw someone up near the ridge of where Liz's place should be. *I must be getting paranoid* he thought to himself. *I better get to Liz's place soon, I definitely need a rest.* About three o'clock he saw new fencing almost down to the river and the land had been cleared for a pasture. *This must be the place, but things have surely changed since the last time I was here.*

Reining his horse to the right, he rode up the hilly land and as he neared the top he noticed more clearing going on to the north with men felling trees and east of the barn which was also being enlarged. A rider approached saying, "Saw you coming up the hill, can I help you?"

"I have been looking for the ranch that is owned by Elisabeth

Connolly. Is this it?"

"Could be, who's asking?"

"Names Todd Morgan, I knew her a while back; I was also looking for Crusty, as well."

"Miz Elisabeth is in the barn; Crusty is up in the north pasture, pointing past the barn. "Name is Hackenfield, Josh Hackenfield. Perhaps you've heard of me?"

"Can't say as I have." The young rider looked dejected but the frown quickly faded to a slight smile. "Ride with me up to the barn and we'll see if Miz Elisabeth knows you." Todd was beginning to wonder what in hell's name was going on and why all the secrecy. They rode together for a short time until they came to the barn where both men dismounted. "Just stay here at the hitchin' post and I'll get Miz Elisabeth." Soon afterward, Liz came out and upon seeing Todd threw her arms around him, gave him a hug and a kiss on his cheek. She said to Josh, "You can go back down to where you were when you met this here hombre." She wrapped her arm around Todd's waist and they walked over to the cabin, and said to him, "We were wondering what happened to you. We hadn't heard hide nor hair about you from some of the mountain men that travel through here from time to time. What have you been up to? Can you stay awhile? Crusty will be so glad to see you. We have so much to tell you."

-26-

An hour later, Crusty rode into the yard and noticed a ground-tied horse. After tying off his horse in front of the porch, he heard Liz talking. He opened the door, stared for a few seconds at Todd before he said, "We have been so worried about you. How the hell are you?"

"Nice to see you, too. I have been doing just fine."

Crusty removed his hat and gloves and said, "If you'll excuse me for a minute I need to get cleaned up." Todd had taken a chair by the fireplace while Liz poured him a cup of coffee. She got an empty cup off the mantel and filled it for for Crusty and refilled hers, also.

Crusty came out of a bedroom and said, "So what have you been up to all these months?"

"I was just starting to tell Liz."

When he finished, Crusty said, "That's a lot for one person. You know, if you want, you can come back here. We could sure use a hard working fellow like you."

"I'd like nothing better than to be with both of you, but I'm just getting into the swing of things where I am. I'll think about it, though."

Liz replied, "Why don't the two of you go and get the horses taken care of while I finish making supper." He and Crusty

123

left, slapping each other on the back. Crusty took his horse over to where Todd's was and said, "I didn't recognize the horse when I rode up and upon seeing you sitting here in our home, I was shocked when I walked in the door."

"I'm thankful I had the mare. The roan that I had all those years was stolen out of my barn while I was taking a walk of all things. The roan was getting up there in years, but it was like losing a friend; the mare is slowly getting to know me; she's a good riding horse. We've covered a lot of ground since I started riding her."

Crusty showed him a stall where he could put his horse and indicated the place where to put his saddle, blanket and bridle. Todd wiped down Misty with some fresh straw, curried her, and gave her some grain. Crusty poured fresh water in the trough. She whinnied as if to say, "Thank you."

"You'll be staying in the spare bedroom we just finished building," Crusty said, as he closed the barn door before they walked back to the cabin.

Liz had just finished putting a pot of venison stew on the table along with fresh baked bread, a crock of fresh churned butter, and a pitcher of buttermilk, something she knew Todd probably hadn't had in a very long time. She also took a second covered pot out the door and set it on the side of the porch along with another loaf of bread and rang the dinner bell. The three of them sat down for dinner, Liz said grace before passing out plates with heaping amounts of stew. Todd said, "Why do you put a second pot out on the porch?"

"We make dinner for the ranch hands, ring the bell and one of them comes over and gets the food for the rest of them. There is a bunkhouse behind the barn."

"That's nice of you to do that for them. I sure hope they

appreciate it."

"I'm sure they do and to reciprocate, they do the hunting and help me out in our rather large garden from time to time."

Crusty spoke up saying, "After you left last year, we decided that maybe we should clear timber, build some pastures and get some cattle. So Liz and I rode back to the Henderson Ranch and over to Timber Creek as well. When we got to Henderson's, Mr. Henderson wasn't all that well; seems he was injured when he and some of the others were out rounding up strays. I asked him if we could buy some yearling cattle and a two year old bull from him. He said he'd sell us twenty-five head, but he didn't have a bull. He told me that maybe Charlie Cooper had one. After we visited for a while and picked out the cattle, Mr Henderson asked us to have dinner with him and stay the night.

"The next day, both Liz and I rode over to Timber Creek. Mr. Cooper was really glad to see us and asked how you were doing. I told him that we had parted company and that you were headed for the Yellowstone, but we hadn't heard any more about you since you left. Since Mrs. Cooper wasn't there, Liz walked down to the gazebo to relax while Mr. Cooper and I talked business about buying a bull. He told me he had a young one that he had planned on selling in the spring, but he said we could buy it for $100 since we were just starting out. We stayed for supper and he put us up for the night. The next day, he said he'd have a couple of his cowhands help us get the cattle back here; we couldn't refuse his offer. One of the men you met, Josh, decided to stay on while the other fellow decided to go back. We have been doing right well since we got the cattle and the bull and had a fairly good spring with twelve calves born. As you know, cattle need range to roam and good grass and that prompted us to enlarge the old pasture; we are making two new pastures to the north and east of the old one. Liz's mine has provided us with the money we needed to keep the ranch from going broke while we build it up. We hope that with new settlers passing through, they will want to buy a beef cow."

"Hard work just follows you" said Todd. "Just think, you could have gone with me and had an easy life." They all laughed and then got down to some easy talking. While Liz sat in her rocker by the fireplace knitting, Crusty and Todd cleaned off the table; Crusty took what was left of the venison stew, put it in two tins and set it on the porch for the dogs, who were eagerly waiting for their supper.

Liz said, "I hope you enjoy the accommodations; we both get up early and have breakfast for everyone, then we all go out to start on our chores. Don't feel that you have to get up when we do; this is time off for you. After you do get up and have your breakfast, come find one of us. I am usually in the barn while Crusty is cutting down trees and working on the new pasture."

"Sounds good to me. If you don't mind, I think I'll turn in; Goodnight!"

"Pleasant dreams."

-27-

Once again, he dreamt about the lady in the field of wildflowers. He woke later than he had in months and still felt tired. He decided after having two cups of coffee and a couple of sourdough biscuits that he found sitting on the side of the stove that he'd sit on the porch and relax in the sunshine like he did at home. Just before noon, he walked over to the barn to find Liz and Josh building new stalls. Liz said, "You must have been more tired than you thought. Are you okay?"

"I'm still tired, but I thought I should get some fresh air and sat on your porch with the dogs for a while. I remembered you saying that you'd be in the barn, so I decided too mosey on over here to see what you were doing."

Sarcasticly, Josh said, "Seems like they'd appreciate you helping out rather than having you sit on your ass doing nothing."

Before he could answer, Liz spoke up and said, "Josh, mind your mouth. He's a friend and if he wants to sit in the sun all the time he's here, that's his business, not yours."

Todd spoke up, "You know Josh, ever since I met you yesterday, there's been something about you that bothers me and if I were you, I'd not try to provoke me into a fight. You just might be sorry with the outcome. Understand?"

Josh stood there for a few minutes pondering his answer.

Todd said to Liz, "Thanks for putting my horse out. Is there anything I can do to help out?"

"Would you take a look at the horses out in the pasture? We need to know which ones will make good breeding stock and which ones won't." Josh was about to say something, but Liz gave him a look that would have killed anyone else. He just shut his mouth and went back to work.

"Sure, I'd be happy to." He walked out the Dutch door at the end of the barn where the pasture was and closed the bottom half. He stood for a few minutes looking over the horses and where Misty was grazing. Upon seeing him, she trotted over and he petted her before walking toward an Appaloosa mare standing not more than fifteen feet away eyeing both Misty and Todd. The mare was skittish, but eventually, she let him touch her. He ran his hands over her body as he walked around her. She was fourteen hands at least, shiny coat, long mane, good teeth and obviously good eyesight. *She'd do* he thought to himself; next he walked down through the pasture to another horse while the other two horses followed him at a distance. He did the same thing with that horse and on it went through a good part of the afternoon. He had looked at over twenty horses and better than half of them would make good brood mares while the rest would make good trail or work horses.

Instead of going back into the barn, he climbed over the fence where he was and walked back up the hill toward the cabin. He stopped at the water pump and pumped the handle a couple of times splashing the cold water on his face and drank some. He decided to make dinner for Liz and Crusty and the ranch hands, too. He went out to the garden to find nice ripe tomatoes, green beans, carrots and potatoes that he dug up using a shovel that was sitting next to the fence. He put everything in a bucket and took them over to the pump to wash them off. Misty was by the fence so he set the bucket down and went over to her. He scratched her behind her ears and rubbed her forehead before giving her a couple of carrots. She whinnied and made him think she had died and gone to heaven, but he knew the more time he spent with her, the more she would become a faithful horse just like the roan had been. She sauntered away and he walked over to the cabin with the pail full of cleaned vegetables.

He decided to roast the potatoes on the edge of the fire; next, he cut the carrots in two and put them in another pot and added water. He went out to the porch and sat in one of the rockers and snapped the beans and set them in a separate pot and added water to it, just covering them. He took the two pots and set both of them on the hearth. He went out to the smokehouse and found a nice roast and brought that back into the cabin, cut it in two and set both pieces in a large roasting pan with some water, added a pinch of salt, pepper and some butter from the covered crock that was sitting on a marble slab on the side of the table.

He set the pan on a rack just above the flames in the fireplace adding a couple of half-split logs underneath it to build up the heat. He hung the two pots on hooks and gently pushed them over the flames to boil. He also decided to make biscuits and he set about making an extra-large batch of them. He would put them in the beehive oven that was next to the fireplace about forty minutes before he guessed everything would be through cooking. When he was finished, he decided to sit on the front porch and relax. He hoped that met with Josh's approval, if not that was too damned bad and if Josh said another word to him, he'd pop him one and maybe by then, he would get the message.

The aromas were wafting over the yard as Crusty and the other two ranch hands were walking down to the barn yard; Liz had stopped doing what she was doing and had Josh round up the horses and put them in the paddock next to the barn and make sure they all had enough feed and water. Liz met Crusty over at the water pump and they took turns washing up before walking arm in arm over to the cabin. Todd had everything ready for them when they came inside. He had even put some fresh flowers in a vase on the table. The coffee pot was simmering on the fireplace; just before he sat down, he put the roast and the second pot of vegetables outside with a dozen biscuits in a small sack sitting on top of the lid, then he rang the dinner bell.

Henry Watersmith made his way over to the porch to pick up the food, and then went back to the bunkhouse. He set everything on the table for him, Tinkham Goode, and Josh. Josh started to complain about this fellow named "Morgan" to the others when Henry said to him, "Josh if you were smart you'd give him a wide berth. From what Crusty told Tink and me, he isn't someone you want to piss off. He was a sharpshooter during the insurrection, he actually fought on both sides, and he could hit a target dead center at 300 yards. Once he mustered out, he worked for the same ranch you worked on. He must have been there before you came. He was really good with horses and he knew almost every horse on Timber Creek Ranch and they knew him. He's done more in his lifetime than most men or women will ever do."

Josh replied, "Bullshit! He's got everyone snowed. I've known men such as him and he doesn't scare me none. Before he leaves here, he'll know who I am, you can bet your last dollar on that."

Henry looked at Tink and they both said in unison, "Suit yourself, it's your funeral." After they finished dinner, Tink took the empty pot over to the pump, washed it out and set it on the porch before returning to the bunkhouse.

Todd stayed an additional two days; he rested and it gave him renewed energy. On his last night, Crusty said to Todd, "We have a surprise for you. When we were visiting with Mr. Cooper, he wanted you to have four horses. You can pick out any four from the herd in the pasture."

"That was mighty generous of him to do that. I had thought about raising horses where I am and doing what y'all thought of here, but instead of cattle, I'd be selling horses to settlers. I noticed that you had two young stallions in that bunch, a black and a mix-breed Appaloosa. I would gladly buy one and still take two each of work horses and broodmares. When I leave here, I am going to Lander to file a land claim and two mining claims. While there, I also plan to buy a buckboard so the work horses will be exactly what I need. Besides my trapping and mining, I need to do other things as well."

"We hadn't thought about selling either of the stallions."

"I'll leave my two brood mares here with you and come next spring or early summer, I'll be back to get them and with any luck one of them might just foal a stallion, then I wouldn't have to buy one. I have plenty of work to do for the rest of this year on my place. I need to get it fenced, plus I still have to make a living. I only go mining when I am out trapping. I haven't told anyone but the two of you about that and I'd like to keep it that way. Crusty replied, "OK, It's a deal on the brood mares."

To Liz, Todd said, "you've obviously filed claims and had an assayer determmine the value of the gold you found. Who is the best person in Lander to see about my gold, my claims, and filing for a land title?" She said, "I'd take your gold dust and nuggets, assuming you have some nuggets, to McDavitt & McIntosh on Main Street in Lander. They have a very good reputation and have been quite fair with me; you should mention my name so they know who referred you to them to file your land and mining claims. I'd see August McDavitt, he's a lawyer and his office is on Second Street. He's a brother to the other McDavitt, Plan on spending about $200 dollars for the legal work. It will be money well spent. Make sure you say that you want a quarter to a half section, that's about 160-320 acres in addition to the original 50. I know you only wanted to file on fifty or so acres, but you'd be better off with more than you need right now. If you ever wanted to increase the size of your acreage and you didn't do it the first time out, you might very well find that someone else has filed on the property right next to yours. That's what almost happened to us, but we got wind that speculators were in the area looking for prime land especially up near where my dad's mine was. Crusty and I made a quick trip to Lander and August McDavitt helped us file on four additional half-sections that surround this property. As luck would have it, the lumber mill in Lander wanted our timber; so we signed a contract with them to supply timber for the next three years. Our quick actions saved my dad's mine, gave us room to grow and sent the speculators looking elsewhere."

"I simply want to protect what I took over as abandoned property, not become a land baron. I guess I have a lot to think about before I get to Lander so that I know what I am talking about. My head is swimming right now. I think I'll take a walk before I turn in and I will see you both in the morning before I leave."

When Todd walked out on the porch, he noticed a shadowy figure over by the corral gate. The person unlatched the gate and threw it open and then went behind the barn. Todd quietly walked over to the gate while the person was in the corral, closed it and re-latched the gate. For added strength, he took off his belt and looped it twice around the gate and the post next to it so that the gate wouldn't budge as the horses started bunching up next to it.

The person came around the corner of the barn and shouted, "Someone is stealing the horses. Help! Help!" He confronted Todd and said, "You? I knew you were up to no good as soon as I met you. I ought to shoot you where you stand or have Crusty hang you for being a horse thief, you sons-a-bitch."

Tink, Henry, Crusty and Liz came running out into the yard to see what all the commotion was about finding Josh holding a gun on Todd. Josh said, "I caught this here hombre trying to run off your horses, no tellin' who else is out there waiting to help him get away with them."

Todd's response was, "When I came out onto the porch, I noticed someone over by the corral gate. The person appeared to unlatch it and swung the gate wide open. I walked over here and quickly re-latched the gate. I used my belt to secure it to the post so that the horses would not be able to push it open no matter what. I have no idea who that person is or was, but I have my suspicions."

Crusty replied, "Tink, Henry, will you put the horses in the paddock and make sure the gate between the paddock and the corral is secure? Josh, I think you have some explaining to do. Todd was in the cabin with us until three or four minutes ago. What you accused him of doing would have taken him ten or so minutes to undertake, so you're wrong about him. Besides, he'd have nothing to gain by stealing his own horses, now would he?"

Josh stood there silent and didn't know what to say. "You know Josh," Todd said, "I have had enough of your insinuations and I want an apology."

Josh, again stood silent a few seconds, said to Todd, "Draw, you son-of-a-bitch."

Todd was close enough to feel his breath when Josh gave his challenge. He didn't hesitate as he punched him in the nose followed by an uppercut with his other fist as Josh fell to the ground. Todd stepped on his gun hand, wrenched the pistol away and threw it in the watering trough. He picked Josh up off the ground and held him up against the side of the barn and said, "I told you once before you little piss ant that if you got in my way, I'd make sure you didn't do it ever again. You don't listen very well and if you ever challenge me again, you'll wish you didn't, comprende?" Todd pushed him away.

Half stumbling, Josh went over to the water trough to fish out his pistol and to wash the blood away from his nose and chin. He muttered something under his breath as he walked back toward the bunkhouse.

Todd said to his friends, "Sorry about what happened, but I can take only so much and he pushed me to that point. It's best that I leave in the morning."

"You don't have to leave on account of him," Crusty said, with Liz nodding in agreement. I'll keep Josh busy cutting trees. You certainly deserve some rest, amigo."

"And I appreciate your thoughtfulness and the hospitality, but I'm getting homesick for my place. I'll be back in a year or so to get my horses and I promise, I'll stay for a few days then."

Next morning, Todd got up when Liz and Crusty did, had breakfast and before he went outside, gave Liz a peck on the cheek and a hug, thanked her for their hospitality once again, left and walked over to the barn. Inside, he dusted off his saddle and went to the stall where Misty was and saddled her. Next he went out to the paddock and got two of the horses that he could use as work horses, put a rope halter on each and brought them up to the paddock gate, unlatched it and led them out and closed the gate behind him. He led all three horses over to where Crusty was standing and ground tied them. He tied his bedroll, saddlebags and a large sack of food for himself behind his saddle. They both mounted and Crusty took him up to a new trail that had been cut through the forest and said, "I'll keep Josh busy all day with me up in the pasture, clearing brush; sooner or later, he'll settle down. He is a hothead sometimes and you let him off easy; any other man would have killed him."

"I have my suspicions that he wanted to let the horses loose and then bring them back to you so that you'd be indebted to him. Something is eating at him and I hope he doesn't give you any real trouble. I know you will be able to handle him, but if not, kick his sorry ass off your property before he does harm to you or even worse, to Liz."

Crusty nodded in agreement and pointed off in the distance

to the northeast, "Follow this trail until you reach that pass up there where the pines separate, rein to the left and follow the trail down to the bottom of the hill. You will come out to a valley and due east is Lander, about a half-day ride. You should be there by tomorrow morning. Take your horses to the livery and tell Butch that you're a friend of mine and to take good care of them. I'd make sure that you take your saddlebags, bedroll, sack and the rifle with you and stay at the Mayfair Hotel; ask for a second floor room that faces the back of the hotel so that you can get a decent nights sleep; Also, the Country Squire Restaurant has good food."

Todd shook his friend's hand, thanked him for his hospitality and advice, and headed down the trail with the two horses in tow.

-29-

The new horses kept up the quick pace that Todd had set for himself on his way to Lander. Arriving without any incident along the trail he needed to find both The Mayfair Hotel and the livery that Crusty suggested. He passed one of each along the main street, but a small sign caught his attention **Parker's Boarding House.** He turned down the side street and came upon a freshly painted Victorian manor house. After he dismounted, he tied all three horses to the hitch rail. He walked through the gate onto a nice slate pathway with a flower border and a lush green lawn beyond that. He walked up the stairs, wiped his boots on the woven door rug, and knocked on the door jamb. A young girl about nine years old came to the door with her mother right behind her who said, "May I help you?"

Todd took off his hat and said, "Yes, ma'am, I saw your sign as I was riding down Main Street and was wondering if you had a room that I could rent for about a week?"

"I have a single bed on the second floor toward the back of the house. $10 for the week including breakfast and dinner. You can also board your horses in our barn out back for an additional $3."

"That's very reasonable, I'll take it," he replied.

138

"Take your horses around back and my daughter Megan will show you where you can put them, where the feed bin and water is, and where the paddock is also. Once you have got your horses settled, come to the screen porch and have a seat. I'll get the information that I need and you can pay me."

"Yes, ma'am," he replied. He walked back down the steps and through the gate which closed behind him, untied all the horses and led them around to the rear of the house. In the barn, Megan sat on top of several hay bales waiting for him. He walked in through the open barn door and said to her, "What stalls can I put the horses in?"

"Well the last two stalls on this side and the single stall over by the paddock door are available; the feed is in the tack room behind me and you can put your saddle, blanket and bridle in there also. I'm really good at feeding the horses. Sometimes I even get to sneak a carrot or an apple out to them, but please don't tell my mother or I'll get in trouble. I just love horses and someday I hope to have one of my own."

"I won't tell her and I am sure you will have your own horse someday." She went skipping out the door into the yard. After he finished rubbing down and currying the horses, he grained them, found a couple of empty buckets, went to the pump, filled both with fresh water and poured it into the troughs that were in each stall.

He scratched each of them behind their ears, went out of the barn door closing the bottom half and secured it. He found the little girl playing with a black lab puppy in the yard between the barn and the house; he walked up the back stairs, knocked on the door frame and walked into a large screen porch.

"My name is Priscilla Parker, but everyone just calls me Priscilla. Please have a seat. Would you like some lemonade?

I just made a fresh batch."

"Yes, that would surely quench my thirst. I have been riding since early this morning."

"I'll be right back," she replied and brought three glasses and a pitcher of lemonade on a tray and set it on the round table between them. She called for her daughter to come get a glass of lemonade; she handed the next glass to him and took a pad of paper and began writing down his name, where he was from, nature of his business in Lander, how long he planned to stay and did he have any preference for meals; she then wrote down Room 4, $10 plus $3 for three horses.

She had him look it over and sign it; she wrote all that again on the bottom of the page and tore off the bottom half and gave it to Todd. She told him, "Breakfast is at 6 am and supper at 6 pm; if you are not going to be here for breakfast or supper, please let me know so that I don't have to set a place for you at the table. If you wear spurs, please remove them before you come into the house. I change the bed linens every Wednesday and dust your room the same day. I have six other borders beside you, three of them, like yourself, will not be with us long and the others work in Lander.

"Can you recommend a lawyer?"

"I suggest that you see August McDavitt, he's a very fine lawyer and he'll take good care of you. Just tell him I sent you to see him. He's usually in his office by 9am on Monday, Wednesday and Friday; on Tuesday, he's usually in court here in Lander and on Thursday, he goes to South Pass City to take care of the folks down there. Since this is Tuesday, he should be in the office tomorrow morning. Dinner will be in one hour so why don't you go up to your room and get yourself settled in. Use the stairs in the kitchen and at the top of the stairs, the room is to your immediate right and the key is in the door lock. I'll introduce you around at dinner time if that's OK with you?"

"Fine with me. After dinner, is it alright if I just sit on the front or back porch and enjoy the night air?"

"The front porch is where most of the others retire too."

Todd took his leave and gathered up his saddlebags, rifle, and rucksack before walking up the stairs to find his room and deposit his things. It had a single bed along the wall opposite the door and next to a side window that overlooked the rear porch roof; there was another window that faced the barn and he could see the pasture to the left of the barn with a watering trough and several shade trees of Maple, Aspen and Pin Oak along one side of the fence. There was a dry sink with a wash basin on it, a pitcher of water, two glasses, a small bar of soap and two towels, one small and one large; on the side opposite the back window was a chair and a small table with a lamp.

He was introduced to everyone during dinner: two older ladies and four men; one of the men looked familiar to him, but he couldn't place him. Dinner consisted of roasted chicken, mashed potatoes, green beans, biscuits followed by coffee/tea or water and a chocolate cake with buttercream frosting. When everyone was finished eating, one of the ladies helped to take the dishes out to the kitchen while the rest of the folks took their leave. A couple of the men went out to the front porch with Todd. Small talk centered around the influx of new settlers arriving daily on their way west to California or Oregon.

After a while, he excused himself and retired to his room where he opened the window on the side that overlooked the porch roof. He could hear the night birds singing to each other as they lulled him to sleep.

He woke early, about 5 am, and washed up before breakfast. He quietly walked down the rear stairs into the kitchen where he found Mrs. Parker preparing breakfast. She said, "Did you sleep well Mr. Morgan?"

"I did indeed, a very restful sleep, I might add." He proceeded to help her carry the food into the dining room and set it on the table. He sat in the chair he had used the previous night and poured himself a cup of coffee while he waited for the other boarders to arrive. After grace was said, platters of ham, eggs, crisp potatoes with grilled onions, and biscuits were passed from one person to the next. She also brought in a large pitcher of milk and then a large coffee pot. Breakfast was over by 7 am and the folks who worked in town left for their jobs; two of the transient boarders were leaving today and they went back to their rooms to retrieve their belongings. He helped her clear the breakfast dishes before he went out to the barn to let his horses out into the pasture. They needed to run, graze, and frolic for a day or two.

-30-

After he put the horses out to the pasture, he decided that he would walk to town and meet with the lawyer and the assayers. He walked back inside the boarding house and asked, "Ma'am, can you tell me how I find Mister McDavitt's law office and a place where I can buy supplies and a buckboard?"

"Go back towards town and when you come to the main street, turn left and walk down two streets. You'll see the Lander National Bank on the opposite side of the street. Looking at the bank, on the left side of the building there is a door that leads to the second floor. At the top of the stairs you will see a hallway with three doors. Go all the way to the end of the hall and the last door on the left is Mr. McDavitt's law office. To buy supplies, go to Henderson's Mercantile, and as far as a buckboard is concerned, ask either Mr. McDavitt or Mr. Henderson."

"Thank you," he replied before he went back up to his room. He needed to sort out his papers and make more marks on the map. After talking with Liz and Crusty, he had decided that he wanted four sections of land totaling 640 acres. How big that much acreage was, he did not fully understand, but he knew he wanted the cabin as the central point. He would explain to the lawyer that he planned on raising horses and some cattle, along with the farming of grains, and the rest, he would leave as a forest. He also wanted to file three mining claims. He felt that if he worked those areas a couple of times a year, he could get enough gold to pay for supplies and buy more horses and cattle to build up a decent size ranch. Once he had everything together, he walked down the front stairs, out the door and up the road toward town.

As he was walking along he gave some thought about Mrs. Parker. *She reminds me a lot of the lady in my dream. Good manners, nice hair, just the type of lady I'd like to get to know; just wishful thinking on my part.* He reached Mr. McDavitt's office about 9:45 am. An attractive young lady was sitting behind a desk and asked, "May I help you?"

"I'd like to speak with a Mr. McDavitt."

"I have an opening at 11:30 this morning, can you come back then?"

"Yes," he replied. He walked out the door, down the steps and at the bottom of the stairwell, there was an entrance to the bank. He had the letter of credit from Hanson and now that he had decided to start up a ranch, he would need to open up an account so that he could buy additional items. The bank manager, Mr. Johansen, was very cordial and helped Todd set up an account. While he was talking with him, Todd asked if he knew where he could purchase a buckboard. The manager told him, "Hiram Bender is the best wagon maker in this area. His place is about two miles northeast of town. Simply follow the main road north and as the road splits, take the right fork, about a mile or so until you see a sign that says "Bender" on it. Ride up to the barn, Hiram will more than likely be inside working. He has a bell attached to the wall, just pull the string attached to it once and he'll come out. After you have talked with him and decided about a wagon and the cost, all you'll have to do is let the bank know the amount and the funds can be transferred from your account to Hiram's. We'll give you a letter telling Hiram that the transfer has taken place and you can drive away in your new buckboard." Todd had a lot to do but first he had to keep that date with the lawyer. He had about forty minutes or so until he had to be back at the lawyer's office. He decided to walk around town and see what Lander had to offer.

Then, at the appropriate time, Todd arrived at the lawyer's office. Once Todd was seated, he explained who recommended him and what he wanted.

Mr. McDavitt replied, "You shouldn't have a problem filing the mining claims," and gave him the necessary paperwork to fill out. "May I assume you have some gold from the areas you prospected?"

"Yes, I have some and I will need to have it assayed; turned into cash."

"I'll arrange to have it assayed for you. The land claim may pose a bit of a problem. The cabin and twenty acres have already been filed on. I did the paperwork on it several years ago. Lucas Johnson from Ohio filed an original land grant on that property. If any of his heirs show up some day to claim the property, you may be out of luck and all the hard work you put into it will be lost."

"I never thought about that," Todd replied. On the wall behind Mr. McDavitt was a large map showing what land had been surveyed by the government, filed on, and what was still available. Mr. McDavitt pointed out other possibilities. While Mr. McDavitt was talking, Todd was half listening and looking at the Homestead map at the same time. He noticed that there were still some sections available near town. Actually, one was next to the boarding house and one further down the same road next to the river *with good bottom land and just a mile or so from the boarding house* he thought to himself. He put it out of his mind and continued to listen to where he could own some property up near the Teton Range. "Section 99 is further up the canyon and on the same stream that runs close to where you are now, but it is mostly forest. It has maybe ten acres or so of cleared land; Section 172 is more northwest, half the acreage is flat land, about eighty acres or so, the other half is in thick forest and has a bold running stream as well; plenty of possibilities there. A third possibility for you would be to file for a quitclaim[21] deed on the so-called abandoned property you are on, and as I stated previously, if the owner or his relatives came back to claim it, you would have to go to court and convince a judge that you improved on the property. You would probably have to have the Langstrom's and the Indian provide testimony for you, but there is no guarantee that the courts would award it to you."

Todd replied, "I really hate to start over as it would delay my plans. What about the field and the vegetable garden that I have already planted? If the current owner or his kinfolk come back to claim the property, then I am out the grain, hay, and vegetables. Making it through the winter without them would put me in a really tough spot."

"You can stay at the cabin and harvest the fields when they come in and gather the vegetables that you planted. In the

---

[21] Quitclaim - https://en.wikipedia.org/wiki/Quitclaim_deed

meantime, however, you could start building a new cabin or a barn and pasture on your own section. No one could encroach on you there or try to make you move off your own land. Do you get along with the Indians and other folks in the area?"

"My neighbors are just fine, we get together from time to time; I have met with both the Shoshone and Sioux tribes, I guess you could say we are friendly with each other."

"That's a plus in your favor. I have been told by others that if your neighbors accept you then you shouldn't have any challenges on property that you file on."

"I need to think about what you have told me. Do you have an opening later this afternoon or tomorrow morning so that I can give you an answer at that time?"

"I have a working lunch today from 12:30 to 2 pm, but I am open the rest of the afternoon. Go have lunch, fill out the mining claim forms and think about what I have told you regarding the homesteading claims. Just in case I get held up in the 12:30 meeting. I will see you back here at 2:30 pm, When we are done, I will take you over to the assayer's office. Tell Lucy at the front desk to pencil you in on my calendar from 2:30 pm until the end of today."

Once done, he went just a few doors down the street from the bank to a small café, *Los Frijoles de Mexicana*. He asked for a table in a back corner, ordered coffee, a glass of water, two burritos with chicken, refried beans, and a small salad. He sipped the water and began to mull over what the lawyer had said. He thought to himself, *I have put in a lot of time fixing up that cabin, adding the side barn, all that cultivating with the hay field and vegetable garden only to be told that all my hard work, may be down the drain and I would have to start over; then again,*

I would have the rest of the summer to improve the new land and in five years, under the Homestead Act,[22] *it will be mine and mine alone.* In-between bites of food; he took a napkin and drew out plans of what he could do with his own land. He could build a barn much like Liz's father had done when he first homesteaded his property and when the time came, should he take a wife, build a cabin. He would also have plenty of time to till new acreage for hay fields and he could fence in enough pasture for the horses while he lived in the abandoned cabin. He would still be able to go trapping in late fall and early winter, especially where his mining claims were.

He decided to file for Section 172. It might be a bit farther to the west, but from the map on Mr. McDavitt's wall it only looked like three miles from where he currently was. The miners would be just over five miles and Moon's place would be about six miles away.

---

[22] **The Homestead Act of 1862** was passed by the U.S. Congress. It provided for the transfer of 160 acres (65 hectares) of unoccupied public land to each homesteader on payment of a nominal fee after five years of residence; land could also be acquired after six months of residence at $1.25 an acre. The government had previously sold land to settlers in the West for revenue purposes. As the West became politically stronger, however, pressure was increased upon Congress to guarantee free land to settlers. Several bills providing for free distribution of land were defeated in Congress; in 1860 a bill was passed in Congress but was vetoed by President Buchanan. With the ascendancy of the Republican Party (which had committed itself to homestead legislation) and with the secession of the South (which had opposed free distribution of land), the Homestead Act, sponsored by Galusha A. Grow, became law. In 1976 it expired in all the states but Alaska, where it ended in 1986.

-31-

He asked for another cup of coffee and made out the list of items he needed from the mercantile, eight - two over two glass windows, sixteen hinges, eight snap locks, twelve heavy duty barn door hinges, four rolls of barbed wire, two bolts of heavy muslin fabric, a thirty inch cooking grate, two pot hooks, ten bags of cement, six laying hens and one rooster, two long-handled shovels, one short-handled shovel, two mining pans, fifty pounds of oats for his horses, and ten pounds each of oat, buckwheat and rye seed and three pounds of corn seed for planting, fifty pounds of #16 nails, fifty pounds of ten inch spikes, a two-person buck saw, two double-bladed axes, a pick ax, a miner's hand chisel, two sharpening stones, two ten inch pulleys, 200 feet of sisal rope, a wash basin, a sixteen foot by twenty foot waterproof tarp and a framing hatchet. He also needed six pairs of leather work gloves, a heavy duty work coat, four pairs of blue jeans, two each of cotton/flannel and woolen shirts and two sets of long johns. When he got to the fort he would pick up the food he ordered at the trading post.

On yet another napkin he drew the design of a buckboard wagon. He decided that he wanted one that was four feet wide by ten feet long, removable sides sixteen inches high, double

149

springs and a shelf under the seat for blankets or to hide a rifle and a secret well where he could put his gold. He hoped he'd not have to pay more than $250 for it and that it could be built over the next four or five days. The waitress asked if he needed anything else and he replied, "No thank you; your food was very good and I'll be back. How much do I owe you?"

"Your bill comes to $1.40." He took $2 out of his pocket and said to her, "Keep the change."

"Muchas gracias, Senor," she said with a big smile on her face.

It was 2 pm by the time he walked back to the lawyer's office and thought to himself *I could sure use a nap right about now but I have to get this legal paperwork done first. I'll catch one when I get back to the boarding house.* The door to Mr. McDavitt's private office was open when he came in the office door and Mr. McDavitt saw Todd walk in. He motioned for Todd to take a seat and said, "Give me a few minutes to finish my writing and we'll get started." After a few minutes, Mister McDavitt set aside what he had been working on and said, "What have you decided?"

"I want to file papers on four sections with Section 172 as the starting point under the Homestead Act."

"Lucy, will you get a copy of the Homestead Act and the attached papers for four sections, and bring your notary seal with you. As soon as Mr. Morgan has signed the paperwork you can notarize the forms. I would like you to hand carry them over to the clerk's office and get everything recorded this afternoon."

Lucy replied, "Whenever you're ready." Todd read the Homestead Act and signed where he was instructed to do so;

Lucy came in and notarized his and Mr. McDavitt's signatures on the homestead papers and on the mining claims. She put on her wrap and left to go to the court house.

"When she gets back, I will give you a notarized, signed copy; Lucy will keep the second copy for our files here. The charge will be $155 and when I take you over to the assayer's office, we will stop downstairs at the bank where you can sign a draft to have that amount taken from your account and I'll deposit it in my account. I want to assure you that if there is ever a question as to the legality of this transaction or if anyone tries to cross file on your mining claims or on the sections; I will defend you in a court of law. I need to get some writing done, would you mind waiting out in the front office until Lucy returns?"

"Not at all. I might take a short nap in one of your comfortable leather chairs if you don't mind."

"Pick any one you want; she won't be back for at least an hour."

After Lucy came back, she handed one set of papers to Todd, while she filed the second set in the cabinet behind her desk.

Todd and August walked the five blocks to McDavitt & McIntosh, Assayer's. Upon entering the building, there was an armed guard sitting at a desk in the spacious vestibule. "Nice to see you Mr. McDavitt. Your brother is expecting you and Mr. Morgan. If you have any weapons Mr. Morgan, please remove them and I will hold them for you. When you leave, I will give them back to you." Todd did what was asked of him; he took off his sidearm, the bowie knife out of his boot and a small derringer from his topcoat. The two men looked at him and Todd said, "You have to be prepared when you are in strange territory."

The guard replied, "I guess you have a point there." He put the weapons in a drawer, locked it and put the key in his vest pocket. Behind him there was an ornate staircase that led up to the second floor. August said to the guard, "I'll take Mr. Morgan up to my brother's office, so you won't have to." August pointed out various offices as they walked toward the grand staircase. After they reached the second floor, he took Todd to the front of the hallway where a set of windows overlooked the main street down below. To the right of the windows was an office and on the door in gold lettering was printed **Flaherty McDavitt**. August opened the door and ushered Todd into an impressive oak- paneled waiting room furnished with a highly polished mahogany sideboard and four well-appointed leather chairs facing at angles around a square mahogany coffee table with a beveled glass top in the middle on top of ornate wrought iron legs. He motioned for him to have a seat. "I'll see if my brother is ready for us." He knocked on the office door that had **PRIVATE** printed in gold lettering. A voice from inside said, "Come in." August entered the office and said to his brother, "Are you ready for us yet?"

"Yes, by all means, have Mr. Morgan come inside." August motioned for Todd to come with him as they entered a large office with floor to ceiling windows with ornate ironwork covering them on the outside that overlooked a lovely garden below. A rather tall, thin man looking out the window turned and warmly welcomed Todd first, then his brother and said to both, "Please have a seat. I was just admiring how beautiful our garden looked today and how much I would love to be outside on this beautiful day fishing, but work comes first."

Todd thought to himself *A man after my own heart, but if I wanted to go fishing, I might just stop what I was doing, grab my fishing pole and go and get my supper.* "What can I do for you Mr. Morgan?"

"Well, sir, I have been doing some paning for gold up in the foothills of the Tetons and just filed on those claims with the help of your brother. I have some small sacks of gold and I wanted to find out their quality and value; then I wish to convert them into money. Your firm came highly recommended by a friend of mine, Miss Elisabeth Connolly."

"Ah yes, Miss Connolly is an excellent customer. We have had the pleasure of dealing with her and her late father, rest his soul. Let's see what you have and then I'll be able to tell you the quality, weight and value." Todd removed the two rabbit skin pouches from the inside of his outer coat, placed them on the desk and said "Each pouch is from a different location, would you please do each one separately."

Flaherty took both pouches over to his work table where he poured the contents of the smaller of the two onto a scale and it read 298.96 grams. Then he placed that into a crystal dish and set it aside, writing down the weight on a piece of paper; he then took the second pouch, which had the nuggets in it, and repeated the procedure that he did with the first pouch and it weighed 1105.63 grams. He wrote down the weight of the second pouch before he poured it into a bigger crystal dish and set it aside. He took the first dish, placed an eye piece over his left eye, carefully picked up a grain at a time and looked it over. He placed about fifteen of them in a separate small dish and used a magnet to see if any of them were attracted to it, none were. He brought out a bottle labeled Nitric Acid and unscrewed the eye dropper top and added some to the dish. The dust did not dissolve. At this point he said, "I am almost done. If you wish, there are some liquid refreshments over on the sidebar, please help yourselves."

Todd and August went over to the sidebar, poured their drinks and sat back down again. Mr. McDavitt followed the same procedure with the second dish and next to each of the numbers he wrote down, 20 carats; 22 carats. He went back to his desk and retrieved a book and a scratch pad from his desk. He wrote down $20.67 per ounce and using the book, converted the grams to ounces, multiplied the number and wrote down for the first bag $113.69; second bag $392.73. He left all of that on the work table, returned to his desk and said, "The gold that you found is of high quality, your first bag is rated as 20/24 carats[23] and weighed 5 ½ ounces; your second bag is rated as 22/24 carats and weighed 19 ounces. The current market price for an ounce of gold[24] is $20.67. Your total for both bags comes to $506.42 less our 8% fee, leaving you with a grand total of $465.91. I will write you a check and you can cash or deposit it at the Lander National Bank & Trust Co. If you prefer we can do a draft and you can deposit it in your account at any bank. What is your pleasure?"

"I'll take a check," Todd replied. Flaherty said to him, "Each time you come here from now on you will be assigned to one of our assistants on the first floor. That person will do exactly what I have done and you will have the choice of a check or bank draft.

We have enjoyed doing business with you and hope that we

---

[23] Wikipedia was used for answers to questions on Quality of Gold, Carat weight, etc.

[24] Google provided text on the value of an ounce of Gold from 1880-1935, the price of gold for the time period was set at $20.67 to $21.00 per ounce.

will see you again. Have a nice day." He stood up and both Todd and August did the same. He shook Todd's hand, showed him to the door and said, "If you will please go downstairs, our guard will give you back your weapons. August, please have a seat, we have some additional business to attend to."

Todd said to Flaherty, "Thank you for your time and you will be seeing me from time to time; to August he said, Thanks for your help today," before leaving the office.

-32-

Once he arrived back at the boarding house, he went in through the front door and started up the stairs. Mrs. Parker was sitting in the living room knitting and said, "You look like you have the world on your shoulders Mr. Morgan, why don't you rest before dinner?"

"That's exactly what I had in mind."

"I'll have Megan knock on your door around 5:30 so that you'll have plenty of time to get up for dinner."

"Thank you, that would be nice." He opened both windows for a cross-breeze before lying down on the bed and was soon fast asleep.

After dinner, he wandered out to the barn to see his horses, Misty looked lonely; the other two mares seemed content. He stepped into the tack room, but found no feed and hoped the horses had enough graze during the day; he carried two buckets out to the pump, filled them and poured the water in their troughs. He promised himself to buy some carrots and a bag of apples at the mercantile tomorrow. He made sure that all the windows were closed as it looked like storm clouds were gathering. Before he left, he scratched behind their ears and walked out of the barn. He made sure the barn door was closed tightly and walked back to the house. He'd inform Mrs.

Parker in the morning that there was no feed for the horses.

He got up after 9 am and knew that he was too late for breakfast. Looking out the window, he saw that it was raining; the kind of rain you want if you're growing hay, grains, and vegetables and wondered if it was raining back at the cabin just like it was outside. He put on his blue denim shirt and tucked it into his blue jeans before strapping on his holster. He shook out his rain poncho from his saddlebags and took his hat with him as he went down the back stairs. No one seemed to be around, but the coffee pot was on the stove with vapors coming out of the spout. He found a couple of biscuits that smelled like cinnamon in a baking pan sitting next to the stove. He poured himself a cup of coffee and took the biscuits out on the back porch. He put the cup down on the cross member that the screen was attached to and looked toward the barn. While he was enjoying the rolls and his coffee, Mrs. Parker drove into the yard in an old buckboard that looked like it was about to fall apart. In the rear of the wagon were three sacks of grain. She pulled up to the barn door, jumped down, and quickly opened the door to unloaded the sacks of grain and closed the door before getting back up in the wagon. She turned the team around and parked the wagon on the side of the barn. She unhitched the team and walked them one by one through a side door into the barn. Shortly thereafter, she emerged from the barn and sprinted across the barnyard to the porch stairs. He noticed that she was dressed in faded blue jeans, a denim work shirt, old cowboy boots and a wide brimmed hat.

"Never seen a lady in pants before, Mr. Morgan?" She said abruptly. Before he could answer she had already gone into the house and was out of sight. He thought to himself *A bit abrupt and yes, I have seen women wear men's clothes before.* After finishing his coffee and biscuits, he put the cup in the wash basin before going out to the barn to saddle his horse. He took out his pocket knife to open the grain sack marked OATS and used a scoop to measure out enough for all the horses in the barn and poured it into their feed buckets. Before he left the barn, he strode over to his new horses and gave each of them a scratch behind their ears, a habit he has done since he got them. He led Misty out into the yard and closed the bottom half of the barn door before riding out of the yard toward town.

First on his agenda was to go to the bank to deposit the check from the assayers' office. While at the teller window, he asked for two hundred dollars in cash, enough for the wagon maker and the general store. After he completed his business at the bank, he rode out of town toward the wagon maker's, following the directions that were given to him. He found the sign he had been looking for and rode up the winding lane toward a large barn; he dismounted and ground tied his horse. He pulled on the bell cord on the side of the building. After a few minutes, Hiram Bender came around to the front of the barn and said, "Can I help you young man?"

"Mr. Bender, my name is Todd Morgan. The bank manager said you were the best wagon maker in these here parts. I am in need of a wagon, but if you don't have one already built for sale, I would like to have one built to my specifications."

"Well you've come to the right place. Come with me and I'll show you my operation." Todd followed him into the barn where there were four wagons in various stages. Mr. Bender said, "What type of wagon are you looking for?"

"Well, I need a buckboard[1]. One that is sturdy enough for

ranch work up in the hill country."

"I don't have any for sale at the moment. It would take me a week to get the wood that I would need and another two weeks to build it."

"I had no idea that you'd have ongoing projects. I was thinking that you could get it done in a week and I'd be gone. Having to wait three weeks is longer than I can stay. I do want it built right though. I would like one that is 60 inches wide, 120 inches long, with sixteen inch removable sides. I would like double springs on each side of the front and rear axles, a shelf under the seat and a hidden box under the floor. I also need to have two horses trained to the harness, as well."

"Training the horses is no problem, I do that for several of my clients, but it costs $20 extra. Let me figure up the cost of the buckboard for you. He grabbed a pencil, a sheet of paper and took a book down from the shelf near his workbench. "Take a look around, it will take me a few minutes to figure up a cost for you."

Mr. Bender pulled up a stool and began to write down what he'd need to build the buckboard. The book he used had dimensions on all kinds of wagons, materials needed to construct a wagon and miniature plans. He flipped through several pages until he found a buckboard that looked much like the one Todd had described. He waved Todd over to his workbench, showed him the picture and said, "Is this about what you had in mind?"

"That's exactly what I want." Mr. Bender wrote down the specifics: length, height, two five inch wide wheels for the rear with double springs, two three inch wide wheels for the front with double springs, a 60 inch wide seat set on bow springs, a buggy whip holder, hand brake, metal bracket for a shelf ten inches wide by fifty-two inches long, storage box nine inches deep by fifteen inches wide by eighteen inches long with hinged door and wooden knob (barely visible), hemp rug and leather harness for a two-horse team. Then he looked up the costs, added in his profit, the total came to $97 plus $20 for the training of horses. "If I knew you Mr. Morgan, I wouldn't ask for a deposit, but I don't. I'll need half up front and the balance when you come to pick up the buckboard."

"I anticipated that you might, I have the cash and I need a receipt for my records. When I come to pick it up, I will pay you the balance."

"I just need your signature or your mark on this paper. I will order the parts for your wagon this afternoon when I go into town. I will be using a mixture of locust, oak and pine on your wagon, if that's alright with you."

"You're the wagon builder and you know what's best. I'll bring the horses out to you just as soon as I can." He shook hands with Mr. Bender before he went out the door he came in and rode back to town.

<h1 style="text-align:center">-33-</h1>

Once Todd arrived back in town, he noticed a dappled gray gelding in front of one of the saloons *If I didn't know better I'd say that's Josh Hackenfield's horse. I think I'll walk down to the saloon, peek in through the windows to see if it is him or not. If it is him, I know why he's here. I don't need this kind of trouble here in Lander.* He tied his horse at the rear of the saloon and walked through the alleyway toward the front of the building. He was about to turn the corner when out sauntered Josh, slightly drunk. Todd stayed in the shadows to avoid being seen and thought *Now what do I do? Sooner or later I am bound to run into him and he'll want another chance at me.*

Todd walked back to his horse and rode out of town the way he came in and took a road that connected to the one that went past the boarding house. He thought to himself *The wagon won't be ready for three weeks, possibly longer. I'll take the horses out to Bender's farm early tomorrow morning and then I can make my way back to the fort. I can pick up my supplies and the supplies for Moon and the miners. I'll have to let Mrs. Parker know that I'll be leaving tomorrow and will be back three weeks from Monday and see if she could reserve a room for me. Then I won't have to worry about getting a room when I get back.*

Hopefully, over the next few days Josh will figure that I'm not here in Lander and move on.

He let Mrs. Parker know that he had to change his plans and that he would be leaving tomorrow just after breakfast. "I'll be back three weeks from Monday; can you have the same room I am in now available for me when I return?"

"That shouldn't be a problem and I am sorry you had to change your plans. I'll have to give you a refund for the days that you are not staying to finish out the week."

"Just keep it and when I return, if I have to pay more for keeping the room available, I'll settle with you then. Is that OK, with you?"

"That will be fine." He made sure all the horses were well fed and watered. On Saturday, he arrived at the dining room table just in time for breakfast consisting of fresh picked blueberries sprinkled into the pancake batter, sausage, scrambled eggs, coffee and buttermilk. After breakfast, he helped Mrs. Parker clear the dishes and took them out to the kitchen; then he went back up to his room, gathered up his belongings, came down the back stairs through the kitchen, down the porch stairs and over to the barn. He saddled Misty and tied on his bedroll, as well as the rucksack, before sliding his rifle into the scabbard. He looped a rope halter on each of the work horses to take to Bender's farm and with them in tow, he rode out of the yard and turned left. He decided to ride around the town to the north and pick up the road that led to the Bender farm.

Once he arrived, he found him in the corral training a horse. He reined up and said, "Here are the two horses that I need you to train to the harness; I will be back three weeks from Monday to pick up the buckboard and the horses. I have to get back to my cabin. If you are going to be late in getting the wagon finished, send a telegram to Ft. Washakie c/o Corporal Miller, Post Commander's Office and when I start back this way, he'll make sure I get it when I come past the fort.

Mr. Bender replied, "Just tie them over by that oak tree next to the barn and I'll take care of them when I get done with the horse I am working with now. Have a safe trip back to your home."

Upon arriving at the fort, Todd reined up in front of the trading post, dismounted, and tied Misty to a post. Inside the store, the sutler was behind the counter with his back to him. Todd said, "Hanson, can you get my supplies together so that I can leave here in the morning?"

"Nice to see you too, Morgan and no, I can't get it ready until later tomorrow."

"Why not?"

"If you took the time to look around the fort you would see a lot more people here than when you left. I have been busy filling their orders since the influx began."

"I had noticed that there seemed to be a lot of covered wagons and people milling about as I entered the fort. What is going on anyway?"

"Where have you been? One of the trappers found gold up in the hills beyond where you live and news like that spreads fast."

Almost apologetically Todd replied, "If you show me where my supplies are, I'll pack the horses and then I can be on my way. Is that alright with you, Mister Hanson?"

"Give me a few minutes to finish what I am inventorying and I will show you where your supplies are stored. Your horses are over at the post stables and you should stop in to the post commander's office to see if you owe them anything. When you're done there, come around back, knock on the door twice and I'll let you in to retrieve your supplies."

"Thanks!" He went down the stairs, untied Misty, and walked over to the post commander's office and ground tied her. Upon entering, he saw Corporal Miller talking with a settler about land grants and where he had to go to file. Todd found an empty chair and sat down to wait his turn. Corporal Miller approached him and said, "Nice to see you again Mr. Morgan and as you can see we are quite busy. The commander is in; did you want to see him?"

"Actually, I did, but with all that's going on I don't want to take up his time. I also wanted to find out what I owe y'all for the feed and caring of my horses."

"Well, they have been here for two weeks, with feed and care that will be $3.50." Todd took out the money and paid the corporal; who in turn handed him a receipt. The corporal rose and knocked on the colonel's door.

The commander replied, "Come in."

"Mr. Morgan would like to speak with you, sir."

"Have him come in and take a seat."

Todd entered and took a seat in front of the colonel and said, "I hope your maneuvers a few weeks back were successful."

"They were, but you're not here to talk about that are you?"

"No, sir, I wanted to let you know that I met with the Sioux about three weeks back and at the time they were very friendly, even welcoming me to stay with them for a few days. They taught me a lot about furs which will be helpful to me over time. I do worry, though, that with a gold rush and with a possible land grab, there may be trouble if the settlers and miners try to set up camps on Indian lands and it could lead to bloodshed. If that happens, the Indians will get all the blame. Personally, I took the time to file on three mining claims for myself and on four sections of land under the Homestead Act. I will be marking my property lines just as soon as I get back to my cabin. I will, as always, be law abiding, but I will defend my property from squatters, claim jumpers, wayward miners and settlers. Though I suppose I'll have to a bit lenient on the settlers and miners."

"First off, I want to congratulate you on doing the right thing by filing legally for a homestead and the mining claims. I wish everyone was as conscientious as you are, but I fear that we will have trouble. Until I get a new company of soldiers in a month or so, I will be stretched thin in keeping the peace between everyone. I know you have your priorities, but when you have all your claims and land marked, will you take a letter to the Sioux Chief for me. I want him to know that we will do our best to inform the settlers and the miners as to where they can and can't settle and/or look for gold. But as I said, we can't be everywhere all the time. Matter of fact, it would be nearly impossible to accomplish that feat. The letter will state that if there is any trouble they should let you know and you in turn will let us know. Would you do that for us? For your country?"

"I will. Will y'all be able to settle any arguments that may develop?"

"Like I said, we'll do our best."

"Can I ask a small favor of you?"

"What might that be?"

"If a rider comes through here looking for me, please don't tell him anything about me. His name is Josh Hackenfield and I think he'd like to kill me."

"What did you do to him to make him so angry with you?" Todd related the story.

"So you can see why the less you say about me, the better."

"I'll pass the word along so that no one mentions your name or makes it known where you live. You have to inform Hanson though."

One last thing, "May I stay in the barracks tonight?"

"Certainly. You know the sergeant, just let him know I said it was alright."

"Thank you, sir." He stood up, walked out the door and closed it behind him before he headed over to the livery. He took the horses to the back of the trading post, tied them off and walked up the stairs, knocked twice on the door and waited for Hanson to come out to the back porch. When Hanson came to the door, he said to him, "I need to talk with you for a few minutes if you don't mind."

"You're not changing your mind again, are you?"

"No, nothing like that, I just need to ask a favor."

<h1 style="text-align:center">-34-</h1>

Once Todd got to Moon's cabin, he knew he only had about a mile to go to get to the miners' cabin. Once he reached their cabin, he found a sign on their door, 'Gone to our mine.' As he continued up the road toward his place, he saw several horses in his pasture and the barn door was wide open. *Something isn't right here* he thought to himself. He tied Misty to a tree and wrapped the halter ropes of the other horses around his pommel. He walked around to the side of the cabin where he found Molly with a rope tied around her neck, gaunt, panting and tied to a porch post. He scratched her behind her ears, she perked up a bit, but he could tell she hadn't been fed in a couple of days. He walked up the stairs, knocked on the door and waited. A scruffy looking man opened the door and said, "Kin I 'elp you?"

"Well up until three weeks ago this was 'my' cabin, this is 'my' dog and I don't see my Indian friend here either."

"We run off that no account Indian. We would have killed the sons-a-bitch, but that wouldn't be neighborly, now would it? You wouldn't be Morgan by any chance would you?"

"Morgan's my name, what's yours? You still haven't told me why you're in the cabin?"

"Don't smart mouth me, you squatter. This here place was

my daddy's and I and my brothers came up here to claim it back for our family. We set your things over there by those trees, but you know how critters get into things left on the ground and all," he replied sarcastically.

"I'll take my dog, gather up my things and be on my way."

"Sorry to disappoint you, but we found that there dog just a wanderin' in the woods one day and she stays here, but you can get your things off of our property, pronto." He was in no position to argue and he remembered what August said to him, "If you file a quitclaim deed on the property and any family or kinfolk come back to claim it, you may not win in court despite all the improvements you made." At this point, he's glad he filed for the other four sections and if he had a mind to, he'd file on all the sections that surrounded this cabin and then we'd see who had the upper hand. He gathered his things off the ground and tied them on top of the bundles already burdening the mare. He only had another four or so miles to go before he'd be on his new property; Come first thing in the morning, he'd be posting No Trespasing signs on his new property.

Using the map that August gave him, he followed the trail until he found the stake showing where his land was and how to identify the different sections. He dismounted and held the reins to his horse and stood at the corner of Section 172 and knew he had his work cut out for him. His first priority was to set up a temporary camp and corral where the horses could graze. He would build a temporary lean-to where he could sleep, dig a fire pit for warmth, cook his food and keep his coffee hot. Before he left Lander he went to Henderson's Mercantile like Mr. McDavitt suggested and purchased sixty-four foot stakes, a can of black paint and a quarter inch wide paint brush. August had said, "When you get to your property, print the following on the stakes: Section 162, 163, 172, 173 MORGAN and hammer them into the ground at the four corners of each section. Every hundred feet or so down your property line, do the same thing. These will mark your boundaries until you can put up fencing to identify the corners. When you have the fencing up, pull the stakes and nail them to the fence posts so that anyone can see where your property line is.

"On the mining claims, paint MORGAN, plat map 97 on the one in the arroyo; plat map 106 for the one in the draw, and of the one that hasn't been surveyed yet, just put your name. Drive the stakes in the ground and then pile rocks around each stake, but leave enough of your name and the plat number showing so anyone can see that it is your property. Make sure you carry with you at all times the notarized copies that we gave you so that if anyone challenges you, you can show them proof of ownership for your sections and the mining claims. Any trouble you have with any of the properties, notify the nearest law and let them handle it." August had also told him, "When you walk your land after staking it out and using the maps we provided you, mark every identifiable tree, creek, boulder, overhang, beaver dams or ponds, open land, the eventual fence, cabins, barns, outbuildings already on the property, anything that will prove you own the property, then sign and date it. When you come to Lander again, bring one copy to our office so we can put it in your file just in case an ownership issue comes into question; put the other map somewhere safe for your own peace of mind."

He had a good supper and slept well. When he woke in the morning he added some kindling to the ashes in the fire pit to reheat the coffee so that he had some energy. The first thing he was going to do was paint the stakes for two of the sections before he set out staking the property. He decided to use Misty and after putting on the pack frame, he tied the bundles of stakes on the frame and found the first government marker. From there, he started walking and guessing the length and width of all the sections combined; each section was roughly eighty acres long and twenty acres wide and since he had title to four sections, that was eighty by eighty.

As the sun was sliding behind the mountains that first day, he figured he got one and a half sections staked; tomorrow he would start where he left off and get done as much as he could and finish it up on the third day. Making his way through the forest, he noted several caves, crossed three creeks and eventually came to the clearing where his makeshift lean-to was. When he got there yesterday he remembered to haul his supplies up into the trees . He made sure that all the horses were hobbled, had sufficient grass and were near one of the creeks for drinking. After looking over the site, he decided if he went 200 yards south from where he was, he could build a barn with a decent-size pasture next to it. Just after sunset, he went back to where he had planted the garden just north of his former cabin and took tomatoes, dug up several potatoes, and other vegetables.

If the men in the cabin heard him harvesting the vegetables that he'd planted, he could expect a visit from them at any time. He would be ready for them. Once he got back to his campsite, he got his fire going and put two potatoes in the coals to roast; he took his frying pan and fried up some of the green tomatoes along with several strips of rabbit meat from a rabbit he snared earlier that morning. As the Sioux indians taught him, he had scraped the skin clean and dried it in the sun on a huge boulder near the campsite, then rolled it skinned side out to protect the fur. The more he did, the better he began to feel, and under his breath said *One way or another, I've got to find a way to get Molly back, otherwise she will starve to death.*

Every time he moved down the line while staking the property, he took the time to make markings on the maps as he walked along. The maps were filling in nicely and there would be no question if he was ever challenged as to what land he owned, no matter what. When he was finished he decided to take a nap in the tall grass by one of the creeks. He woke suddenly when he heard voices coming from the woods that surrounded his campsite. He crawled over to where his rifle was and from there he crawled to where he could see who was coming onto his property.

One of the voices said, "This here looks like a good place as any to hunt, even if it is staked. We'll pull up those stakes and no one will be the wiser. These new sodbusters won't know what to do next and by the time they run to the fort and get back here, we'll have driven our stakes into the ground. Those soldier boys will just tell them they must be mistaken and to find another place to settle." Todd watched them as they systematically removed some of the stakes and threw them into the woods. Another man said, "We'll come back tomorrow, drive our stakes in the ground and hunt us up some game."

Fortunately for Todd, neither man went any further into

the forest and didn't find his campsite or the horses. He decided he would have a surprise waiting for them when they returned.

He had retrieved the stakes that had been thrown into the woods and put them back where they belonged. The men that had taken over the cabin put four of his eight traps, two of the ropes, a tarp and his clothes in the pile. He thought it would be better if he had a cold camp tonight; tomorrow was going to be very interesting.

He woke early just as the first tinges of sunlight were breaking through drifting clouds. He quickly gathered up three of the large steel traps and went to where he found the trail they had come in on, guessing that they'd come back the same way today. He placed the traps both on and off the trail; about fifty feet down the trail, he dug a pit about two feet deep and covered it with branches and leaves and scattered the dirt off to the side of the trail in the brush. If anyone stepped in it with the spikes he had sharpened and pushed into the ground, it would do some real damage to their feet and legs. He made a man size snare that would drag a man off his feet in a matter of seconds and have him hanging upside down and swinging back and forth until someone cut him down. He wished he had a twelve gauge shotgun loaded with buckshot; it made for an interesting spray pattern, especially when you were shooting at a varmint's backside. Instead, he had his Sharps with him and his Winchester as backup. If they didn't get the message after he fired in their direction, they were not only dumb, but stupid too. He went back to a huge dead oak that was near where they would be coming in and waited. He dozed off for a while, but came fully awake when he heard a horse nicker and men talking. It was time for the show.

Sure enough, like clockwork, the same four men started to walk along the trail and the lead man, the big fat ugly bastard that he encountered at the cabin door, stepped into the bear trap. The jaws nearly broke his leg in half and while two of the others tried to pry it open, the fourth man went forward to the left about twenty five feet or so and he stepped into the second trap. Now two of them were caught just where Todd wanted them, both screaming in unbearable pain, cursing and cussing.

He could hardly contain himself and decided to set up a spray pattern first with the rifle firing at the rear of the trail, then in the front of the other two men who were trying to help their friends out of the traps. They were so confused from all the rounds whistling over their heads, they didn't know which way to run to get out of the way. Finally, he took aim with his Winchester and zeroed in on the fat man's right shoulder and fired. Between the pain caused by the bear trap and the wound in his arm he was one hurtin' son-of-a-gun. Finally, one of the men said, "We give up, just let us go. We won't ever come back."

Todd yelled back at them, "You're damn right you won't. Now get off my property and if you don't leave the territory by the end of the day, I'll track you down and kill you in your sleep. Now start walking and leave those horses where they are tied. They are your payment for trespassing on my land."

"You can't be serious we won't get anywhere without our horses."

"You should have thought about that when you decided to trespass on my land, now git." He laid down another barrage of gunfire just to make sure they understood who was in charge.

"Okay, okay, we're going. Just give us a chance to get outta here."

"Make sure you pass the word, I don't put up with trespassers, squatters, cattle rustlers or horse thieves and if anyone of your kind causes any more trouble, I'll shoot to kill the next time, whether it's you or them."

The two men who were not injured were scared shitless and managed to get the first man out of the trap and sat him up next to a tree trunk while they went and got the second man out of the other trap. The second man limped along, while the other two half-carried and dragged the first fellow out of the forest whose arm was now dangling from his side and bleeding profusely. He watched them go and decided after a half hour or so he'd track them and fire a couple of shots over their heads to make sure they were moving along in the right direction. That afternoon he took a nice long nap and nobody bothered him.

-36-

Todd had been checking every couple of days to see if the miners had returned and when they did, he gave them their horse and supplies. He also mentioned to them, "If you ever see Moon in your travels tell him to come find me. He has a home here with me."

"Why? What happened?" Gus asked, wondering what he was talking about.

"When I came back from Fort Washakie, I found your note on the door. When I got back to the cabin, there were some kinfolk in it from the man who built it. I only saw one man, but there could have been others in the cabin. He told me they ran off Moon and took my dog as their own. I could have fought for the dog, but figurin' that I was outnumbered, it made no sense to try. While I was in Lander, I filed on four sections under the Homestead Act."

Gus replied, "Well, if that don't beat all. We knew the trapper that built that cabin and he told us he had no kinfolk to speak of. He was an orphan and when he was old enough, he ran away and never looked back. He just kept coming west until he found that spot where he built the cabin. Since we're back, we can go there in force if you want and take the cabin back."

"Three weeks ago, I would probably have taken you up on

176

that offer, but now that I have my own property. I'll just stay there and do the best I can to make it my own. I'll need one of you to watch my place for about a week. I have to go back to Lander to pick up a wagon that I'm having built and get the supplies that I ordered. While I am there, I can get any additional supplies that you may need as well."

Turk spoke up and said, "One of us has to go to Lander and have our gold assayed. Why don't we ride together and Pete can stay here while Gus stays at our place. With all of these new settlers moving through this area, we have got to stick together or they'll attempt to take over our homesteads. I hear tell there are a lot of squatters among the new settlers. We also heard up in the mountains about a settler who scared the bejesus out of some squatters who were hunting on his property without his permission. I don't suppose you know anything about that, do you?"

With a smile on his face that could have cut a fog in the morning he replied, "I can honestly say that the story is true, but I'd rather not say who that was."

He and Turk left the following Sunday morning and they expected to get to Lander early on Tuesday morning. Todd hoped by the time he got there that Josh had moved on. Turk was staying at The Mayfair Hotel while Todd had already made arrangements to stay at Parker's Boarding House. They both agreed to meet at the Mexican restaurant on Thursday at noon for lunch.

Before going to the boarding house, Todd went to Henderson's Mercantile and gave him an additional order to the one he had placed a few weeks ago. He added three steel traps, a moldboard plow with disc harrow,[25] six additional rolls of barbed wire, a come-along, forty pounds of wire staples, two wire pliers, a short handled ax, an adz, framing hammer and some other small tools. He placed a separate order for two rolls of sixteen gauge wire fencing with a two by four inch spacing and one galvanized watering troughs. He recently purchased a mule from some settlers on their way to California. He put an extra pack frame on it and an extra pack frame on Misty; he'd just have to put the saddle on the wagon seat next to him on his way back home.

When he finished at the mercantile, he went to the Morningside Café and had breakfast; afterward Todd rode over to Mrs. Parker's. Like the first time, he went up the front stairs and knocked on the door. When she came to the door, she looked even prettier than the first time he saw her. Seeing that it was Todd, she invited him into the parlor and said, "I was expecting you last night and began to worry that something had happened to you. I should have known that you'd be here sooner or later."

Todd replied, "Since I saw you last, a lot has changed. If you can get me a cup of coffee and if you have a few minutes to spare, I'll explain."

He was anxious to see how the buckboard had come out, so on Wednesday afternoon he borrowed a horse from Mrs. Parker so that Misty could rest and graze in the pasture. When he arrived at the Bender farm, he saw his horses in the pasture. He reined up just outside an open barn door and yelled out, "Mr. Bender are you in there?"

Hiram replied, "Who goes there?"

---

[25] https://smallfarmersjournal.com/disc-harrow-requirements/

"It's Todd Morgan, Mr. Bender."

"Tie your horse around the side of the barn and come in the side door. I'll be with you in a few minutes. Your buckboard is over in the far corner." Todd did as he was instructed and upon seeing the buckboard, thought it looked like a piece of artwork. The length was just like he imagined it, the seat sat a bit higher because of the double-wishbone springs, the shelf underneath was hanging from black wrought iron straps on each side of it, the secret storage box was hidden very well, so well in fact, he couldn't tell where it was until he lifted a thickly woven hemp floor mat that had been put on the floor where a person's foot would rest. Instead of a door pull which he had expected, there was lip about four inches long just barely above the floor boards for opening it.

Looking inside, he saw that it was crafted like a jewelry box and lined with smooth cedar boards. The sides were the required height on the rear of the wagon and instead of one solid board, it was made of two boards equally spaced and fastened with three inch by one inch wide black wrought iron straps to two by two inch posts. They dropped into matching holes in the floorboards so that the sides could be easily removed and the wagon would have a flat surface all the way across. Underneath the wagon were two equally spaced wrought iron straps about ten inches tall and twenty-four inches wide to hold the two sides when they were not needed. The wheels on the back were wider than the front ones and the double springs gave the wagon a sturdy look about it. He was thrilled and could hardly wait to harness the horses to it and drive it back into town. Hiram, seeing him looking over the buckboard said, "How do you like it so far?"

"It looks great and I'm hoping it rides as nice as it looks."

"It does. I had the horses pull it for the last few days to get them used to it; if you'll give me a hand we'll get it outside, get the horses harnessed and take it for a ride. You have to get used to driving with a team and I'm guessing that you may have used shorter buckboards where you worked before. This one's bigger and you will need to understand the difference in maneuvering it and how to make it work for you when you need it the most. They got the wagon out into the yard, got the horses hitched and took it for a ride. Hiram drove first pointing out things about it that Todd didn't know. When he had gone about a mile or so, they switched places and Todd drove back to the barn. Hiram went inside and brought out a new black buggy whip and put it in the hole on the driver's side. He set a sealed bucket of wheel grease under the seat and said, "Keep the wheel hubs greased on a regular basis and you'll never have trouble with them, if you don't, you'll have trouble someday when you need the wagon the most. I get several wagons in here that need repairs to the hubs because they weren't taken care of properly."

Todd promised he'd keep up the maintenance on the wagon. He took a check from his pocket and gave it to Hiram, saying, "I can't thank you enough. I've put a little extra on the check, take your wife to dinner sometime when she least expects it. Again, thanks for building 'my' wagon."

"It was my pleasure and nice to do business with you. If you come by this way again, stop in and see me."

"I will." He tied the horse to the rear of the buckboard and drove back into town, smiling.

<h1 style="text-align:center">-37-</h1>

On Thursday, Todd met Turk at the café and they both ordered flank steak, black beans, seasoned rice and lemonade to drink. While they were eating, Todd said to Turk, "Have you ever considered selling your cabins and barn to a settler, then filing for a homestead on one of the sections near my property? The reason I ask is that you'd be closer to your mine and you'd have me for a neighbor. When you were gone, I could keep an eye on your property and when I was gone you could do the same for me."

"My brother had mentioned that very same thing to me before I left. Do you know who could help us file under the Homestead Act for land that the government is offering?"

"I used a lawyer, Mr. August McDavitt. He's very thorough and his brother is an assayer."

"We know the other McDavitt; his company assays our gold and turns it into money for us. After lunch, why don't you and I go see if he is available later this afternoon. I need to go back to the hotel for some shuteye."

August was busy until 3 pm, so Lucy penciled in Turk's name and what he wanted to talk about.

Todd remarked that he had to take care of some business around town and he would come back to the hotel at 2:30 and wake him for his 3 o'clock appointment. When they parted Todd went over to Henderson's Mercantile and purchased a wide brimmed Stetson, two new denim shirts, one with buttons straight down the middle, the other with fake buttons on one side and the real ones on the left. He could just button it part of the way, leaving the top part open like a tunic. He also purchased two pairs of Levi jeans, two pairs of long-johns, a pair of extra-long socks and a pair of work boots, then paid for everything and decided it was time he got that haircut, shave and a bath he had been putting off; he'd have just enough time before he met up with Turk.

He looked and felt like a different person when he walked out of the barber shop, so much so that he passed a man that looked like Josh, but the man only nodded his head as he walked by him. Todd quickly walked down the steps and turned the corner into an alleyway between two buildings and said to himself *If the guy looked like Josh, it probably was.* He walked to the end of the alley, turned and went the opposite direction that Josh was headed. He came out on Howell Street and walked back toward Main Street and looked up and down the street, but he didn't see Josh. He crossed the street to the other side and walked up a block to the hotel where Turk was staying. He walked up the stairs and down the hall to his room and knocked on the door. Turk came to the door and said, "Can I help you?"

"We're supposed to go see Mr. McDavitt at 3 pm."

"If I bumped into you on the street Todd, I wouldn't have recognized you. Maybe I ought to get a haircut, shave and a bath before I go back to see my brother and Pete, they'd never know it was me." They both laughed and Turk said, "Give me a minute and I'll be right with you."

After introductions were made at the lawyer's office and seats taken, Mr. McDavitt pointed to the sectional plat map and said to Turk, "The following sections are available where Todd has his place, Sections 161, 164, 171, 174 and 176. You say you have a brother and a friend who are living on your current property with you. Why don't each one of you file for a section and slightly improve each one to meet the requirements of the Homestead Act?"

"The only problem is that I am the only one who came to Lander," Turk replied.

Mr. McDavitt offered a solution, "I will be at Fort Washakie by the middle of July to settle a land dispute. I will be staying with the post commander, he and I are old friends from West Point. You could meet me there and I am sure there is a notary at the fort. Would that meet your needs?"

"You bet it would. In that case, I'd like to file on Section 171. Could your secretary check on our mining claims that we filed about three years ago over at the courthouse? I'd be happy to give her the claim numbers."

"Lucy, will you bring me a set of Homestead papers and get out your notary stamp please." Lucy brought in the necessary paperwork, Turk read it and put his signature on the pages where he was told; Lucy notarized it and August said, "The courthouse had to close early today because of a town meeting tonight. Lucy will file the paperwork in the morning once the courthouse opens. If you can come back by here around 10 am, she'll have the documents for you. While she is at the courthouse, she'll check and make sure your mining claim is still on file. I am going to give you two maps, the same as I gave Todd. He'll explain what you have to do with them. I'll give you maps on the other sections as well. Meet me at the fort and we will finish the paperwork there. That will be \$155 and you can pay Lucy tomorrow. Do you have any questions?"

"I don't have any right now. If I think of any, I'll ask you before we leave for home."

"I will be in South Pass City tomorrow on business so I won't see you again until we meet at the fort. Thank you for doing business with me. I will represent you in all things that pertain to your property."

"In that case, I'll just write any questions I have on a piece of paper and give them to your secretary in the morning."

Turk said to Todd as they were walking over to the mercantile, "Do you think you'll be ready to go home by the day after tomorrow?"

"I don't see why not. I'll ask Mr. Henderson if they can get the supplies I ordered on the buckboard by tomorrow afternoon. We can have him put the stakes you'll need for all the properties on the buckboard as well."

"Now I'll have time to get that haircut, shave and a bath. While I'm here at the general store, I might as well get some new clothes, too. When they were finished, Todd walked back toward the boarding house; Turk walked toward the barber shop.

-38-

Todd wanted to see Mrs. Parker's reaction to the way he now looked. He walked up the front stairs and used the door knocker that had been recently installed. Megan came to the door and said, "My mother will be with you in a moment. She turned around and ran back down the hall; Priscilla came to the door and said, "I am sorry, but we are full up this week. You might try The Mayfair Hotel in town, they may have some rooms available. He removed his Stetson and she gasped, "It couldn't be. You found out where I lived after all these years and now you show up on my doorstep you no account son-of-a-" As she reached down beside the door frame and came up with a double-barrel shotgun and said, "Get out of here before I blow you to kingdom come."

"Priscilla, it's me, Todd Morgan, please put that shotgun down before someone gets hurt. I got a haircut and a shave, I just wanted to see the expression on your face, but I got more than I bargained for." She just stood behind the screen door for a few moments. He could see that the initial shock was taking effect as she dropped the shotgun and began to collapse. He quickly opened the screen door and caught her before she fell, picked her up into his arms, and took her into

185

the parlor setting her in an overstuffed chair. She composed herself and said, "I'm sorry, but you shocked me so much with your appearance. You looked like my no account husband who ran off eight years ago."

"I hope you won't hold that against me."

"No, actually this will be fun introducing you all over again at dinner."

"May I take you out to lunch tomorrow? I will be leaving the following day to go back to my homestead."

"That would be nice. Would you mind if I pick out the restaurant? A friend of mine from church just opened a new place and I'd like to try it out."

"That's fine with me and by the way, I won't be up in time for breakfast tomorrow. I need to sleep in, I haven't had a good night's sleep in a couple of weeks; as a matter of fact, I might not get up until it's time to go to lunch."

True to his word, he woke around 11 am and was thirsty. He went over to the bureau and poured himself a tall glass of water from the glass pitcher, drained it and then poured another one. He looked out the window to see all his horses and the mule frolicking or grazing in the pasture next to the barn. *Good* he thought to himself *come tomorrow you'll be wishing you were in the pasture, but there will be work to be done getting all the supplies back to the homestead.* He lay back down on the bed for a few more minutes. He felt like he could sleep at least another couple of hours. Reluctantly, he got up, picked up the washcloth and the bar of soap and went over to the bureau. He poured water into the basin and began to wash his face, neck and chest, and under his arms and then dried himself off. He pulled out one of the new shirts and wished he had asked Priscilla to press out all the folds and wrinkles, but it would have to do as it was.

He decided to put his derringer in his watch pocket instead of wearing his gun belt. He smoothed over his hair, grabbed his new hat and went out the door, locking it behind him, and went down the front stairs. When he got to the landing, he could see her standing next to someone and she said, "I am not ready to make that kind of commitment." The man walked away from her and stormed out, slamming the front door, rattling the glass. Todd cleared his throat before he finished walking down the remaining steps into the front hall. She looked up, frowning, which quickly turned to a smile as soon as she saw him and he said, "Are you ready to go to lunch?"

"Let's take the surrey and on our way back from the restaurant we can pick up my daughter, Megan, at school." He went out to the barn and got the Appaloosa mare, harnessed her and led her over to the surrey. He drove the surrey out to the front of the house, got down, and went through the gate to walk Priscilla out to the surrey. He helped her up into the seat, then walked around the back of the wagon before getting up next to her. As they set off for the restaurant, he said, "Just tell me how to get there."

Later that afternoon after they arrived back at the house with Megan in the back of the surrey, he pulled into the yard behind the house and in front of the barn. He jumped down and helped Megan out first, then her mother. Jasper, the puppy, ran and jumped up on Megan; he wanted some attention. She petted him for a few seconds before going into the house. She knew she had to get her homework done first before she could play with her dog. Priscilla said to Todd, "I want to talk with you in the barn, but first I have to get Megan settled. Will you put the surrey on the side of the barn, then take the horse to the pasture and let her loose?"

"I'd be happy too. I will meet you in the barn in a few minutes." She changed into blue jeans, a button down shirt and boots. She looked every bit the part of a ranch wife. Once in the barn, she pushed a couple bales of hay together and took a seat waiting for him.

When he came in the barn, she said, "I want to explain about my meeting with the man you saw storm out of the house this morning."

"You don't have to explain a thing to me."

"I want to, please sit down." She explained to him that when she first came to Lander, she didn't know what kind of work she could find or do. She also needed a place to stay with a child and none of the hotels or saloons with rooms would rent to her.

"I went to the parsonage and spoke with the minister about my plight and he and his wife put us up in their home. We stayed with them for the better part of a month. I had some money saved, but that would run out before too long. I borrowed a horse and rode around town to find out what, if anything, could be bought or rented for a reasonable price. I came down the road out front and saw this Victorian in disrepair with a sign out front that simply said "FOR SALE" and to contact the bank for more information.

"I went to the bank and asked to speak with the president. He told me the owner had moved back to St. Louis and he wanted it sold as soon as possible. He told me the house had ten bedrooms, a large dining room, formal living room, a parlor, indoor plumbing and a hundred sixty acres. Some of it was fenced while the rest of the land was undeveloped. The owner wanted $5000. I didn't have that kind of money, but I had close to $2000. He asked me what I would do with such a big house. I told him I would fix up part of it for me and my daughter to live in, and the rest of it I would turn into a boarding house. We haggled a little bit, I can be quite persuasive when I put my mind to it, and we settled on $4100. I put $900 as a down payment and I could pay the bank $38 a month with 1% interest until the principal balance was paid off. The parson spoke at church on my behalf and asked if the parishioners would help me clean up the place so that I could live there and start my boarding house.

"Over the next four months, men, women and even some of the older children would come by and help, and what you see today is pretty much how it ended up. One of the older men from church comes by every now and then to fix anything major for me and in return, I feed him lunch. The bank manager, Mr. Johansen, took a liking to me, but my feelings for him are not mutual. He was the man in the parlor this morning. He thinks he is in love with me and wants to marry me, but I don't love or want to marry him. I was married once before to a demonstrative person and Mr. Johansen has the same type of personality. You are the first man that I have met, other than my regular boarders, who is not only kind to me, but my daughter as well and that means a lot to me. Blushing, she said, "I, I am attracted to you. Please don't think that I am being too forward or throwing myself at you. You have your life, a hard life and I would never—"

"I have been having a dream every so often of a lady with reddish-brown hair, a nice smile and features similar to yours. She is in a field of wildflowers running towards me but I always wake up before she gets to me. I must say that it is uncanny that you could be that woman. Even though I hadn't met you until just a few weeks ago, I have strong feelings toward you, Priscilla. I didn't want you to think that I was being too forward either. I wouldn't ask you to give up what you have here, but I need my space, if you know what I mean. I have never lived in a town and I've done things that no man would ever burden a woman with. So, for the time being, let's just be friends and over time we will see what develops." She slid off the hay bale and stepped over to where he was standing and gave him a kiss on his cheek. Todd thought to himself, *She sure smells nice and she is very soft to the touch.* She turned and quickly ran out of the barn, leaving him standing there to ponder what just happened.

The following morning, Turk arrived in time for breakfast. Todd had said his goodbyes to Megan the night before and had given her a doll he had purchased at Henderson's. He said to her, "I know she's not much, but she will listen to you laugh, dry your tears when you are sad, and be there when you need a friend."

"Thank you, Mr. Morgan, I'll give her a nice name and keep her on my bed all the time." After breakfast, Todd asked Turk if he would mind going out to the barn to get the three horses and the mule ready, and he would join him in a few minutes. He helped clear the table and after putting the dishes in the wash basin, he pulled Priscilla into the pantry and slid the pocket door over so they could be alone. He pulled her close and gave her a deep, tender kiss before whispering in her ear, "I'll be back for you." She kissed him back, wiped away a tear, fixed her apron and slid the door back into the wall, looked to see if Megan had come downstairs. She hadn't and just as she was about to go out into the kitchen, he pulled her back and gave her another kiss. "I don't want you to stop, but I also don't want Megan to see us. Your friend will wonder what happened to you, so you'd better go. Do come back to me, I love you."

As he walked out of the back door and down the steps he had a smile from ear to ear, but before he entered the barn, his expression changed. He began formulating a plan in his head. After he saddled Misty, he put a pack frame on the mule and tied the extra one on top of that; Turk had already put harnesses on the other two horses.

He said to Turk, "If you are ready, let's go to the mercantile and hitch up the horses to the buckboard, transfer some of the supplies to the mule and my horse, and we'll be on our way."

-39-

She stood in the doorway, wiped away a tear that had formed in the corner of her eye, touched her lips and gave a little wave as he rode out of the barnyard. Megan had just come into the kitchen and upon seeing her mother said, "Why are you crying?"

"It's nothing, really."

"Are you sure Mom? I mean…"

"I'll be alright. Are you already for school, teeth and hair brushed; dress on straight?"

"Yes, Mother!"

"We better get you out to the front of the house so that you don't miss the school wagon."

They walked hand in hand out to the front gate and waited. She could see Todd just turning the corner onto Main Street making his way to the mercantile. Oh, how she wished he would come back for one more kiss.

After tying everything down on the buckboard and before leaving the mercantile, Todd gave Mr. Henderson an envelope to give to August McDavitt when he returned from South Pass City. The letter read in part… *I have a plan, please bring the Homestead papers for Sections 36 and 41 with you when you come to Fort Washakie. I will meet you there and explain. Todd Morgan.*

They headed northwest toward the mountains, as they were travelling along, Todd explained his plan to Turk.

Turk replied, "I think that would work for all of us. We'll have to see what my brother and Pete think about what you are proposing and what Mr. McDavitt has to say when we go to the fort to see him."

Bypassing Fort Washakie, they stopped at Shoshone Joe's for the night. Todd explained to Joe what happened to the faithful dog and why he wanted to get not one, but two new dogs. A lab and a border collie, if Joe had them. Joe said one of his bitches just had a new litter of border collie puppies that would be weaned in about seven weeks and he'd keep one for Todd. As to labs, he only had two females, one tan and one reddish-gold. Todd chose the reddish-gold one. He paid Joe for both dogs, took the lab and said he'd be back in about nine weeks to pick up the border collie.

In the morning, they readied the horses and arrived at Turk's cabin about three in the afternoon, finding his brother Gus mucking out the stalls in the barn. After dismounting, Turk gave his brother a big 'bear' hug, while Todd set about unloading the supplies that Turk had bought while he was in Lander. He said to them, "I am sure that Pete would like to sleep in his own bed for a change. I will send him along just as soon as he helps me unload the heavier items. I will see all of you at my place two weeks from Monday."

Gus couldn't get over how youthful his older brother looked after he had gotten a shave and haircut and said half-joking, "I think before Pete gets back here, I'll shave and you can trim my hair. Then we can prank him." They laughed and took some of the items into the cabin.

Todd found Pete dozing in the sunshine on top of a large

granite boulder. As Todd got close, Pete woke and nearly fell off the boulder. He said, "I thought y'all had decided to stay in Lander. Now I can get back to the cabin and sleep in my own bed."

"I just said the same thing to Gus and Turk," Todd replied. "If you'll help me get the heavy things off the buckboard, you can leave. I really do appreciate you watching my place. Did you have any problems?"

"Not really, but around the third day or so there was a wagon train of about a dozen wagons passing through and they asked if they could camp down by the creek, so I told them to go ahead. Their leader, a Mr. Peters, I think his name was, asked if anyone had homesteaded this area. I told them that it was and he said they would just continue on in the morning until they found a place like this where they could settle down.

They were very friendly, but you could see the fear on the faces of their womenfolk and some of the younger children. I am guessing that they hadn't seen anyone who was bearded and dressed in buckskins carrying a rifle and a large knife strapped around his midsection. If they are going to live out here in the wilderness, they'll have to get used to the way we dress and look. Those hunters never came back."

After Pete left, Todd looked over his property deciding where to put a cabin, barn and corral. Once he had that figured out, he hoisted his food supplies up into the trees. He walked over near the stream and built a firepit with enough area around it to eventually put in a table and four chairs for relaxing by the fire after a long day. He added kindling and a couple logs to the firepit to cook supper and boil his coffee before he retired for the evening.

The morning came too early as Todd rolled out of his

doubled blankets to a slightly overcast sky. He put kindling on the ashes, adding a split log to the firepit while he made a fresh pot of coffee and ate leftover ham and beans for breakfast. After using the outhouse that he had constructed previously, he next led the horses and mule to a patch of wild grasses and hobbled them so they wouldn't go too far.

He decided that he'd start cutting loblolly pine until he thought that he had enough to build a barn and eventually a two-room cabin. That took the better part of the day and once he had them all down, he started to trim the branches. Some he'd use for fence posts while the rest he'd either use for kindling or firewood. He was sore after using muscles he hadn't used in over a month and decided that tomorrow he'd clear the sites that he had picked out for the cabin and barn.

He cleared the brush, cut the trees on it and using the mule, he pulled out any stumps that remained before using the mold board plow to loosen up the soil and graded it so that the buildings would sit on a level surface. He decided to place the cabin where it would face southwest to take advantage of the afternoon sun. He was going to put one of the windows that he bought on the wall that faced the barn and corral and the other window on the side that faced a road that he had cut through a stand of trees and graded from the front edge of the section line. He curved the road in such a way so that as you rode past the entrance, you couldn't see the cabin or the barn.

On the third day, he hitched Misty to the buckboard and started to follow the stream stopping every now and then to gather rocks from the creek bed and put them on the floor of the buckboard. When he thought he had enough of them, he went to each hole that he had dug for the corner footings and piled the rocks next to each hole. He mixed cement with the sand from the creek bed and put the rocks in the holes for added strength. He'd have to let the footings cure before he could begin putting the logs he had cut for the corners and for the foundation of the barn. He set about squaring them up first before notching the logs until he had them all done. Later in the afternoon, he stopped to have something to eat, drink, and to rest his back. While he was sitting against a tree stump, he took a piece of paper out of his shirt pocket and wrote down what he had already explained to Turk and what he wanted to say to Gus and Pete about his idea and how he thought it would all work out. Once he finished writing out what he wanted to say, he decided it was a good time to take a nap while he was facing the sun. He called the dog over to where he was, she laid down next to him and they both fell asleep.

Just before sunset, he woke and took the dog with him to gather the horses and mule. He brought halters with him and put them around the mule and each horse's neck before taking off the hobbles. He led them back to where he had a tarp stretched between four trees and tied each one to a separate tree.

He had placed several oil lamps around his work area so he could continue to work at night. He used an adze to trim the side of the logs that would be on the inside of the cabin. Just before midnight, he could hardly see straight. He used the outhouse and when he came out he gathered six of the oil lamps and set them all on the table by the fire pit. He took one and hung it on a broken limb of a tree near enough to the temporary barn; he hung another where he intended to bunk down for the night and extinguished the flame on the other four. The dog curled up next to him and they both were sound asleep within minutes.

Over the next several days, using the work horses, pulleys and ropes, he worked alone and was able to get all the logs set into place for both the barn and the cabin. Rather than build the barn first which wouldn't happen until his three friends were coming in a week to help him, he decided to build the cabin. Once the ridge pole was set, he began nailing the roof rafters and notched logs in place on top of them. He secured a plank door and cut out where he intended to put in the windows. Tonight, for the first time in a very long time, he would sleep in the cabin on the wood floor.

The following morning, he had set some snares to catch his and the dog's food to last them a couple of days. He had named the dog 'Happenstance' and she became a good friend, guard dog and a joy to have around. He checked the snares and caught two rabbits. After he skinned them, he put the furs in the cabin for safekeeping. He cut up one of the rabbits for the dog; the other he put on the grill to cook along with some of the corn he had taken from his original garden.

The following day, he decided to build a bed wide enough for two people, table for four with two benches and a dry sink so he could prepare his food inside the cabin before he took it out to the fire pit to cook. He said to himself after he was done for the day, *one of these days I'll have to build a fireplace and a chimney so that I don't always have to cook my food outside. Right now though, I have to finish cutting a few more trees for the barn so that when The Langstrom's and Pete come over to help me, I'll have what I need for the corner posts and connecting beams. If we could get two sides roughed in, I'll be in good shape.*

He said to the dog, "Stay." The dog just curled up on an old blanket that Todd had put on the porch with a watchful eye towards where the horses were. He opened both windows and the night air was just right; he shed his clothes and crawled into bed. He pulled up the quilt that Priscilla had given him to keep him warm so that he'd think of her tenderly as he fell asleep.

-40-

Todd knew he had to get to his mining claims and mark them before someone else did. It would be the last time during the summer that he would have to look for gold until the end of September when he planned to start trapping again. He also had to see Walking Many Places and his father, Standing Tall, and give them the letter from the post commander. He knew he would be gone at least a week and he hoped that maybe Turk would stay at his place while he worked on staking out his section. He was getting overwhelmed with everything that needed to get done in what seemed like a short amount of time. *Certainly no time for resting on my laurels, but If I don't take some time off, I won't be worth a tinker's dam and my plans won't work out like I hope they will.* There was no place to go swimming, so he stripped down and sat in the stream that ran along the south side of his property. After he got use to the cold water, he laid down and let the water washed over him. Once refreshed, he toweled off and got dressed. He found a nice place in the tall grass with the sun beating down and went to sleep; the dog was close by.

Early Monday morning, Gus and Turk arrived to an overcast sky. It was a good day for working without the blazing sun at their backs. Todd had all the logs set where they needed to be. Before they arrived, He took the time to build a table with two benches and had placed it down by the creek next to the fire pit. The night before, he made another late night raid on his 'old' vegetable garden for potatoes, onions, string beans, a dozen ripe tomatoes and a bushel of carrots. The other day, he shot a deer, cut the meat into roasts and steaks, and used some to feed the dog; he put the rest in burlap bags high up in a tree near where he shot it and scraped the hide as soon as he got back to the cabin. He put the potatoes in the hot coals to cook and set the roast in a roasting pan with a little water, pinch of salt and pepper to slowly roast while they worked. The coffee pot sat on a flat stone at the edge of the firepit. About an hour or so before they would break for supper, he put a small pan of onions on the edge of the grate to simmer. Once they had taken on a golden hue, he could pour them over the meat just before they sat down.

As they worked along using both work horses, ropes and pulleys rigged on opposite sides of the barn to sturdy oaks, they got the four corner posts erected and the cross beams set in place. They steadied them with long, thin trees stripped of their branches and nailed to the side of a tree for support for each side. They even went so far as to get the roof joists in place on each end and in the middle, using eight inch spikes to secure them to the center beam. This was much more than he had hoped for and by working in pairs they got the job done a lot quicker. It was helpful that he had cut and notched the logs that they were going to use.

In the late afternoon, they all took the time to get cleaned up before they sat down to eat supper. The venison roast with the caramelized onions was perfect, baked potatoes, sliced tomatoes, sourdough biscuits, coffee and refreshing cold water to drink rounded out the meal. During supper, Todd explained everything to Gus and Pete and finally said, "So you see if each of you take over one of my sections that I already filed on along with Turk's, you'll have more than enough room to do what you want with the land. Each one of you will have to put some sort of structure on a section, but with the adjoining sections you'd be able to have a cabin, barn, pasture, and a storage shed to meet that requirement of the Homestead Act. I have bought enough barbed wire to completely enclose the original four sections and enough wire mesh fencing for the corners. I never really wanted all that land in the first place. What do you think? If you're in agreement, do we have a deal?"

Turk spoke up for his brother and Pete and said, "We are all in agreement, but until we meet with Mr. McDavitt, the sections are still yours."

"Absolutely!" Before the Langstrom brothers and Pete Boyd were going to leave, he asked Turk, "Could you stay here at my place starting the day after tomorrow? I have to go see the Sioux chief and deliver a letter from the commander at Fort Washakie. The commander doesn't want or need any trouble with the Sioux, especially with all of these new settlers and prospectors moving in, and quite frankly, none of us do either. I'll be gone about a week and that would give you enough time to stake out your section and walk the property to make the marks you need on the map that Mr. McDavitt gave you."

"I don't see why not," Turk replied. They all shook hands. Gus, Turk and Pete mounted their horses and rode back to their cabin. Todd hadn't felt this good since he pulled Priscilla into the pantry, but she was more appealing. *Maybe things will come together after all* he thought to himself. He took the tin plates and eating utensils down to the creek, swirled some sand and using a clean rag washed out the pans, then the eating utensils and finally the coffee cups; he took them inside the cabin and set them upside down on a small table to dry. He went back outside, walked over to look at all the framing that had been accomplished today. Once he got back to the cabin, he sat down and propped his feet on a couple of unsplit logs in front of him. It was time to rest. Happenstance came over and Todd scratched behind her ears as she lay down by his feet. They both seemed content as night overcame twilight. Yawning, he said, "I think it's time for me to get some sleep. I'll leave you right here to keep an eye out for the both of us," and with that said, he went inside the cabin, sat on the edge of the bed and removed his boots. He lay on top of the covers, put his hands behind his head and drifted off to sleep.

It was the last week in June; he had planted a small garden of potatoes, onions, carrots, turnips and four tomato plants. He fenced it in with some of the wire fencing. *At least* he thought to himself *I'll have some vegetables during the coming winter months; more importantly, I need to finish tilling those forty acres and get that hay mixture of rye and buckwheat seed in the ground., Even if the hay comes in late, I should have enough for the horses and the mule during the winter. Once I have it all harvested I can let them graze on the stubble. Tomorrow, Turk will be here and I'll be able to get done what I need to regarding my claims.* As he was having a cup of coffee, he took a piece of paper out of his pocket along with a pencil and wrote down what he needed to take with him on the trip.

-41-

Todd rode north and then headed west along the Continental Divide until he came to the stream that he'd only seen frozen over this past winter. When he got to the top of a plateau, he looked out over the land that had turned into a beautiful carpet of waving green grass with yellow and white butterflies flitting over the red, yellow and blue wildflowers mixed in with the purple sage. The aspens and box elder were full with leaves, while squirrels jumped from tree limb to tree limb, and sparrows, warblers and king birds hunted for seeds, bugs and worms. They flew up into nests well hidden in the trees and sang their joyful songs; an occasional antelope came into view and bounded away at the sight of him.

However, guessing where the draw was became a challenge. Checking the map he had drawn and the compass he had brought with him, he figured he would have to climb higher up and look down over the valley rather than looking up. After all, he had made it so that if a person or persons were riding by and looked up, they wouldn't see a thing, but he had to. Riding back and forth, looking out over the valley, he remembered that off in the distance was a mountain peak with a crooked top and guessed it would have snow year-around.

He took the binoculars from his saddlebags and scanned the horizon to see the mountain top. Upon seeing it, he followed his line of sight, but he still didn't find it. *Maybe I should ride back down to the valley floor and look up using the binoculars.* Once down on the valley floor, he scanned the forest and became frustrated at not seeing what he was looking for. *I should have made more blaze marks on the trees* he thought as he turned the horse around. He took a drink from his canteen and said to the horse, "This is harder than I thought. You and I are just going to have to ride back and forth until I see something that looks familiar." He finally saw the faint outline of the lean-to that he had built. Once he got there, the stream was running full, though not gushing, as it had been a dry summer so far, and in the winter it was iced over and partially covered with snow.

He tied off the horse and mule and walked to the back of the draw to find just the right place where he could build a new lean-to so that it faced south. Any wind that came up would be blocked by the back wall of the draw. He cleared out the dried pine branches and set them aside. He could use them as kindling if he decided to have a fire tonight. He took the shovel and dug an adequate fire pit. He didn't have that luxury during the winter, and mounded the dirt around the sides, took some rocks out of the creek bed and lined the fire pit, then set a flat rock just over the edge so that his coffee pot could be kept heated during the day and night if a fire was in the pit. He took the rest of the supplies and the pack frame off of the mule, then hobbled her and Misty, while he went off to find suitable timber to cut so he could build an adequate lean-to and use the limbs to make a new corral for the horse and mule.

He decided to build the corral first so that he could put Misty and the mule in it. He put his saddlebags under the saddle and spread out his sleeping bag and extra blanket. Tomorrow morning would be soon enough to build the new lean-to. There was plenty of grass and wild flowers for the two of them to crop; he was only going to be here a few days before he left for the other claim. He found plenty of dead wood, gathered more than enough and piled it next to the fire pit for future use.

Standing back, he surveyed everything. It all looked good. He decided to pan for gold and walked up into the draw where the creek ran next to the corral. He took the empty squirrel skin pouches that he had made, a pan, shovel and his canteen with him. He'd been panning about an hour or so before he got his first piece of gold about the size of a 10 pound nail head. He shoveled some of the sand and gritty dirt from the creek bed and, systematically using an empty coffee cup, scooped some in the pan and swished it around until he found some gold flakes or if not, he'd just pour the grit back into the creek and let it wash away.

After three hours of working in one spot, he decided to take a break and took out a biscuit and had a drink of water from the canteen. Looking down, he saw that he had a tiny amount of gold dust and several flakes about the same size as the first one. He stood, stretched and listened to what sounded like a herd of horses. He quickly ran to the edge of the clearing where he could look down into the valley below and saw a large herd of mustangs being led by a mottled palomino stallion at least sixteen or seventeen hands high.

If the Timber Creek ranch hands could see this, they'd be awestruck he thought. He watched them for over a half hour before he went back too look for more gold. He walked up the draw to where water was sliding down between a cleft in the rock face that went up at least twenty feet. He remembered what he should have brought with him, the pick ax. He did the best he could with the chisel hammer, just chipping away here and there, but surprisingly enough, he found a small gold seam between the boulders to the left of where the water was gushing out. Now he wished he had the pick ax more than ever. He chipped enough of the rock to see that it went very deep into the ground out of sight and that in itself was a good thing, at least from the standpoint that if anyone found the lean-to, they may not come back here or wouldn't know enough to chip it out like he had.

He decided to hide what he had already done. He took the shovel with him and walked a good distance away from his campsite looking for six to eight small aspen saplings and three or four spruce trees just right for transplanting. He'd cover the holes with earth and leaves and hoped that over time no one would find them. He brought the aspen and cedar saplings to where he wanted to plant them in the draw and made it look like they had been there all along. He also decided to plant more cedar saplings in front of the lean-to and fire pit to hide the campsite. He'd rope the back of the draw off from the horse and the mule so they wouldn't eat the leaves or the bark, exposing the cleft.

He took the rocks with the gold and put them in a satchel that he had brought with him. *This is quite a find* he thought to himself *quite a find indeed.* He went back down the creek a bit and sifted the sand and grit until he had about a thimble full of gold dust and one nugget the size of an acorn. He decided to have a small fire tonight if only to have a little warmth for himself, to heat the biscuits, jerky, and coffee. So far this had been a successful trip.

In the morning, he took four of the stakes and drove them into the ground at each of the four corners after pacing off the size of the claim. He piled rocks around each one so that his last name showed above the pile. He made sure the fire was out and the ashes were cold. The fence poles were stacked next to the opening used for a gate and he had removed the rope in the back part of the corral. Using a pine branch, he brushed out his shoe prints on the ground in the rear of the draw before he scattered pine straw, leaves, and twigs. He thought to himself, *If only a nice gentle rain would come along and make it look like no one has been here at all.* The clouds had started to drift in from the west and that could be a good sign. The earth needed the rain, badly. He had at least twenty-five miles to go to get to the next claim; hopefully he'd be there before nightfall. The arroyo was near Bull Lake and like the claim in the draw, it too would take some work finding it.

Priscilla certainly had to get her work done today as she had neglected cleaning out the rooms that were last used by the temporary boarders. She was going to strip the wallpaper and paint the rooms instead of wallpapering them all over again and move the furniture around in the rooms. The town had recently sent her a new property tax bill and it had gone up considerably since she opened the boarding house. The town was growing and most everyone at the town hall meeting agreed to give the sheriff a raise and for him to hire a deputy. The sheriff couldn't cover the whole area by himself and still keep peace in the town at the same time. The Town Council voted four to one for the increase in property taxes and for the sheriff to hire a part-time deputy until such time that he needed someone full time. Some of the residents grumbled about the tax increase. Rather than start a discussion about the merits of such an increase, they gave everybody a three month reprieve on collection of the tax increase. She wondered if Todd had to worry about property taxes upcountry; she'd ask him when he came to Lander the next time.

How thoughtful Todd had been to give Megan a doll before he left to get back to his ranch. Megan had aptly named her Molly and made sure that after she made her bed in the morning to put the doll on top of the pillows. She would occasionally say to her mother, "I want to make sure that Molly can see the sun" or "I want Molly to be comfortable while I am in school." Her daughter's happiness was her first priority so she hoped Todd would accept Megan as more than just a little girl who came with her mother.

She fantasized about visiting him up at his ranch, but like he had told her, "When I go back home, I'll be working from sunup to sundown. I am all work and have little time for myself, even for only a few minutes." She worried that he did too much and someday it would catch up to him when he least expected it. She'd make sure that the next time he came to town and stayed at the boarding house, he'd have time to rest and be able to be with her or at the very least take her out for lunch.

Since she was beginning to have feelings for Todd, she decided that the advances Johan was making weren't to her or Megan's advantage. Oh, she'd be cordial, but Todd was different. He made a fuss over her daughter and Megan had said just the other night before she went to bed, "I like Mr. Morgan, he's a nice man." She would agree with her daughter on that count; he was a nice man, but she really didn't know all that much about him other than he was a trapper and had worked on a ranch near Green Springs called Timber Creek. Perhaps she could have August McDavitt find out more about him or maybe Parson Samuels would. She wanted to know as much about him as possible so that she could make him feel more comfortable when he came back to Lander the next time.

There were times when Priscilla wished that Todd was there to keep Johan from bothering her; he was persistent, she'd give him that, though it was not his most enduring quality for sure. Every time she went into town and he saw her, he made it a point to walk past her with a leering smile or on other occassions he purposely would cross over to the side of the street she was on and try to engage her in conversation. When Megan was with her, he made sure that he always had a candy stick to give her so that she had to say thank you and would smile back at him. He was becoming more of a nuisance and she decided to limit the days of the week when she absolutely had to get something in town, and before Megan got home from school.

-42-

Todd had ridden several miles and decided to let the horse and mule graze for a while; he could use a break himself. As he sat on a weathered stump, he took a drink from his canteen and started to think about his past. *If I'd been on a cattle drive, I would either be riding drag and eating their dust or riding beside them to keep them from straying off, no rest, ride all day and if we made thirteen miles that would be a good day; my face would feel like sandpaper and the dust would be up my nose, making it dry as hell and tough to breathe. I wanted to be my own boss. Here I am in a peaceful valley, long wavy grass, a meandering stream with fish swimming in it and all I can think about is getting to the next claim.*

He let the horse and mule graze a few more minutes before he gathered up the halter on the mule and mounted his horse. He rode over the next ridge with eyes straining to see Bull Lake off in the distance and how far it might be. Using his binoculars, he saw what looked like a blue dot almost due north. He decided that it was to far to go today, he dismounted just inside the tree line and walked the horse and mule down to the stream where he hobbled them before taking off the saddle on Misty and tied the reins behind her neck; he undid the packs, set them on the ground and removed the pack frame on the mule. The valley looked peaceful enough with plenty of grass. He took the tarp and threw it over a fallen tree and used several large rocks to anchor it on the ground behind it. He found two long sticks and jammed them in the ground and tied a rope between them, then took the other side of the tarp and dropped it over the rope to form a temporary lean-to; using his bowie knife he dug a small fire pit about four inches deep in the gravel soil. He placed the saddle and saddle bags well up under the tarp before unrolling his bedroll, and decided to take a nap while the sun was still out.

"I got your back, partner," he heard a voice saying. Slowly opening his eyes, he saw a campfire. *What's going on?* he thought as he rubbed his eyes before clearly seeing that there was a fire in the fire pit and the outline of a man sitting opposite him craddling a coffee cup in his hands. He sat cross-legged with a Hawken 50 caliber lying across his legs and wore a rabbit skin hat on his head. "Saw your campsite as I passed by yonder ridge about an hour ago, safety in numbers I always say. So I moseyed on down here to find you a tossin' and a turnin' in your sleep and you were mumbling something about shooting them Yanks as they rode past you. Name's Jacob Johnson, but my friends just calls me Jake. What's yourn?" He asked.

"Todd Morgan."

"You that young fellow that trapped and damn near killed those hombres who went hunting on your homestead awhile back?"

"Yes, and I'd do it again to anyone who thinks they can trespass on another man's property or take something that isn't theirs and get away with it."

"You're nearly a legend to us trappers and miners. Thanks

for sticking up for us. We appreciate you settin' the record straight. Ever since you done that, there hasn't been any poaching of trapper's skins or claim jumping and that's a good thing. I hope you don't mind that I used your coffee pot and made coffee, I haven't had any in a coon's age and it sure tastes good. I shot me a turkey a ways back, we can share if you haven't et in a while."

"I haven't. You pluck them feathers, Jake, and I'll get us a few potatoes and onions from my supply satchel. While you're doing that, I have to go and get my horse and mule, and bring them closer."

"I already did. They were right friendly. They're over there by my horse and mule on the picket line that I strung just on the other side of this here campsite further up in the trees."

"You said something about safety in numbers. What did you mean by that?"

"Like I said, saw your camp from up on the ridgeline pointing to the northeast. There was a band of Indians riding single file opposite from where I was, watching me. I slowly made tracks down here to your camp. They stopped and faced this way before they rode off toward the north after a few minutes."

Todd said, "After we have supper, I'll take the first watch and you can take the second."

"That's fair enough, partner."

During the night, a wolf howled off in the distance and just as he was going off the watch, Todd heard the cry of the cougar and the horses whinnied and stamped their hooves. He settled them down and stayed with them till he didn't hear it again. Jake said he was awake, had to do his business over in the brush, but he'd be back in a minute. Todd put a couple of new logs on the fire and set the coffee pot back on to heat up. Jake could use a cup or two. Then he settled into his doubled blankets and nestled up to the saddle. His last words were, "If you get sleepy, nudge me and I'll take over for you.

Jake replied, "I make do with whatever sleep, I get."

-43-

As they were breaking camp, Jake said, "I think it's going to be a cold, hard winter this year. You might want to consider getting your trapping done early."

"Thanks for the information, I might just do that after I get back to my homestead and get everything squared away there. Hope to see you again sometime."

"Same here," Jake said as he took the trail to the northwest.

While Todd was heading due east,the trail was a bit easier to follow than over the mountains to the north. He crossed a trail left by the Indians thinking *Must have been the same ones that Jake saw. I will have to keep an eye out for them. I have to make contact with Walking Many Places before I go back to my homestead. Once I get to the claim, I will have to set a signal fire.*

Todd entered the area where the arroyo was and thankfully, the blaze marks could be seen just a short ride up the hill. He said to the horse, "Looks like a few bear prints in the soil, but they are old. Perhaps man-bear came to see if I was here and not finding me, went on." The horse just shook its head as if to say, "That's alright with me, I don't like bears." He dismounted and tied the horse and the mule to a tree. He cut fifteen small trees, trimmed them and set about constructing the corral. Next he dug a shallow trough on the side where the stream

214

rushed past so that the water would flow in and out keeping the water fresh. Once finished, he unsaddled the horse and led her to the corral where he took off her bridle. He walked back to where the mule was and took off the supplies and pack frame before he led her over to the corral and removed the tether.

He walked around the area and gathered several dead tree limbs to make an impromptu lean-to since he was only going to be there a day or two at the most. Once finished, he threw two ropes up and over stout tree limbs to hoist up his supplies out of the way of critters. When the necessary chores were done, he dug a fire pit, added kindling and started a fire to heat up water for coffee, a can of beans and a couple of biscuits for his supper. When supper was over, he sat there for a while, drinking his coffee and enjoying the warmth of the campfire. He had gotten a good night's sleep the previous night and tonight he thought he would probably stay awake most of the night. There wasn't anyone to help him keep watch, but after a few hours, sleep overcame him.

He woke just as the sun was rising, stood, stretched and walked over to the corral to check on Misty and the mule. He found them cropping grass or drinking water. After he came back, he added kindling to the embers to heat his coffee. He noticed the thunderheads boiling up in the western sky. They reminded him of the storms, he encountered growing up in the hills of Tennessee and at Timber Creek, twelve summers ago. Thunderheads like what he was seeing often erupted and caused a forest fire of major proportions. He hoped they brought rain instead, which was much needed in the surrounding area. He'd keep a watchful eye on the sky just in case.

While he was panning for gold in the creek that ran next to the corral he saw a flash of lightning up towards the mountains. If it was dry lightning and not the type that brought rain, he'd head straight down the hill to Bull Lake from where he was, *'bout two miles* he thought to himself. *I better stake the property before I forget to do what I came up here for in the first place.* He took four stakes with him and hammered each one into the dry earth and piled rocks around them, leaving only the **Mor** showing above the rocks. There were two swift flowing streams, one to his right that he had just come back from and the other along the western edge of the arroyo. *Might be the only saving grace if there is a forest fire,* he thought to himself. Afterward, he picked up his shovel and pan, and walked back to the stream, but on the western side this time to see if any gold was there. He had a good view of the valley and hills that surrounded him. He managed to get a thimble full of flakes and dust before he continued to move up the creek bed trying different places. The pickings were as plentiful as he had ever seen. After a couple of hours, he decided to look in the boulders where the water was coming out of. Could there possibly be a gold seam underground and the water flow was bringing the gold dust and flakes up to the surface and filtering itself down the creek bed? He made a mental note to come back here on his first trapping trip in late September and to bring with him the pick ax and a long-handled shovel.

He had promised himself a nap around midday, so he walked back to his campsite and set the shovel and pan down before walking over to the corral to check on the mule and Misty. He whistled for them and they came down to the fence where he scratched them behind their ears and poured some oats on the ground. Once he had them taken care of, he went back to where his blanket was, laid down with his hands clasped behind his head on the saddle and fell asleep. A few hours later, he woke to a sharp crack of thunder close by. Groggily, he sat up, rubbed his eyes, smelled burnt leaves and realized it wasn't the campfire. He heard another thunderclap off in the distance. Not knowing exactly where the forest fire was or how fast it was burning, he got the horse and mule settled down. He saddled Misty first, put on the saddlebags and the bedroll and tied them down. He hooked the canteen over the pommel and the Sharps in the scabbard and tied her to a tree. The mule was next. First the pack frame, supplies satchel and the satchel with the gold ore in it *and don't forget the coffee pot,* he said to himself. He went over to the fire pit, picked up the pot and poured the contents over the fire pit and tied the pot on the frame with a piece of rope. He could see a glow in the sky over his right shoulder and said to himself *If it comes this way, I'll be in a tent come the winter.* He didn't dare ride the horse down the hill not knowing the terrain all that well. He would just have to walk slowly down to the lake with the horse and the mule in tow behind him. "At least the lake will be between me and the fire and we can all rest," he said looking at the the smoky air.

Once he was on the other side of the lake, he picked a spot where he could tether the horses and watch the fire in progress. It crested the top of the hill where they had just been a couple of hours ago. As it advanced, it seemed to have a mind of its own following the gulley's snakelike curve down the hill, spreading out once it was about a half mile or so from the lake. Fortunately, the lake and the gently flowing streams on both sides of the arroyo kept it from advancing to where he had camped. The smell of burned brush, trees, dead leaves, and grass was overwhelming, but Todd had wetted his bandana and tied it around his nose and mouth and using two of his shirts, did the same for the horse and mule.

outskirtsThe people in Lander couldn't help but see the glow in the sky just past sundown and knew the fire was a bad one. There was nothing anybody could do to stop it or help the folks who lived up there. They could only hope and pray that it wasn't as bad as the one back in '68 when a forest fire sparked by lightning continued unabated for several weeks inching closer and closer to Lander. The farmers and ranchers took it upon themselves to cut down trees, clear brush and till the earth, creating a 100 foot wide ring around the town and part of the surrounding countryside thus saving most of the homes in and near the of Lander. Only a few cabins were lost, but more importantly no lives were lost and they had saved the town from total destruction.

Priscilla prayed that nothing terrible had happened to Todd. She knew he lived up near the mountains and he had said he was going to make a trip to stake his mining claims. She longed for him to be with her, maybe she could convince him to move closer to Lander. Megan saw tears on her mother's face and said, "What's wrong Mommy?"

"Mr. Morgan lives up near the mountains and I hope nothing bad happens to him. The smoke we've smelled comes from the glow in the sky we saw several days ago."

"Molly told me not to worry about that old fire anyway and that Mr. Morgan would make sure that it won't hurt us. I just know he'll be alright." The child's innocence gave her hope; she gave her a kiss on her cheek while Megan wiped away her mother's tears.

Mr. Johansen, the banker, continued to be persistent, inviting her out to lunch on several occassions and she continued to decline because she didn't want to encourage him. She was worried that if she continued to rebuff him, he could make trouble for her at the bank if he wanted to. She decided to talk with Parson Samuels about Johan. After she dropped Megan off at school the following day, she stopped by the parsonage to talk with him. The parson was a good listener and after Priscilla had explained everything to him, he said, "Does Mr. Morgan know how you feel about him?"

"I'm sure he does, we've gone to lunch, talked about what's important to both of us, and I have shared with him things about my past." She left out the part of kissing him; she did not want to give the parson the wrong impression.

"You said you shared your past, but has he shared his?"

"He told me that he had done some things that no man would ever burden a woman with, but I can honestly say I don't know what it's about. I didn't want to pry. He suggested that we be friends and see how things worked out over time. "

"It bothers me some that he didn't tell you about his past. He could be a deserter from the war, wanted by the law or any of a hundred other possibilities. I shall check around, I don't want you or Megan to get hurt in any way. Now about Mr. Johansen, he does have a stable job, has his own house and is well liked. What would it hurt if you at least had lunch with him, or if you like, the misses and I could join you if you feel that uneasy around him."

"Even if he is stable, I don't want to give him false hope that I am interested in him in any way. He has the same demeanor as my former husband."

The pastor said, "Since Mr. Morgan is 'living' up in the

mountains and you have no idea when he will come calling again, I suggest you meet Mr. Johansen at least half way. It's worth a try. Why don't you think about what I have said the rest of this week and give me your answer after church on Sunday."

-44-

Lack of sleep was beginning to take its toll on Todd. As he rode south toward his homestead, he slumped forward several times on the horse's neck. Finally, he stopped to let the horse and mule crop grass and drink from a stream and he walked upstream, laid down on the bank and splashed water on his face, took his bandana off soaking it in the clear, cold water and tied it around his neck to let the coolness help keep him awake. He drank heartily, filled his canteen, walked back to a tree and sat down to rest and fell asleep. He woke a couple of hours later and was refreshed. The horse and mule had not wandered far, he gathered the reins, tied the rope tether to the pommel, mounted and pushed on. He arrived just before sunset, and managed to get the saddle, saddle bags, and blanket off Misty and the things that were on the pack frame off the mule, before putting them with the other three horses in the temporary corral. Turk was down by the stream when he rode in and said, "We worried that the fire caught up with you by Bull Lake and we wouldn't see you again."

"We got out just in the nick of time to watch the fire's destruction; the animals and I are exhausted and right now I just need some sleep. Can we talk in the morning?"

"Sure, I was just getting ready to eat supper. Do you want to join me?"

"As much as that sounds appealing, I think I need sleep more."

"I'll be in just after I clean up after supper and I'll sleep by the door. Would you put my blankets there for me?"

"Sure, I'll see you in the morning for breakfast." Todd used the outhouse before going inside the cabin. He shed all his clothes except his long johns, took a healthy swig from his canteen crawled into his bed, pulled the comforter over his head and was fast asleep in seconds.

Turk had done a lot while Todd was away. Not only had he walked his section marking down all important landmarks on his map, but he staked the property and had started to dig fence post holes in the corners and along the fence line. In the morning, while Todd was still sleeping, he took one of the work horses, hitched her up to the buckboard, took two more rolls of barbed wire, a hammer, a roll of the sixteen gauge wire fencing, the come-along, and enough staples to get one side done by mid-afternoon and hopefully, start a second side before he quit for the day. He left a note for Todd tacked to the outhouse door, "Gone to the east side of my section, come find me after you get up."

Todd woke mid-day, made his way to the outhouse, saw the note on the door and thought *Turk knew I wouldn't miss a note from him if it was attached to this door.* When he came out he went to the stream which had slowed considerably since he had left. There was barely enough water running for the horses and the dog. *Speaking of which, where was the dog?* He did not remember seeing her when he rode in; maybe she was out chasing rabbits or squirrels in the woods. "I'll ask Turk when I see him, but right now, I need to have some coffee and some hot food." He set about getting the fire going in the firepit and noticed that rocks were placed by the back of it to deflect the heat. His frying pan was hanging off a nail put into the side of the table top. He filled the large coffee pot from the creek using a coffee cup to make sure he got enough in it to last at least a few days.. The chicken coop had been moved to this side of the barn and the space in front of it was fenced with heavier gauge wire fencing including the area above it. The wire fencing was buried at an angle in the ground so that a fox or weasel couldn't burrow under the fence to get to the chickens. A new gate into the area next to the chicken coop had also been built.

After breakfast, he decided to walk rather than ride over to find Turk and found him about halfway down on the back side of his section. Turk was sweating in the midday sun and when he saw Todd, he decided it was time to take a break. He sat on the back of the buckboard and poured one of the canteens he brought with him over his head to let the tepid water run down his back and chest, then hung it over the side of the buckboard that wasn't in the sun; from the other canteen, he took a long drink, stood up and walked to the front of the wagon and set that canteen under the seat in the shade. Todd said to him, "You've done a right amount of work and at the rate you're going you'll be finished by the end of the week, I 'spect."

"With any luck, I'll have my section fenced over to where section 172 is and I can get the corner done so that my brother or Pete can continue to fence down past 162, put a corner fence in and continue that over to the corner of 163. You'll be able to start fencing the back part of yours once the corner posts are in."

"I guess I have my work cut out for me. By the way, do you know what happened to my dog?"

"I knew that subject was going to come up. After you left, the dog would go off and not come back for hours at a time, but at night she'd be right by the door looking for food and after getting it, she'd settle right in her spot and go to sleep. Yesterday, she was gone by the time I left the cabin. So far she hasn't come back. By the way, I used the last of the venison, but I did put some snare traps out so maybe we'll get lucky and catch a rabbit or two. Did you also notice how low the water in the stream is getting?"

"I did notice. So far, it has been a dry summer, but we have a long way to go before the snows come. I think I'll walk back through the woods and try to figure out what's going on.

He took Turk's horse so that he wouldn't wear himself out and rode along the stream bed toward its headwaters. After he had gone about two miles, he saw what the problem was. Beavers had created a pond and that restricted the water flow. He thought to himself *Those critters are helpful at times, but this isn't one of them. Come tomorrow morning, I am going to set a few traps and see how many of them, I can catch and then I am going to pull that dam apart. I'll take the branches that were cut by the beavers for firewood. Wouldn't it be nice if I got my beaver quota right in this area, then I could concentrate on other animals during the fall and winter months.* He made his way back down the stream bed and noticed what he thought was a wolf trailing him part of the way. He made a mental note to set traps for them, just as he had at the old trapper's cabin. Maybe the forest fire had driven some of the animals out of the mountains. It was a little too early for a single wolf or even a pack of them to be down this low unless game was getting scarce and that would be a problem for all the trappers.

-45-

Over the next few days, Todd trapped six beavers in the large pond that they had created. He decided that he would take the dam apart slowly so that all the water stored behind it didn't rush down all at once. He also wanted to have more time to dig out the pond he had started a month ago for watering his horses, mule, and eventually his crops when it hadn't rained enough. Today he was going to build a channel facing the downward flow of the water to capture most of the runoff over the next week or so. He tore enough branches away to let about a quarter of the pond make its way down the stream bed. The rocks in the stream bed would filter the water as it rolled along.

The dog still wasn't back and he began to worry that the black wolf he had seen more than once had something to do with his dog's disappearance. But he was more concerned with work at the moment. Looking for the dog would have to wait until he finished fencing the front of his section and down the lane he had cut through the forested parcel.

Turk spoke with him one afternoon before he headed back to his cabin and Todd reminded him that the following Wednesday they were all going to Fort Washakie to meet with Mr. McDavitt. "That's five days from now. I'll meet you at your cabin early."

"We'll see you in five days. I hope the dog comes back," Turk said as he rode off. Todd had thought out a plan: *In the mornings, he'd work on the fence; afternoons, dig out between the corner posts of the barn for a stone wall foundation on each side of the barn; early evenings, he would continue to dig out the pond and when he was too tired to do any more, he would take a break and sit at the table, have something to eat, and rest beside the firepit before it was time for bed.* Again, the sky became overcast. It didn't rain, but the winds blew at a steady speed for much of the day and into the night. The horses were restless and he decided that maybe he would have to pull a watch outside tonight; he wished he had the dog and it became obvious that she wasn't coming back until she was ready to.

When Sunday morning arrived, it was crystal clear not a cloud could be found in any direction, no wind and cooler weather, a good day to get some of the barn done. He had dug around a width and a length; he made the trench about a foot and a half deep and about a foot wide. He took the buckboard and rode nearly all the way to the beaver pond looking mostly for flat stones or rectangular ones. He didn't really want the big round ones, they'd fit in the space, but then he'd have to find a matching one to make it level. When he was done with the stone wall foundation, he would start with the split logs, rough side out. and if things went right, he would be done within three or four weeks.

Around mid day, it became cloudy and by late afternoon, a gentle rain began the type that soaks nicely into very dry ground. The native grasses were turning brown from lack of moisture, but hopefully, the rain would turn that around. The horses and the mule just loved the fact that the dust that had settled on their backs began washing off, like a good bath in the middle of the summer. Since he couldn't continue to work outside, he retreated to the shelter of the cabin. He took one of the chairs from inside, put it in the doorway to enjoy the clean, rain-washed air, and began writing a letter to Priscilla.

Dearest Priscilla,

Oh, how I have missed you. It is hard to believe that a month and a half has gone by already, yet in some ways it seems like I was just there yesterday. You must have worried when you saw the glow in evening sky. I assure you that we all made it out safely. We watched sadly during the night into the early morning hours the destruction it brought upon the land. I am guessing that over 5000 acres of aspen and loblolly pine were destroyed, many animals displaced and new growth timber completely burned to the ground. We can all be thankful that Mother Nature saw fit to contain it between two swift flowing streams and the north shore of Bull Lake. Had she not done so, I might not be writing this letter to you. I hope that you and Megan will have a good summer. With luck, I hope to be able to come to Lander by the end of July or no later than the middle of August, and that we have some time to spend together. 'Waiting is such sweet sorrow' and if your heart leads you elsewhere, it is I who is to blame, not you. I have done a lot to my homestead and I will explain all when we see each other again. Please say hello to Megan and her doll for me. I am sitting here in my cabin listening to the rain on the roof, much like I did the first time I stayed at your boarding house. Since the rain isn't letting up, it will be a good time for me to get some much-needed sleep. I use your comforter every night that I am here; it brings back such peaceful memories for me and keeps me warm, especially on chilly summer nights.

Love, Todd

He folded the letter and when he got to the fort, he'd ask for an envelope from the orderly in the commander's office. He would give it to August and ask him to deliver it for him. He opened the window closest to the corral, The horses were quiet and enjoying the rain as much as Todd was. He went to sleep, half asleep anyway, just in case the horses needed him during the night.

-46-

After the rain stopped, it was as if someone had used a wide paint brush to change the landscape from brown to green with wild flowers of every shape and color dotting the canvass. The peepers were in full chorus most days and the cicadas in perfect rhythm every night; still the dog had not returned.

It was the day they were heading to the Fort to meet Mr. McDavitt. Todd saw Pete first, then Turk and Gus as they came out of the cabin across from their barn, waving and getting on their mounts. He said to them, "We'll have to ride at a steady pace in order to arrive before noon. We can check in at the post commander's office to find where Mr. McDavitt is and if he isn't available, we can go to the trading post and get some extra supplies and any news that we've not heard about."

At the Fort, things were as hectic as they were the last time Todd had been there, maybe even more so. The Langstrom and Pete hadn't been there in nearly a year. They were amazed that the Fort had been enlarged; the buildings were now made of stone and the trading post still had high prices and were out of some of the things they would like to have bought. They'd wait, because they knew Todd had planned a trip to Lander either the end of this month or the middle of next and he could pick up their supplies there. Each one of them bought a roll of sixteen gauge heavy wire mesh fencing, each roll weighing close to fifty pounds.

Fortunately, Todd had brought his mule and they had brought their work horse with them. Any other supplies would have to be put on their horses for the ride back home. Mr. McDavitt was conducting the land dispute in the commander's office and he left a message for them that he'd see them at 3 pm, here in the office. They had about two hours to kill, so they went to a small restaurant on the outside of the Fort that had recently opened. They all ordered steak, mashed potatoes with gravy, green beans, corn bread and lemonade to drink for a change. Turk and Gus ordered apple pie for dessert. Afterwards, they rode down by the river and lay in the tall grass by the water's edge, just passing the time until their appointment.

Mr. McDavitt was usually punctual, but a lawyer had not been seen in these parts in a couple of years and he was overwhelmed with questions. He finally got around to seeing Todd, the Langstrom's and Pete Boyd at 4 pm and said, "My apologies for making you wait. I had no idea that I would be inundated with so much work while I was here. I actually have to spend a few extra days to get everything taken care of before I have to go back to Lander. Let's get down to business."

Todd spoke first, "When I came to see you a few months back, all I could think about was to file on the four sections and that would be the end of it. The more I thought about it, the more I realized that four sections were too many. Six hundred and forty acres is a lot of land, and after talking with Turk, Gus and Pete about homesteading I got to thinking if

I could transfer my title to Sections 162 and 172 to Gus and Pete that would solve my dilemma. When Turk came with me the last time I was in Lander, he filed on the section right next to mine and if we can do what I am proposing, he'll actually be right next to his brother's section and the other section is partially behind both of theirs and that could be for Pete. I knew that there may be some legal issues, but I am confident that it can happen. What do you think?"

August replied, "Well, at least you had the time to think it through. Some folks usually don't get enough land, settling for too little or in a rare case like yours, too much, and then they can't meet the Homestead Act requirements. At the end of five years they end up losing everything. You, on the other hand, pose an interesting question and a dilemma; what to do if you do get too many sections? I need to look through my law books for a past precedent and send a telegram to the office that handles Homesteading for the territory. I know I will get some sort of answer by tomorrow. Can all of you come back tomorrow afternoon, say at 1 pm? I know it's an imposition to ask you to come back, but I am sure we can resolve this by then."

Todd replied, "I'm sure we can stay with a friend of mine just a few miles from here for the night, but we must have an answer by tomorrow so that we can get back to our homes." He excused himself from the others and said to Mr. McDavitt, "I need to talk with you privately about another matter, if you have a few minutes."

"I have about fifteen minutes before my next appointment. Let's you and me walk some so that I can smoke my cigar and enjoy this beautiful weather."

"I shouldn't take more than five or six minutes of your time.

First, I would like to ask a favor, taking out the letter. Would you please deliver this to Priscilla Parker when you get back to Lander?"

"I'd be happy to."

"I asked you to bring the paperwork for Sections 36 and 41. Did you do that?"

"I did. What have you got in mind?"

"I'll be honest with you, if things go like I expect them to, I plan on building a sizeable herd of horses and I'll need that land in Lander. I believe that sooner or later the railroad will lay down track on the outskirts of the town. It will make it easier for me to ship my horses from Lander. Whereas, if I continue to live and work Sections 163 and 173, it will add costs to get my stock to market, cutting down on my profits. I have considered both sections, each has unique qualities, but the one with the river frontage offers better bottom land to grow hay and grains; the other is perfect to house my horses. I would not want it known who settled on Section 36 and 41 until the time is right. Can we get that done?"

"You are certainly thinking ahead about all of this. As far as I can see, we can get it done without any problem"

"I was hoping that you could just hold the paperwork for a little while and not file it with the courthouse until I take a look at those two parcels when I'm in Lander in about a month. When I see you next, I would like to make out a will in case anything happens to me. I have someone in mind who means a great deal to me and I want to make sure that, should I meet my demise, she gets all my property."

"I'm sure that can be arranged Todd and I want you to know I am confident that we will be able to make the switch in ownership of those two sections up next to you. I just want to make sure how to word it correctly." They shook hands and Todd left to join the others. They were going to Shoshone Joe's for the night. With little time to spare before his next appointment, August continued his walk out to the main gate puffing away on his cigar and enjoying the sunshine.

<h1 align="center">-47-</h1>

The following day, they all shook hands and Section 172 was now owned by Gus Langstrom; Section 162 was now owned by Pete Boyd. "We can't thank you enough, Mr. McDavitt," the Langstrom brothers said to him. Pete was less cordial, but did shake Mr. McDavitt's hand, especially after Gus poked him in the ribs.

"I was confident that there would be an amicable solution, I just wanted to make sure of how to word it. Now remember what I have told each of you, once I get back to Lander I will have the parcels recorded in your names, thus absolving Todd's legal right to them. If any questions should arise over the ownership of the parcels in question, please refer anyone to me."

"Fellas, I'll catch up with you in a few minutes. I have got to see Mr. McDavitt on another matter," Todd said to his three friends.

"We'll meet you over at the trading post," Gus replied.

Todd said August, "I need to add a post script on the envelope for Mrs. Parker." August took it out of his coat pocket and handed it back to Todd. He wrote on the back of it, 'I won't be in Lander until the end of August. I have much work to get done before fall gets here.' He then handed the

235

envelope back to August, who put it back in his coat pocket.

Todd met up with the other three at the trading post. They all purchased a few extra supplies they needed and securely tied the heavy gauge wire fencing onto the pack frames of the horse and the mule, which was also carrying two extra rolls of barbed wire. Todd said to them, "I have to swing by Shoshone Joe's to pick up a new puppy. I'll catch up with y'all on the trail."

It was apparent while Todd was gone that Happenstance hadn't come back. While he was gone, nothing had bothered the horses, chickens or the rooster for that matter. He bought a dozen buttermilk biscuits at the restaurant after they had their meal. He put the supplies and biscuits in the cabin; the wire and barbed wire under the covered pile next to the barn.

It was near sunset before he got everything put away. He decided that tomorrow, he would start fencing across the front of the section, leaving a space for the lane leading up to the cabin and the barn. He would need to get the pasture completed before fall, but for right now it was important to get the puppy settled in and for him to get a good night's sleep. He woke just past midnight from the sounds that the horses were making. He put on his boots and grabbed the rifle by the door. Once outside, he went over to where the horses were tethered and tried to settle them down. He looked around the area and when he turned to his left and looked into the forest just past the cabin, he saw three pairs of eyes looking back at him. He didn't hesitate and fired rapidly in their direction, hearing the yelps and then silence. He'd check in the morning to see if he had killed any of the wolves. He sat on the front porch for an hour or so before he returned to bed. Morning came and he made his way to where he saw the eyes looking back at him. He only found splatters of blood and bits of fur. It was time once again to set some traps.

At breakfast he had a bowl of oatmeal and three cups of coffee, afterwards he used the outhouse and began to systematically clear all the trees except those that would offer shade for the horses that he planned on raising here on the ranch once he got everything in place. Over the course of the next week, he pulled the stumps, tilled the soil, and raked it smooth before he spread a mixture of buckwheat and rye grass seed. He was hoping for a late crop and next year if he was lucky, he'd get in two cuttings, maybe three. This year, however, he'd be happy with just one and then he could use the field as a temporary pasture during the late fall.

The following week, it was time to finish building the pond. It finally looked like an actual pond with banked sides and a wooden platform half on the bank and half overhanging the water. On the afternoon of the third day, he lifted the board on the small dam he had built at the edge of the channel next to the stream bed to fill the pond. He dragged two of the downed trees into the creek bed to help divert most of the water into the channel that led directly into the pond. He rode Misty to where the beaver dam was and removed more of the branches, allowing more water to flow down the creek bed.

As far as the wolves were concerned, he didn't have any further trouble with them. The dog never came back and he could only think that one of those pairs of eyes were hers.

One day as he was working on the inside of the barn the border collie alerted him that someone was coming. He quickly went out a doorway at the back of the barn and walked quietly to where he could see a rider. The rider reigned up, got down off his horse and walked slowly toward the barn. "Can I help you?" Todd said to the rider who was caught off guard. He started to turn with his hand on his pistol, but saw the rifle leveled at him and decided it was best to remove his hand from where it was. The tall man said, "Pat Hendrickson is my name, and I am the U.S. Marshal over in Sweetwater County. I understand that you used to work at Timber Creek Ranch and you know the folks at Sweetwater Ranch. Is that correct?"

Todd replied pensively, "I guess it could be, why?"

"I have been looking for Josh Hackenfield for over three months, but every time I get close, he disappears. Your name was mentioned to me in Lander by August McDavitt who said that you had a run-in with him. Seems he cheated at cards and had a run-in with Jarvis at Timber Creek. He hired on with Crusty and Liz to help get a small herd back to the Sweetwater Ranch. Shortly after your visit at the ranch, he told Crusty that he was going to find you, but before he left, he pistol whipped Crusty and stole some gold. I am guessing that he has been looking for you ever since."

"Have a seat Marshal, let me pour you and I some coffee and I'll tell you what I know about Josh." Todd told his story to the marshal and said, "As far as I know, he was in Lander two months ago, and he may still be there. I don't get many visitors up here and I seriously doubt he knows where I live. I told the post commander at Fort Washakie and the Trading Post owner that if he ever came looking for me, they didn't know me. I suppose, though, he could find out by other means, but I hope not. When I was visiting with Crusty and Liz, I warned him that if he ever came after me, I'd shoot him on sight."

"I hope for your sake he doesn't find you. By the way, I have a letter for you, it's a couple of weeks old, though."

"Why don't you stay the night? I've got a rabbit stew cooking over at the fire pit. Your horse looks like it could use some rest and you'll definitely get a good night's sleep up here in the foothills."

"I accept. Is there anything that I can do to help you while I am here?"

"I am laying down floor boards in my new barn and building stalls as I go along. An extra pair of hands would surely help." Over dinner they talked about Crusty, that he would be alright and that Liz was with child due next March. Quizzicaly, Todd asked, "How did you get into the law business?"

"I had been a rancher for a long time, but after my wife died during childbirth and the baby as well, I just couldn't do ranching any more. Charlie Cooper and others encouraged me to become the sheriff in Green Springs and eventually I was asked by the district judge to become a U.S. Marshal. As they say, the rest is history."

Todd had the marshal sleep in his bed so that he'd get some restful sleep. He sat at the table after supper with a cup of coffee and a lantern, reading the letter that Priscilla had written.

Priscilla explained in the letter that she had talked with Parson Samuels about him and Mr. Johansen. The parson's suggestion was to accommodate Mr. Johansen, yet keeping him at a distance and with the help of a few of the ladies from church, she would keep him off balance, especially when he saw her and crossed the street so that she had to talk with him. The ladies from the church, always joined in on the conversation and before long he excused himself saying he had something else to do. She, Megan and Molly, the name that was given to the doll, had worried about him when they saw the glow in the sky and was relieved when his letter had arrived.

I am disappointed that you have to put off the time when you'd be back in Lander, but I understand that you must get things done around your ranch. I remember your kisses and dream every night of doing it again. I can't wait until you get back here by the end of August and your room will be all ready for you. Do be careful and try to take some time off every now and then so you don't get so worn out.

All my love,

Priscilla.

He had worked hard all day, and after reading the letter decided that now would be a good time to get some sleep. He had already put his bedroll in the barn. Before the marshal left, he would write another letter to her.

-48-

The marshal decided to stay an extra day. It certainly was a change from the day-to-day grind of riding many miles and coming up empty handed at nearly every turn. He said to Todd, "I think when I get back to Rock Springs where my office is, I'll look into getting a small place of my own. Working here has given me more energy than I have had in months."

"Will you be going back to Lander?"

"Yes, but first I have to see the post commander at the Fort."

"Would you mind delivering a letter for me when you get to Lander?"

"I'd be happy to. Now let's see if we can't finish laying the rest of the floor boards and if time permits we'll get the last three stalls done also. When we're done for the day I'll take you out to dinner."

"That sounds fair to me," both of them laughed.

Without the unexpected help from Marshal Hendrickson, the flooring, stalls, barn doors, windows and, the doors on each end of the hayloft would not have been completed.

Tomorrow, Todd decided, he'd take the day off. He had shot a deer yesterday, skinned it, and placed the roasts, steaks and ribs up in the cache he built next to the barn. Come this winter, the cache would prove very valuable. He also wanted to build a smoke house and a cold house to keep things cold during the late spring/early summer months.

Tonight they'd feast on venison steaks, roasted potatoes, green tomatoes, sourdough biscuits and coffee. Over dinner Todd said, "When you go past Sweetwater Ranch, please give my best to Crusty and Liz for me. Tell them I'll see them next spring for sure."

"I will and if you ever get over to Rock Springs, stop in and see me."

"I'll do that."

After the marshal went to bed Todd sat in one of the chairs gazing at the fading fire in the fire pit. He lit a lantern and said to the dog, "I think I'll name you Mike, just like my friend in the war. He, too, had my back just like you do." The dog just lay next to him while he wrote a letter to Priscilla.

Dear Priscilla,

I can't begin to tell you how much I have missed you and if I had my druthers, I'd be there sooner rather than later. I have had some help for the last couple of days and we have accomplished so much. I plan on spending at least ten days in Lander, if you can stand me for that long. I will have a new friend with me, so if you have space in the barn, he can bunk there. He prefers the outdoors over sleeping inside and his name is Mike.

In about a week I plan to go to one of my claims and stay for a week. Hopefully there won't be a forest fire to contend with this time. Please say hello to Megan and 'Molly' for me. I have a story to tell Megan after I arrive. I would say that I am jealous of all the special attention that you are getting from Mr. Johansen, but that won't do me or you any good, since I am not there to make sure that he minds his manners. Keep me in your prayers and look to the northwest every now and then, pick out the brightest star and look downward. That's where I am!

Love always,

Todd

He handed the letter to the marshal, and they said their goodbyes. Then Todd saddled Misty and called to Mike as they went up to the beaver pond; it was time to remove the remainder of the beaver dam, and, move the brush far away from the sides of the stream so that it flowed naturally from then on. He thought to himself, *This should fill the pond to a level that I want and any rain that comes along will help also.* As he was riding back, he decided to take a detour and swing by the old cabin. As he approached, the horse reared.

After getting her settled down, he took out the rifle from the scabbard, and tied her to a tree. He walked the last 100 yards to the cabin. He nearly tripped over a mound of earth about a foot high and three or so feet long; next, he made sure he called out, "Anyone in the cabin?" No answer came back; he called out again louder this time, but still there was no answer. As he neared the back of the cabin, he noticed that the door was almost torn off its hinges, the barn doors were both open and there were no horses in the corral. He said to Mike, "I guess they took my advice and left as soon as they could; good riddance. The vegetable garden was ready for picking and the hay field for its first cutting. He remembered what Mr. McDavitt said, "You can harvest what vegetables you planted and you can cut the hayfield as well." Todd went back to Misty carrying a few carrots, fed them to her, remounted and went back to his place to get the buckboard, a scythe and burlap sacks for the vegetables. Thinking out loud he said, "This is my lucky day."

He picked nearly a bushel each of carrots, tomatoes, and potatoes, and a peck each of radishes, squash and corn. Even though the season was over for them, he also took the pea plants with him. If he planted them in September, he might get a late crop when the cold weather returned. He hobbled the horses near the back corner of the hayfield so that they could graze and have water, stripped off his shirt, put on his work gloves and started to scythe the field. Day after day he continued to cut the hay and finally, after six days, it was finished. Now he'd have to gather it in. He piled it on the buckboard as high as he could making seventeen trips in all. Once back at his ranch, he bundled the hay and using the pulley, hoisted eighty-five bundles up to the hayloft. The rest, he put on the floor of the barn or next to the corral that was almost finished. He definitely needed a day off now. He hadn't been swimming in a pond since leaving Timber Creek. He took his clothes off and dove into the cold water and felt refreshed. The dog, mule, and horses all looked at him quizzically while he was enjoying himself.

Pete had come back from the mine while Gus and Turk stayed. He wanted to get started working on his section and asked Todd, "Can I stay with you for a few days?"

"Perfect timing! I am going up-country for about a week. Stay in the cabin and put your horse in the barn. I have moved all the shovels, hand tools, barbed wire and wire fencing into a tack room that I built. I am taking the dog with me this time, but I'm leaving the buckboard and work horses. I recently shot a deer and you will find the meat up in the cache; you will also find some vegetables that I recently picked at the old cabin. They are in the barn as well. Try not to eat them all, I'll need them during the fall and winter months. Please remember to close the barn and cabin doors along with the windows when you go to work on your section and at night. I'll be leaving in the morning."

"I was amazed to see that you got the barn done."

"I had some help for a couple of days and we got a lot of it finished. Just remember to close the windows and doors before you leave during the day or at night."

"I'll remember." Pete replied.

Todd had remembered to blaze one tree with three marks to tell where his claim was so finding it wasn't as time consuming as it was the last time he was here. Since he was staying a week, he'd make sure that he took the horses and the mule down on the valley floor to graze a couple of times, especially when it was time to go fishing in the stream that meandered throughout the valley. It looked like only deer and small animals had been through the site.

He had gotten pretty good about tending to the mule first as she always carried the heaviest load; next Misty was taken care of. He led them to the makeshift corral and put the fence poles back in place to keep them in. The creek was running full and he guessed that it must have rained higher up in the hills that surrounded this area. He set a couple of snares to catch a rabbit for food, but if he wasn't lucky, he would have a cold camp tonight with biscuits, deer jerky, and water from his canteen. He got everything settled in the lean-to and said to Mike, "Stay;" "Guard."

He decided to take a walk to see what game trails he could find and where the best places were to set his traps and snares. He hadn't planned on trapping so early, but remembering what the old-timer had said about predicting a harsh winter this year, it wouldn't hurt to get a jump on it, He made mental notes on what prints he saw and where. He made a complete circle in about an hour. He'd set the traps in the early morning and come back late in the afternoon to check them; in-between, he would do some prospecting and at night he'd clean the skins of the animals he caught that day.

He played with the dog for a while, then checked his snares and found that he had caught a big fat rabbit in one of them; he skinned it, fed some to the dog and roasted the rest over the fire before he settled in for the night. Along about sunup, he woke to the sound of a wolf howling off in the distance. *Kind of early in the year to hear that sound* he thought to himself. In the summer they were like ghosts in the wind, he'd have to see what transpired.

He backpacked the traps and snares, and set out just at sunrise while Mike guarded the camp. To be on the safe side, he brought the Sharps and plenty of cartridges just in case he ran across a grizzly or a mountain lion. Setting the traps just before the sun rose gave him the advantage of catching those small mammals that fed early; the disadvantage was those that fed at night wouldn't be out until later and he only wanted to have to check each area once a day. But if he persevered, his success ratio would increase. He decided to divide the area into four sections, a different one for every other day in hopes of catching a variety of animals. Their coats should be full from all the feeding they had been doing between early spring and now.

Today he'd go north, maybe even up to the area where he met the man-bear. While, he wanted to learn more about him, he had reservations, also. Man-bear deserved to be left alone as much as any of the critters on the earth, but there was so much that man-bear could teach him that spurred him to find out where he might be. After a couple of hours, his traps were set. Now he had some time to find out if the man-bear was in the cave; if not, he'd return to his own campsite.

It didn't look like any large animal had been in the cluster of boulders where he had his first encounter with the man-bear. He investigated the cave; the water was still trickling down the back wall, but strangely enough, it did not flow out of the cave like a creek. It meandered along the base of the boulders, but it did not pool either; it just seemed like a continuous loop, down the boulder all over again. He thought he heard something outside the entrance of the cave and the hair on the back of his neck stood on end. Making sure the safety was off, he put a cartridge in the breach and proceeded toward the entrance.

Carefully, he peered out, first looking straight ahead, then left and right of the cave opening, and finally up. A mountain lion was surveying the area from the craggy rocks above and opposite the entrance from where he was. The cat sauntered down the rock face and began a low growl, enough to send shivers down Todd's spine. Man-bear was not there to save him this time, so it was up to him to take action. His Sharps spoke loud and clear! Within a few seconds, the cat was blown back against the wall from the blast as it had started to make a standing leap with fangs barred and claws extended for a kill. It was his first kill ever of a mountain lion; he had no idea what this type of skin would bring in trade and he hoped he never saw another one all the rest of the time he was here or anywhere else for that matter.

After several days, the trapping had gone moderately well – four red fox, two wolves, gaunt from lack of food he guessed, the lion, one grizzly, one black bear, twelve martens and twenty rabbits. Todd decided it was time, once again, to take the horses down to the valley floor, just a short hike down the hillside, while Mike chased a rabbit in the tall grass and Todd tried his hand at fishing once again. After the horse and mule seemed to have their fill of the sweet grass, he brought them back to the corral. He set about preparing a cooking fire when he noticed that vultures were circling over a not too distant place. Around and around they flew, never seeming to dip below the horizon. He'd check it out soon enough, as long as they weren't circling him, he was okay with them cleaning up nature for the rest of us. He was curious though.

After he had some coffee and ate the fish he caught, he decided to see what the vultures were looking at down in the valley about a half-mile from where he was. He said to the dog, "Stay." He put a tether on Misty and led her out of the corral and ground tied her. He put the rails back in place, picked up his knapsack and slung it over his right shoulder. He cautiously leaned the Sharps against the corral fence and after he mounted his horse, he leaned down to pick up the carbine by the barrel. Holding the rifle in his left hand and the tether in his right, he galloped off to see what the vultures saw.

Coming to the crest of a low hill, he saw a colt lying in the grass, slowly dying from all the attacks made by a pack of wolves who kept taunting it. He thought he saw his old dog, but said under his breath, "It's just too far from where I live for her to be traveling with this pack. Interesting though that a similar dog would take up with a wolf pack."

Todd had a mind to end the colt's misery, but thought best to stay out of it. Mother Nature took care of her own and there was no sense getting involved and bringing attention to himself. As long as the wolf pack kept its distance from him, there would be no problems, but if they didn't, there'd be hell to pay. He decided that he would stay in camp and continue to look for gold, then pack up and head back to the ranch.

Two days had come and gone and he no longer heard the wolves howling off in the distance. The buzzards were gone and the weather was turning more humid, which up at this level in the mountains, meant only one thing, Rain. He brought all the skins into the lean-to, took the tarp and spread it over the top of the lean-to far enough to cover the fire pit; he'd be dry, warm and he would be able to cook his food. He made sure the horses and mule had extra grain, their hobbles were on, and that they were further up in the draw amongst the pines where they would get wet, but not as much if they were standing out in the open. A fog rolled in and drizzle soon followed just past sundown and by the next morning, it was raining at a steady clip, he had no choice but to stay put for the time being. In his dreams, he had decided that Priscilla meant more to him than any one person had a right to, but it was a peaceful dream; she made him happy.

He wondered how he'd ever get used to being around somebody so much, but maybe it was time for a change. He still felt that he wasn't as financially stable as he would like to be. Another year, maybe two, but would she wait that long for him. Despite what she had said about Mr. Johansen, he was there trying to woo her while Todd was trapping and panning for gold in the mountains. Perhaps the Indian spirits would provide the answer, only time would tell.

It rained for thirty-six hours and in the afternoon of the second day, he watched the clouds as they raced southeast toward where his ranch would be. The land there could sure use a steady rain and if not for anything else, just to ease the forest fire threat. Tomorrow he would head home with his skins, gold, and the rocks with the seam of gold running through them.

-50-

Pete was glad Todd had finally returned. "I need to check on our property to make sure there are no squatters on it."

"Or you could post it for sale. Otherwise y'all would be constantly wondering if someone has just moved in. It's hard to believe that folks simply don't understand that if someone is away for a few days, or even weeks and all their possessions are in a cabin or a barn, that someone actually is living there, rather than just assuming that they aren't," Todd replied.

"I'll have to talk with Gus and Turk about doing that. Maybe Mr. McDavitt could handle the legal paperwork for us; we do have to do something. I'll see you before you leave for Lander. I think Gus is coming back here once I get back up to the mine. He wants to start building a barn for our horses and to store our equipment before the cold weather sets in. Can he stay here while you're away?"

"Certainly."

"Be seeing you," he said as he rode southeast toward his cabin.

Todd looked at Mike and said, "I think it's time for you and me to go for a swim in the pond. I'll make sure the dam is up so that some of the water from the creek can run into the pond for a couple of days." Mike just looked back at him and wagged his tail as he started to trot toward the pond, waiting for Todd.

The following day he had to get back to work clearing the eastern edge of Section 173 of brush and small trees. Three days later he had cleared all the land. Now he had to use the plow to cut the soil twenty feet wide from the front edge to the back of the property the same way he did Section 163.

He started thinking *When I get to Lander I will ask the mill owner if I can borrow a log wagon so that I can have the larger trees that I have been stacking by the back of the property taken back to the mill and turned into finished lumber. Priscilla wants to see what it is like up here, and if she can find someone to look after Megan for a few days, she could come with me. I probably would have to make two trips, possibly three to get all these trees. While I am at the boarding house, I'll take the dogs out for a run and casually walk through Section 36 and 41 jotting down what I see on the property so that I have some idea where I could build a house and barn. I'll also ask August what he suggests.*

He planned to spend a good deal of time with Priscilla and Megan while he was in town. He needed to confide in Priscilla about his plans for the future, say for the next two or three years anyway. He smelled smoke in the air, thinking the worst, but couldn't determine which direction it was coming from. He climbed a Loblolly pine as high as he dared to see which way the smoke was coming from. As he looked southeast he had a sneaking suspicion that it was near where Pete was. He shimmied down the tree and ran to the barn. He saddled Misty and told Mike, "Stay," "Guard," before taking his Sharps and a long handled shovel with him.

He arrived close enough to see that Pete's cabin was on

fire. "Pete," he shouted out, but got no response. He tied Misty off upwind of the burning wood so that it wouldn't make her skittish. There was nothing he could do to put the fire out. The only water sources was a small creek that was practically dry and an empty water trough. He saw a horse dead from an apparent gunshot to the head in the corral; he noticed movement next to the barn on the side toward the other cabin. He rushed over to find Pete badly burned on his arms and legs, but still alive, who said in a raspy voice, "They said it was payback for trapping them. Am I going to make it, Todd?"

"Well partner, if you can stand the pain a little while longer, I am going to drag you out of here and over to where my horse is in the shade of that big Locust tree that you are so fond of. Then I am going to leave you there for a few minutes and bring my buckboard back here and take you to the Fort."

"I can hang on." What seemed like hours to Pete was actually only thirty minutes, Todd got back with the buckboard and several blankets as well as the bucket of axle grease to cover the burns on Pete's arms and leg so the burns wouldn't blister. He hoped it also would ease some of the pain. As gentle as he could be, he dragged Pete onto clean blankets and carefully cut off his shirt and blue jeans before laying on a thick coating of the axle grease on his burns. He wrapped him as tight as Pete could stand the pain.

Using a pulley he took from the barn and three ropes, he got the pulley up high enough in the sturdy locust tree, wrapped the ropes around Pete as gently, but firmly as he could. He managed to raise Pete up to where he could get the buckboard underneath him; he lowered him onto the back of the buckboard which had more blankets and several bales of hay on it. He wedged Pete between the bales and told him, "I'm going to take it as easy as I can to get you the seventeen miles to the fort. First, though, I am going to give you some sips of water so that you aren't so parched and then we are off. Alright?"

"Let's go, it can't be any more painful than what I have already endured."

At the fort, Dr. Harris, the post doctor, and his orderlies lifted Pete off the buckboard using the blankets as a stretcher to carry him into the hospital. The doctor said to Todd, "It's going to be touch and go for several hours, possibly days. Why don't you go to the barracks and get some sleep. We'll come get you if need be."

Before he went to the barracks, Todd decided to go see the commander. He walked in the office and saw that Corporal Miller was no longer there. He said to the new orderly, "I'd like to see Colonel Johnson as soon as I can."

The orderly replied, "State your business."

"It's personal." The private looked skeptical at Todd's rough clothing, rose up from behind the desk and knocked on the commander's office door, he entered and said, "Colonel, a Mr. Morgan would like to speak with you, sir; he says the nature of his business is personal."

"By all means, and for an effect on the young soldier, he said, "Have Sergeant Morgan enter, please." The young orderly did an about face with sweat beading on his forehead and a dour look on his face. Todd walked past him into the commander's office and closed the door. The Colonel looked at him with a big smile on his face, rose from his desk and shook hands with him. Just in case the soldier was still listening, he spoke up in a loud voice and said, "How can I help you today, Sergeant?"

Quietly he said, "What can I do for you Todd?"

He explained what happened in detail and then said, "If I'd a known those bastards would come back to cause all this trouble, especially with my friend lying in your hospital and not knowing whether he'll live or die, I would have just finished the job months ago."

"You didn't know and what happened is not your fault. My concern is that this won't be the end of it either. I wish I had the manpower to apprehend the guilty individuals, but they only sent me one corporal and fifteen raw recruits. One of those recruits is sitting out front."

"Can we get a U.S. Marshal or a deputy up where we are? The way it stands now, there isn't anyone and to come here is almost a day's ride from where we are. Otherwise, it'll be a lawless land and that will only bring on more problems."

"I'll see what I can do, but for the time being, you farmers and ranchers will just have to maintain the peace as best you can. That doesn't mean a vigilante force, but you have the right to protect yourselves and your property against all intruders."

"Thank you for your time, Colonel. I wanted to let you know that I didn't get a chance to see the Sioux. Between the forest fire and lack of time afterward, I haven't followed through. I'll try and get that taken care of over the next couple of weeks."

"Do the best you can. I just wanted to let them know that we will try and keep the unscrupulous ones away from their hunting grounds; winter and summer encampments. Is there anything else I can help you with?"

"No, sir, and again, thanks for taking the time out of your busy schedule to see me."

"Any time son, any time." Todd shook his hand before he left the office, and once he closed the door, he stopped by the desk and said to the private for effect and with emphasis, "Private, the next time I come in this office, you better be clean-shaven, hair combed and get that uniform pressed. Otherwise, you'll be pulling KP for a month of Sundays. Do you understand me?" He walked out of the office and over to the hospital to check on Pete; he would have to get back to the ranch by tomorrow.

After he saw Pete, he walked to the telegraph office and sent a telegram to Priscilla.

Mrs. Parker, Parker's Boarding House, Lander, Wyoming Territory STOP Running behind STOP Will explain when I get there STOP Will need a single room on September 5 STOP Todd Morgan STOP

While he was at the fort, he stopped over to the trading post to see if Hanson had any more barbed wire. Hanson said to him, "Sorry to hear about your friend. He's in good hands over at the hospital. I am sure they will do the best they can to get him well; burns on the body are the most painful of all. You need anything else other than the wire?"

"I'm good, just the wire for now. I have my buckboard out back, I can load them so you won't have to. Just take them off my credit."

"Sure. I'll meet you out back in a couple of minutes."

Todd knew that he would have to make damn sure no one trespassed on his property while he was gone to Lander and hoped that Gus came looking for Pete.

-51-

It was over a week before Gus came riding into Stony Creek Ranch, the name Todd gave it just a few days ago. He found Todd pulling stumps along the eastern edge of his section and said, "Pete was supposed to come up to the mine. Have you seen him?"

"Meet me over at the table by the creek in a few minutes and I'll get us some coffee and explain where Pete is." He proceeded to tell Gus what happened and how, despite what the colonel told him, he felt guilty about what happened to Pete.

"None of us expected those bastards to ever come back here and do what they did after all this time, not only to Pete but the destruction of a good horse and our cabin. We certainly don't hold you responsible, either. As the colonel suggested to you, it will be up to all of us to protect our property up here until they can provide us with a lawman. If you can loan me a horse, I will go back to the mine. Turk and I will close it up for the time being and then we'll decide what to do next."

"At least stay the night, get some rest, and leave at first light. Do you need to borrow the buckboard and some tools?"

"Thanks, but we have all the necessary tools up there. We'll just have to make sure it's secure enough as it will be a bit longer before we return. I don't suppose you have any venison do you?"

"Shot one about a week ago. Why don't you go for a swim in the pond and by the time I get done putting the horses in the barn along with yours, the potatoes and vegetables will be done and it won't take but a few minutes to cook a nice steak." Gus grabbed a towel from the peg on the side of the barn and with Mike bounding along, went to the pond for a swim; meanwhile Todd put Gus's horse in the barn, curried it and gave it some grain and water. Once done, he went to get the work horses.

The following day, Gus left and Todd went back to pulling the rest of the stumps. He piled them between the cleared area and the grain field. In late fall, he would use what he could for firewood and the rest along with the brush he'd burn during the winter and scatter the ashes on his crop fields before he tilled the soil. He decided to get the moldboard plow ready so that he could till the cleared area, rake it smooth afterward and get it ready for a mixture of grasses/wild flower seeds that he had been saving to spread over the area. Just as he was about to get the horse moving along, Mike rose up and started a guttural growl, "What is it boy? What do you hear?" He took the reins and tied them around a tree close by, grabbed his rifle and followed the dog. As he neared the end of the barn, he saw a man looking through things around the cabin. The man opened the door, looked in and said to his horse, "I guess no one's home, we'll just make ourselves comfortable."

When the dog growled, the man began to draw his pistol—

"Only if you plan on being buried where you stand, Todd said. Drop that gun of yours and walk towards the barn without the horse. Don't try anything either with a knife or a pocket gun. I always hit what I aim at and right now, you're in my sights." When the man reached the barn, Todd said to Mike, "Guard." He searched the man for other weapons, finding a pig sticker in his boot and a derringer in a vest pocket. He said to the man "Slowly turn towards me." At this point, Todd saw the U.S. Marshal badge on the man's shirt." The marshal said to Todd, "If you'll call off your dog, we can sit a spell and I'll tell you who I am and what I'm doing here."

"Okay, but don't make any sudden moves, my dog is a mite sensitive to strangers. "Stay," he said to Mike, who obediently flopped on the ground next to Todd keeping a watchful eye on the stranger.

"My name is Tom Murphy and I now cover this area for the U.S. Marshal Service. A Colonel Johnson from Fort Washakie contacted our office in Casper. Seems y'all been having some trouble up here and he asked if we could send someone to help keep the peace and take care of law breakers. I was the one they sent. Colonel Johnson told our office that whoever was sent to have him find Todd Morgan. You him?"

Todd relaxed a bit. "I am. Over dinner, I'll explain everything that's happened and why we need a lawman in these here parts. Take your horse over to the side pasture and put your gear in the barn. Sorry, but I only have one bed in my cabin, but the barn is comfortable enough. Hope you don't mind three horses and a mule for company, though."

"Fine by me, I am used to sleeping under the stars. Having a roof over my head will be a change.

"Make yourself at home. I have to get some plowing done before I quit for dinner. Do you like venison by any chance?"

"I haven't had any venison since I left Casper a few months back. Is there anything I can do?"

"Just take it easy,or if you want, you can go for a swim, fish, or take a nap.

"I think a nap would do me a world of good. It's been a while and riding every day gets tiresome."

"Funny you should say that. Pat Hendrickson, the marshal from Sweetwater, said almost those same words to me a few weeks back."

"If you don't mind me asking, why was Marshal Hendrickson up here?"

"He was looking for a theivin', connivin' fugitive by the name of Josh Hackenfield. He beat up a friend of mine and stole some gold from him."

"Do you know if he was successful in finding this person named Hackenfield?"

"Never heard one way or another."

Over a dinner of grilled venison steak, baked potatoes, sliced tomatoes and coffee, Todd explained everything that went on up to and including the fire at the Langstrom cabin. "I've been blaming myself for putting my friend, Pete, in harm's way, even though we had no idea that those men would ever come back this way and seek revenge."

"From what you've told me, you can't keep blaming yourself. It isn't doing you any good and your friend, Pete, needs your support, not your sympathy. Starting tomorrow, I'll be doing a wide circle search from here west, north, east and south working my way outward and with any luck, I'll find those men and take them to the Fort for trial. I plan to use the Fort as my home base until I see where it would be best for me to establish an office. Do you mind if I stay here when I am up in this area?"

"Certainly not, you're welcome anytime. My neighbors,

Gus and Turk Langstrom and Pete Boyd are homesteading on the sections next to mine; they use my place while they are working on theirs, just makes it easy for everyone. We keep an eye on each other's property. I'll be seeing them in a couple of days and let them know that you may be up here while I am gone to Lander. I'll be leaving next Wednesday. It's been a long day and I need to turn in. Mike usually stays outdoors on these nice nights. He'll let us know if anyone or anything is out there that shouldn't be. Pick a space in the barn where you'll be comfortable. I've already closed the windows, just make sure the doors are closed after you are inside. Goodnight, Tom."

Todd dreamt about Priscilla. It had been well over two months since he last saw her. She'd have every right to just keep him as a friend, anything more would be a blessing, but he could still be hopeful.

Before Tom left, Todd said, "You told me that there is someone at the old miner's cabin. Can you describe him for me?"

"He's younger than you and he favors his right side; he looks angry at the world. Why do you ask?"

"Well, I had a run in with that Josh Hackenfield at the Sweetwater Ranch several months back. The man you just described might in fact be him. Do you mind if we ride down there, and if it's him, you'll take a mean hombre out of these here parts and Marshal Hendrickson will be very grateful."

"We can do that, but first I need to get cleaned up and have a good breakfast that will hold me for the rest of the day. By the way, your accommodations were excellent," he said with a smile. After they cleaned up, ate, and saddled their horses, Todd said to Mike, "Stay." "Guard."

As they made their way to the old miner's cabin, he said to the marshal, "I'll circle around and come up from behind. Just ask him if you can water your horse. If it's him, I'll know him on sight and get the drop on him; then you can take him into custody."

"Sounds like a good plan to me. Ever think of becoming a lawman? You sure think like one."

"Not really." As they neared the cabin they saw smoke curling from the chimney, so they knew someone was there. Todd began his ride around the cabin to the far side nearer the corral, while Marshal Murphy called out, "Anyone home in the cabin?"A young man came out onto the porch and said, "Who's asking?"

"It's Marshal Murphy. We met the other day when I stopped to water my horse. I'd like to do the same if it's alright with you."

"Sure, sure, marshal, help yourself. I was just making breakfast. Care to join me?"

"No, thanks, I et before I rode down this way."

Todd stood between the trees where the cache and the outhouse were, getting a good look at the young man and sure enough, it was Josh. Todd thought *Sooner or later we would have met again. What a relief to get you out of here and arrested.*

Marshal Murphy dismounted and walked the horse to the trough, glanced over at Todd, who nodded and when the horse finished drinking, he walked back to the cabin and said to the young man, "I didn't catch your name?"

"Names Josh Hackenfield, perhaps you've heard of me?

"Sorry, can't say that I have, but a friend of mine over in the trees has. Drop any weapons, including that Bowie knife in your belt. You're under arrest for assault and robbery."

Josh just kept muttering to himself before he saw the man from the poker table and said, "Damn you, Slick. Of all the people up here, and there aren't many of them, I would never have thought that you'd be up here."

"Well, Josh, my name isn't Slick. My real name is Todd Morgan. Ring any bells?"

"Morgan, I should have shot you back at the Sweetwater."

"I can honestly say, Josh, that sooner or later we were going to cross paths and have it out. This way the law caught up with you first. You should have left well enough alone, but you thought you were bigger than life and wanted to make a name for yourself. It just didn't end like you hoped it would. Your law-breaking days are over."

The marshal thanked Todd for his hospitality and tied Josh's hands in front of him and his feet to the stirrups. He put a lariat around Josh's horse before mounting his, and rode south toward the fort.

<h1 style="text-align:center">-52-</h1>

odd worked feverishly the rest of the week to get the ground plowed, raked and seeded with native grasses and wild flowers before putting in fence posts along the section lines and strung barbed wire. As much as he wanted to think about Priscilla, he was too exhausted by the end of the day to think about her or anything else for that matter. He was asleep in seconds after lying down on his bed.

Long about Saturday, both Gus and Turk rode in with their pack horses loaded down with tools and gold. They asked Todd if they could store the tools in one of the stalls along with their personal belongings from the cabin once they retrieved them. After doing so, they told Todd that they were going to the fort to see Pete and they would be back by Tuesday, the day before Todd was leaving for Lander.

Upon their return after visiting with Pete, they decided it was time to sell their property and put a sign on the barn: FOR SALE, see August McDavitt in Lander; SQUATTERS AND SETTLERS TAKE NOTICE, NO TRESPASSING! As long as they were staying in the area, they'd check on it from time to time to keep squatters off their property. They would stay in Todd's cabin while he was gone.

They decided to build a barn with sleeping quarters on the

second floor. Once built they would clear enough land for grain and hay, plowing a fire-free zone between the sections.

Todd said to himself, *I can rest once I get to Lander, but for the time being, I have to get as much work done around here as I can.* He selected the logs that he wanted to take with him on the buckboard to the Lander Millwork Company. He would load them on Monday morning using block and tackle; get his clothes satchel ready and put the bags of gold dust and flakes into the well of the buckboard, the bags of rocks with the gold seam in them under the shelf where his rifle was and covered them with an old blanket.

With Josh on his way to the fort to stand trial and eventually prison, he hoped there wouldn't be any other trouble along the way to Lander.

He made eight crude signs. On four he printed:
PRIVATE PROPERTY, TRESSPASSERS WILL BE SHOT!

On the other four he printed: **NO HUNTING OR FISH-ING**

He posted them on all four sides of his property. As much as he wanted to get to Lander, he also wanted to stop and see how Pete was doing. From what the Langstroms had said after they saw him, Pete's burns were healing, but it would be quite a while before he would be walking again. He arrived at the fort and said to Mike, "Guard." He got out of the wagon and walked up the steps of the hospital and said to the orderly, "I would like to see Pete Boyd. He's the fellow I brought in with the burns."

"He is with the doctor, if you can wait a few minutes, I am sure he'll be glad to see you."

"In that case, I'll go see the commander for a few minutes."

As soon as he walked into the office, the private nearly fell off his chair. "You again. I can't catch a break no how; first it's the First Sergeant giving me hell about my uniform, then you gave me a tongue lashing the last time you were here and now you're back. I do the best I can, What is it with you sergeants anyway?"

"Look, son, when a person enters this office to see the colonel, who is the first person they see? You! It's important that you not only look sharp, but you act accordingly. First impressions are lasting impressions and the more you act like a first class soldier, the more you'll feel like one. The last private got promoted to corporal and I have no doubt that someday he'll make sergeant. Now it's your turn. We all started out as privates. If you follow the rules, things will be a lot easier for you and over time, the first sergeant and the colonel will take notice. The sergeant will put you in for a promotion. Now do you get what I am talking about?"

"I never looked at it that way."

"Is the colonel in?"

"He is out of the office. He had to go to South Pass City for a meeting. He should be back in a week. Can I take a message for him?"

"Just tell him I stopped in, nothing special that can't wait."

"Yes, Sir, I mean sergeant."

As Todd was leaving, he saw that the private was brushing off his uniform and smoothing over his hair and when he sat down, he was sitting straighter.

He went back to the hospital and the orderly said, "You can see him now, he's in the second room on the right."

"Thank you." He walked down the hall and knocked on the door jamb. Pete was sitting on the edge of the bed, trying to get up on his own and said, "I can do this!" Seeing Todd he smiled and said, "I thought I'd never see you again."

"Sooner or later I would have stopped by. The Langstrom's told me you were getting better. I have felt so guilty about you getting hurt. I didn't think you'd ever want to see me again."

"You saved my life and I'll always be grateful. You had no way of knowing those men would ever come back this way again and do what they did to me. I certainly don't blame you for any of this. I will tell you though, if I ever see them again, they're mine and mine alone. They'll wish they stayed away; there will be no place where they can hide."

"Well, Pete, I'm on my way to Lander and I'll be gone about two weeks or so. I'll see you when I get back. Don't you give up, you will walk again. Course you probably will only be fishing and hunting the rest of your life, instead of working for a living like the rest of us."

"Wishful thinking. You be careful and I'll see you when you come back."

Todd left; he got up in the buckboard and patted Mike on the head as they headed for Lander.

-53-

He pulled into the Lander Millwork Company and with their help, got all the logs offloaded; he spoke with the owner about borrowing a log wagon to bring in much bigger logs. He'd need a ten-mule team and a deep-sided wagon for at least two, maybe three loads. He told the owner, he'd like to take the wagon on Friday for the first trip. The owner asked him, "Where are you staying while you are in Lander so I can let you know?"

"You'll find me at Parker's Boarding House." Shortly after leaving the mill, he pulled into the boarding house yard, bone tired and hungry. He got the buckboard parked as close to the barn as he could. Next he got the horses into empty stalls and took the two satchels with the rocks in them and hid them under a pile of hay in the corner of Misty's stall. He fed all the horses and gave Mike strips of jerky, put a bowl of water near him and said, "Stay;" "Guard." He took his clothes satchel and a smaller one with him which contained the bags of gold dust and flakes from the hidden storage compartment, grabbed his rifle and went up the back steps. He knocked on the back door frame and said, "Anyone home? Mrs. Parker, are you in there?" A man's voice replied, "Who's asking?"

Somewhat taken aback, "I'm Todd Morgan and I believe I

have a room reserved for me on the second floor."

"Ah, yes, Mr. Morgan, we were expecting you earlier. I'm Mr. Johansen from the bank, we met when you opened your account. Priscilla, I mean, Mrs. Parker is in the dining room with our guests. Let me help you with the door, you have your arms full."

"After I get settled, do you think I could come down the back stairs and get a cup of coffee and a couple of those rolls sitting on the stove? I haven't eaten since before noon."

"That shouldn't be a problem. You know the way to your room, don't you?"

"Yes, I do and thank you for helping me." Mr. Johansen picked up a tray with a plate of cookies and several tea cups on it. He went through the kitchen door into the dining room. Todd went up the back stairs quietly to his room. After he put his things away, he came back down in his stocking feet to an empty kitchen. He took an empty cup from above the stove, poured himself some coffee and took a couple of sweet rolls off the side of the stove. He saw a chicken leg in a roasting pan and took that also. As he tiptoed back upstairs, he heard laughter in the adjoining room. He slept through Wednesday into early Thursday morning. Upon waking, he found his clothes neatly folded on the chair in the corner of the room; a ceramic pitcher with water in it, two glasses, a bath towel, hand towel and wash cloth next to a china washbowl. On top of the dresser, he found a note leaning against the washbowl. He poured a glass of water and sat on the edge of the bed to read the note. *"Todd, I didn't know you had arrived, I wasn't told. I met "Mike" and let your horses out into the corral. I have a lot to tell you. Please join us for breakfast or dinner, whenever you wake. Priscilla."* Todd had a gut wrenching feeling that what she had to tell him wasn't what he wanted to hear, it almost made him sick to his stomach. It was his choice to stay in the mountains and lose the woman he loved over work. He said to himself *What a damn fool I've been. Who am I to think that a fine lady like her would actually settle for a trapper like me?* It was too early to get up, so he lay back down on the bed and drifted back to sleep.

He woke two hours later not feeling all that great, especially after reading the note again. He crumpled it and threw it on the floor. He decided to just go to the café in town and get something to eat. As he was going down the back stairs, Priscilla was cleaning up the dining room and caught a glimpse of him as he was going out through the screen door toward the barn. She quickly put down the dishes and called after him, "Todd," but he ignored her. He couldn't face her just yet. She was not amused by his not acknowledging her. She too went out the door over to the barn to see him. As she was about to enter the barn, he was riding out and almost knocked her over. He stopped, looked down at her and said, "Excuse me, but I have a meeting and I am late already."

"What's wrong?" She inquired.

"Like I said, I have a meeting!"

"We need to talk."

"We'll talk this afternoon and under the circumstances, I think its best that I get a room at one of the hotels in town. I'll be out by tonight." She moved aside to let him pass; a tear was in the corner of her eye. She didn't know what had transpired between the beautiful letter he had written just a couple of weeks back, hand delivered by Tom Murphy, and the note she had left him on the night stand; his abruptness this morning troubled her.

She went back into the house, continued to clean up the dining room, did the dishes and then went upstairs to do some dusting. She noticed that he hadn't shut his door. When she peeked in his room, and saw the crumpled note on the floor and said out loud "That's it! He must have misinterpreted what I wrote in the note. He thinks that I have bad news because he's been away for so long." Crying, she sat on the edge of his bed. "I'll have to right this wrong notion that he's gotten into his head about us. I love him and I'll do anything to keep him."

It was 10:45 when he finished breakfast at the café. He had to get to McDavitt & McIntosh for his 11am appointment. Upon his arrival, the guard said, "Mr. Morgan, we've been expecting you. Please remove your gun belt, that Bowie knife you carry and the derringer. I'll lock them in my drawer. Once Todd did so, he was given a receipt for the items he had turned over. "Since you were here last, we have made some security changes. When you go through this door, you will be escorted by Mr. LaDeux to his office. He has been assigned as your assayer. He'll ask you a series of questions and your answers will be recorded. In the future , you will surrender your weapons as usual, but you'll have to give me a pass code to get through the parlor door and enter his office.. If you don't, we can't allow you into the interior of the building. Do you understand?"

"Yes, I understand." The guard opened the door and Mr. LaDeux stood to the right of the door as Todd entered the interior of the building and said, "Good Morning, Mr. Morgan. How are you?"

"I'm feeling a bit under the weather this morning, but it was important for me to get this transaction taken care of. I understand you have some questions to ask me and you'll give me a pass code for future appointments with you."

"Please have a seat; can I get you some coffee or tea before we start?"

"No, thank you."

Mr. LaDeux asked five short questions and Todd gave him the answers. In-turn, Mr. LaDeux gave him his pass code and said, "Before we start do you have any questions?"

"I'd like to find out if there is another bank where I can put my money in instead of The Lander Bank & Trust Company?"

"Actually, we are starting a private bank for our customers. So many of you have asked that very same question and since The Lander Bank & Trust Co. is the only bank in town, it became apparent that we needed to offer that service. You will have the same privileges as you had there, but we will be paying interest on your money, on a quarterly basis, and your account can't be revealed to anyone else, unless of course you were married. We are awaiting our charter from the territorial governor's office. Mr. August McDavitt has been retained as our legal counsel on all matters pertaining to your private account as well."

"I am interested, but I guess I'll have to wait until you get that charter before any of us can open our accounts."

"Quite the contrary, we are setting up the accounts every time a customer asks. Would you like to fill out the paperwork before we get started on the assaying of your gold?"

"Yes, I would." He was beginning to feel better as the morning progressed.

"I also wanted to tell you that we have new scales to weigh the gold because more and more miners are bringing in heavier amounts." He took the bags of gold that Todd brought with him and set them on the table to his right. He poured the contents of each bag of dust and flakes on a brass plate suspended by three short brass chains and then as before, poured each pile into containers to be tested. There are eight bags in all and their weights are 30.06 oz.; 28.625 oz.; 23.78 oz.; 33.23 oz., 47.47 oz., 32.23 oz., 38.976 oz. and finally 46.625 oz. Mr. LaDeux remarked, "Quite impressive, I must say. I'll test for magnetic properties first, and then the acid test to see if anything dissolves, and finally I will tell you the carat quality. Would you care for any coffee now?"

"Yes, I think I would, just black, please."

"Let me ring for my secretary to bring us each a cup. I find that once I get into my work that I need a third cup of coffee and on rare occasons four cups."

"I've had those days myself," Todd replied.

"Now let me grade the gold. Your carat quality rating is 22/24, an excellent rating if I do say so myself. The rate per ounce that you had the last time was $20.67. Since then,we have been informed that a new rate has been established and will now be $21.00 per ounce[26] until further notice. Your total of ounces is 280.996 and your total is $5,900.92 less our new standard commission of 4.75%, which leaves you with a

---

[26] http://www.wisegeek.com/what-is-the-historical-price-of-gold.htm
Gold was discovered at the South Pass-Atlantic City-Sweetwater district in present Fremont County in 1842. The placers were worked intermittently until 1867, when the first important gold vein was discovered, and prospectors and miners rushed to the area. The towns of South Pass City, Atlantic City, and Miner's Delight catered to the miners. The district was nearly deserted by 1875, and was worked only intermittently afterward. Total gold production was about 300 thousand troy ounces (9.3 tons). In 1962, the district became the site of a major iron mine.

balance of $5,620.62. Shall I deposit all of it in your account?"

"No, I'll take $300 in cash and the rest can go in my account."

"Certainly, give me a couple of minutes to record that in your bank book and on your ledger card for our records. On your way out, we'll stop at the cashier's window and get you the money. Here is your bank book. Please keep it in a safe place and don't let anyone get their hands on it. I see you have brought some other bags with you. What might I ask are in them?"

"I found some ore and what I think are gold seams in them. I would like your metallurgist to take a look at the samples I brought from each claim, but please do not have him mix them together. Let me know what he thinks the potential value is of each, what would be the best method to extract the gold, and their potential carat weight. If you'll sign for these, I'll leave them in your trusted care and that of McDavitt & McIntosh. I will be back in a week for the results. Do you have an opening next Thursday, September 14th around 10 am?"

"I do, and I will see you then." Todd and Mr. LaDeux walked to the cashier's office and the cashier handed him $300 in single and double eagles. Mr. LaDeux escorted Todd to the entrance, pulled a string that rang a bell on the other side of the door. As the door opened, they shook hands before Todd left and Mr. LaDeux said, "I will see you next week and do have a pleasant day, Mr. Morgan." The guard gave Todd back his weapons, he strapped on his holster, adjusted it on his waist and tied it down; he put the Bowie in the sheath on his belt and the derringer in his vest pocket, and said goodbye to the guard as he walked out the door.

-54-

Todd went across the street to Henderson's Mercantile to turn in his supply order and told Joshua when he would like to pick it up.

"It'll be ready when you want it."

He needed to find a pocket watch. Telling time by the sun was fine, but sometimes he needed to know exactly what time it was. He looked around in the store, but didn't find anything that he liked. He would look in other stores until he found just the one he wanted. He was really starting to dread his meeting with Priscilla and his stomach let him know it. He rode to the lumber mill to ask the owner if he had decided about loaning him the log wagon and could he pick up the wagon and the team tomorrow for the trip up to his ranch?

"You can pick it up late tomorrow morning, say around 11 am."

"That's fine with me. See you in the morning."

He rode back to the boarding house, unsaddled and put Misty in the corral. He walked up the back porch stairs. Upon seeing Priscilla, he removed his hat and said, "I guess we need to talk. I can see that I can't be the man you need, however I am not sorry that I kissed you,. When I arrived the other night, I got the impression from Mr. Johansen that you and he were a couple. Upon hearing the laughter in the dining room it got me upset and your note confirmed that. I blame myself for not being here for you and Megan, but I have to earn a living. I had hoped that you'd understand that. I wanted to be here when I had promised, but a lot has happened since I was here last. I'm sorry it didn't work out for us. Like I said this morning, it'll be too hard for me to stay here. I'll pack my things and move into town. I'll have to come back for my wagon and the other two horses tomorrow."

Priscilla was just about to cry, but she held it together and said, "I think you took my note all wrong. I want you, Todd Morgan, not Johan. You have had a lot going on and so have I. I sought out counsel from the parson and unbeknownst to me, he counseled Johan as well. I don't think he did either of us any favors. I have missed you from the time you rode out a few months ago and I savored those kisses to the point where I didn't want to wash my lips for a week. Had I known you were here last night, I would have excused myself from the church meeting we were having and thrown myself into your arms, but Johan didn't say a word. After everybody left, I was looking out at the barn and saw your buckboard. I was so mad at Johan for not telling me that you were here that I could have spit nails. I would leave with you tomorrow, for God knows where, just as long as I knew we'd be together, forever. Please don't leave me for any longer than you need to be gone to get your work done. I want Megan to grow up in a family and I am finding that living and working here isn't working. I have seriously considered selling the boarding house. Recently, I was offered double what I paid for it, but I wanted to consult with you first. Now, I don't know what to do," as she began to cry.

"Please don't cry. Am I allowed to eat humble pie? I guess I did jump to conclusions, all the wrong ones. I was so upset with Mr. Johansen that I decided to put my money elsewhere just so I wouldn't have to deal with him."

"Todd, we have decisions to make." She embraced him while he dried her tears.

"Priscilla, I was wondering if you could have someone watch Megan for a few days. I need to go back to my ranch and get a load of logs to bring to the lumber mill. I may need to make two, possibly three trips and I would like you to go with me."

"I'll ask my friend Mary if she could take care of Megan for me. When do we leave?"

"Tomorrow afternoon."

"I guess I better go and ask her today." She took off her apron and as she passed him to go out the front door, he pulled her into his lap and kissed her lips and neck before saying, "Too bad we aren't married; I'd be doing something other than kissing you."

Blushing, she replied, "You think you're the only one with those thoughts?" She kissed him back. "Now let me go so I can get ready for our trip." He let her go, but he couldn't resist and pulled her back down again and gave her a much longer kiss. She responded passionately without blushing. She got up, smoothed her dress and said before she went out the front door, "Megan will be home soon. She always wants a glass of milk and a couple of cookies before she starts her homework."

"I'll be glad to help her."

She left to go talk to her friend just up the road. Todd ran up the stairs to put his gun away and the rest of his business suit, including his vest and hat.

Soon Megan came bounding up the back steps and said,

"Mom, I'm home." She was surprised to see Mr. Morgan sitting at the dining room table.

"Hi Megan," he said. "Your mom had to run an errand and she asked me to watch out for you when you got home. I understand that you get milk and cookies; then you start on your homework. Is that correct?"

"Yes. Did she tell you that I named the doll you gave me 'Molly' and she has been there for me, just like you said she would. Thank you for getting her; she's the best present ever."

"You're welcome, Megan, and yes, she did tell me in a letter what you named her. I'll have to tell you a story about the name you gave her, but first you need to do your homework." He got a glass and filled it with buttermilk, then got her three cookies from the cookie jar on top of one of the pantry shelves, set them on a plate and said, "I'll be on the back porch if you need me."

-55-

Todd picked up the log wagon the following morning and headed to Henderson's Mercantile to pick up his supply order. While he waited for the order to be put in the wagon, he browsed through the store and picked out a cameo broach for Priscilla, a package of chamomile tea, and some sweet bread. He wanted to make sure that she had a good time and that she learned how it would be if she uprooted Megan and brought her into the wilderness. Once she understood the difficulties one had to endure living there, he'd bring her back to Lander where she could see the advantages of living in a town. His intent was to make a home for her on the tract of land right next to where she currently lived. He would build a house with four bedrooms, living room, parlor, dining room and a big country kitchen. A house where only their family lived, a house where Megan would be happy to come home to after she left to further her education in the east in the not-too-distant future.

He told Priscilla to dress like she had the time he saw her working with the horses, in her checkered shirt, blue jeans, bandana and a hat that covered her hair and face from the sun. He planned on getting to Shoshone Joe's by late afternoon and the rest of the way the following morning. His plan was to get as many logs as possible in the first load so that he'd only have to make two trips.

She told her boarders she would be gone for a few days and that they could either make their own breakfast and dinner or go to one of the restaurants in town. She also reminded them to lock the front door when the last person left, and to make sure the horses were put out in the morning and brought in at night; also to make sure the doors and windows in the barn were all closed. She came out the front door, locked it, and came down the stairs; Mike came bounding around the corner of the house and jumped into the back of the wagon. Todd helped Priscilla up into the wagon as they set off for the Stony Creek Ranch.

Upon their arrival at Shoshone Joe's, Joe remarked, "I am happy to make your acquaintance Mrs. Parker," and welcomed her as if she was an Indian Princess that had come to grace his lodge with her beauty. He welcomed Todd, but not with the same enthusiasm. He escorted them to a tent where they would be staying for the night. After they deposited their satchels, they walked up to Joe's cabin for supper. They enjoyed rabbit stew and sourdough biscuits, a favorite of Joe's. They talked with Joe and his wife about many of the same things that any married couple would talk about after a hard day's work. She saw that out here you made do with what you had, not what you didn't. Todd let her get ready for bed, and went into the tent afterwards to get into his cot on the opposite side of the tent. During the night, she crawled under his covers and whispered, "I haven't had relations since my husband left me, be gentle."

"Are you sure about this?"

"Yes." He made room for her in the narrow cot. He gently

fondled her and kissed her before parting her legs and made love to her. As she climaxed, she murmured something sweet in his ear. He gently caressed her as they both fell asleep holding each other. She didn't want to get up in the morning and wanted him to make love again; she enjoyed the intimacy. He said, "If you wear me out, I won't get the work done that I have come up here to do. We will have plenty of time later today for each other, so let me get our breakfast and after that I will hitch up the team. While I am doing that you can get yourself dressed. We'll leave in an hour." He kissed her intimately once more and had second thoughts about taking her up on her offer to make love again. Instead, he stood up and thought to himself that a dip in the cold pond water at his ranch might be necessary in order to keep his mind focused on work and not on her. Mike just whined at the doorway as if to say, "You have all the fun."

Once they arrived at his ranch, he had her take Mike with her as she walked around his property. He loaded the last log on the wagon just before sundown and took the large tarp from the barn and covered the logs just in case it rained. He threw ropes over the top of the wagon to make everything secure; Mike picked up the end of each rope and ran under the wagon to bring it back to his master. Todd took the rope from the dog and tied a cinch knot on each one he brought back to him making sure they were tight. He went back to the picnic table where Priscilla had prepared their dinner of venison steak, roasted potatoes, biscuits, boiled ears of corn and coffee. For dessert, she opened a can of peaches, his favorite, and put the sweet bread on a plate.

"Just give me a minute while I wash up at the stream," he said. He stripped his shirt off and took a bar of soap and a towel with him. She was staring at his muscular torso when he came back to the table and said, "What? You've never seen a man without his shirt on before? Blushing, she said, "Well of course I've seen a man without his shirt on. I just haven't seen one so handsome or as muscular before, that's all." They both laughed. He savored each bite and she couldn't keep her eyes off him the whole time during dinner. She said to him, "I noticed that you didn't take a break around the middle of the day, is that typical of you?"

"Usually I do, if only for a few minutes. But I knew what I wanted to get done and I just got into the swing of things. I usually work from sunup to sundown nearly every day. I have no other help and, with a wave of his hand, said, I'm responsible for all of this, I'd like to hire someone, but I haven't had the time to do so. I am hoping I can find someone in Lander who wants to work and isn't lazy or a drunkard. I can't continue with the pace that I have set for myself. There are days when I get so exhausted that I just collapse into bed, just like I did at your place when I slept for so long."

"Why don't you come and work for me during the winter months?" She said. "I'll pay a fair wage, you'll get two meals a day, a warm comfy bed to sleep in, and the after-hours entertainment is great, too."

Smiling, he said, "I might think about that, but for the time being, why don't I clean up these dishes while you get ready for bed. I'll meet you in the barn about twenty minutes from now. I have to make sure all the mules are fed and watered; the windows and doors are closed."

"Oh, I've already fed and watered them, the windows are already closed and the only door open is the one you'll be coming in."

"In that case, I'll be there in ten minutes. Now scoot or it will be twenty minutes, I can't seem to keep my eyes off you." She walked over to the barn; he cleaned the dishes, pans and utensils setting them on the table. He brought the lantern with him and Mike followed behind as they went in the barn. He closed and secured the door behind him and said to Mike, "Guard." He took the lantern and turned down the flame and hung it on a peg he had put on the side of the stairs. Then he took another lantern and went upstairs to find Priscilla waiting for him under the covers of the impromptu bed on top of the hay he had made for them. He undressed and stood there in his birthday suit for a few seconds and got under the covers with her. He was as gentle with her as he was the previous night and they slept peacefully after they had made love.

Morning came too early to suit them, but they both knew that if they didn't leave at a reasonable time they wouldn't get back to Lander by the end of the work day. They would need a new wagon and a fresh team so that they could come back for the second load of logs. She rolled over on top of him, her soft flesh resting on his muscular body and gave him a kiss. He put his hands on her soft buttocks, cupped them and pulled her tight against his body. She said to him, "I need some fresh air." She got out of their bed and made her way down the stairs with a blanket wrapped around her to find Mike wagging his tail and going towards the door as if to say, "What took you so long? I've been waiting for one of you to get down here so that I can do my business." She opened the door to find that a thick fog had rolled in and that would make starting early a problem, so she just waited until Mike came back, closed the door again and said to him, "Come!" Up the stairs they went. She had Mike lick Todd on his face and he replied, "Priscilla, your kisses are too wet," blinking, he saw that it was Mike, while she laughed and laughed.

"Think that's funny do you? You're going to pay for that young lady as he pulled her down on their straw bed. He was on top of her, pinning her arms against the straw, kissing her naked body several times saying, "Had enough?"

"No! Why are you stopping?"

"Oh, I don't know, maybe because we have to get going."

"I don't think so mister, a fog has rolled in and it's thicker than my pea soup."

"In that case, I'll just have to keep you busy for a couple more hours until the sun burns it off." He proceeded to rub her inner thighs, fondled her and with each intimate sensation she became hotter and wetter as they climaxed together. They both just lay there, panting, and out of breath. He didn't want it to end, but knew they'd have to get moving if they wanted to get close to Lander today.

-56-

As Todd went out of the barn leading the first set of mules, he noticed that Gus's and Turk's horses were tied in front of the cabin with a deer hanging from a nearby tree. Now he knew where they had been yesterday. He got all the mules hitched, got Mike up on top of the logs, and then came back for Priscilla who came downstairs from the loft and sighed.

"What was that for?" he asked.

"It's so peaceful up here, no worries, why would anyone want to leave?"

"It's back to reality I'm afraid, and besides, we'll be back early tomorrow afternoon and we can start all over again."

"Is that a promise?"

"Yes, unless you keep holding us up by not getting up in the wagon, young lady." Smiling, she replied, "Help me up, won't you?"

He picked her up in his muscular arms and set her on the seat, kissed the side of her cheek before going in front of her to his side. She smiled and he said to the mules, "Get up there Sadie, Maud, get up." The lead mules felt the leather strain against their backs and began to pull the heavy wagon; soon they were in rhythm as they went down the trail. They arrived

286

at the lumber mill late in the afternoon. The mill owner had a new wagon and a team of twelve horses waiting for him. Todd said to him, "By any chance are the logs I brought you about five days ago cut?"

"I anticipated that you might want them, so I had them loaded in this wagon for you."

"Thanks, I should be back the day after tomorrow with more logs." They drove the team around by the river so that no one in town would see them, especially Mr. Johansen. Priscilla asked to stop by the boarding house to pick up some clean clothes, some lavender water, a couple of soft towels, and to check on things. He parked the rig down in front of the section next to the boarding house. Mike jumped down and went for a run in the woods while Todd did a visual check of the property, noting where a clearing was. They stopped for a bite to eat at Priscilla's friend's restaurant before they headed back toward the ranch. With the twelve horse hitch and a light load they would make good time, but they would still have to stop for the night somewhere along the way. He chose a spot near a new community that had recently sprung up practically overnight called Wind River Township.

He picked a grove of aspens and a meandering creek where he could use feed bags for the horses; he wanted to get an early start. He placed feed bags on all of them, then gave each a few carrots, a scratch behind their ears and finally, let each of them drink as much as they wanted out of a water bucket.

He got Priscilla situated and built a fire, mainly for warmth, and gave Mike some jerky, crumpled biscuits, and water. She thought it was a good time to talk and said, "You said a lot had happened since we'd seen you last. What happened?"

"Well, you know about the forest fire; there was a man

named Josh Hackenfield who was at the Sweetwater Ranch when I was there visiting with my friends. He accused me of horse stealing, which was untrue. They were my horses, but he didn't know that at the time. He came at me and I beat him up, stepped on his gun hand and twisted his gun away.

"After I left to come here, he robbed and beat up my friend, Crusty. He eventually came looking for me. He was in Lander and I bumped into him accidentally when I came out of the barber shop but he didn't recognize me. That was the same day you pointed your shotgun at me because you didn't recognize me either. To make this story short, Marshal Murphy was at the ranch and he mentioned that a young man was at a cabin just south of my ranch. We went down to the cabin and I stayed out of sight. When Josh came out on the porch, I nodded that it was him and the marshal arrested him on assault and robbery charges.

"Several months ago, I caught some squatters, trappers actually, on my homestead. They were going to do some hunting on my land. So I set some traps for them and they limped away. About a month ago, they came back, killed my friend Pete's horse, and burned his cabin down while he was still in it. I smelled the smoke and went to find out what it was about. I found him terribly burned, so I got him to the hospital at the Fort and he is still there recuperating. In-between helping the law and helping my friend, I have been trying to get things done around my place before the cold weather gets here and that's what has happened since I saw you last. Actually, recalling all that has made me angry because those trappers that hurt my friend are still out there," he said with a wave of his hand. "I can't talk about it anymore, it's still too painful. I lied to you this morning."

"What lie?"

"I can't make love to you because I am tired."

"I understand. There's always tomorrow morning or later tomorrow night." They both laughed as they cradled each other and fell asleep with Mike standing guard."

Arriving at the homestead around noon, Todd lifted her down from the wagon, then he took the reins and backed the wagon up to the barn where he unloaded all the cut lumber and covered it. He drove the wagon to where the rest of the logs were, unhitched the team, walked them back to the pasture, unharnessed them and once they were taken care of he took the harnesses into the barn and hung them on pegs.

He said to her, "I am too hot to do the rest of the work right now. Why don't you and I go down to the pond for a swim. Afterwards, I'll take a nap and after I've rested, I'll load the rest of the logs. What I don't get done today, I can do tomorrow morning."

"Last one in is a monkey's uncle," she said, as she and Mike ran towards the pond. She was in the pond by the time he got there and her clothes were neatly piled next to a tree. Todd brought two towels and his rifle with him as a precaution and laid everything next to the same tree. He undressed and dove into the pond. He surfaced next to her and said, "Maybe I should name this pond, Sweetwater, after you."

"Why call it Sweetwater?"

"Well, you're sweet and in the water, so Sweetwater fits don't you think?"

"You are so silly sometimes. Why don't we just call it Todd's Pond?"

"It doesn't have the same ring to it." They swam, splashed water at each other, he kissed and fondled her as he guided her over to the side of the pond, hoisted her up on the bank. She lay on her back in the reeds. He climbed out and said, "You've made me very happy these last few days, I don't want this to stop."

"I don't want this to stop either, make love to me right here." She moved back a little onto the tall grass. They were both wet from swimming, but that didn't matter to either of them. She whispered in his ear, "I love how you love me." They felt like a couple of teenagers who had just snuck away for a frolic in the pond for the first time.

After they had made love, she wanted to go back in the pond with him, but he had a feeling. "Something or someone is watching us." He picked up their towels. "Put this towel around you." Then he said to Mike, "Find," and the dog ran off into the brush. Todd gave her his rifle. "If anything happens to me, use it to protect yourself."

He pulled on his jeans and boots and went off to find Mike who had gone maybe 300 yards into the forest between his property and Gus's. He heard thrashing, growling, and finally, the whimpering. Mike came back limping along on three legs while Todd went to find what it was.

He looked under a blowdown and saw Happenstance with two half breed wolf/lab pups. She was gaunt, had many cuts on her body and a torn ear. Her greatest joy must have been those pups. Todd was sad and said to Mike, "She was a good dog, but I should have paid more attention to her and maybe she wouldn't have ended up this way."

He buried her where she lay and took the two pups to where Priscilla was and said, "We'll take these by Joe's on our way back to Lander. He may be able to wean them and train them. I don't want either of them, especially out here."

Priscilla cuddled with both of them; they were so cute. He swept her and the puppies up in his arms and carried all of them to the second floor of the barn, laid her on the hay and said, "I'll be back in a few minutes with your clothes, your satchel, and the quilt you gave me. I need to get started on putting the logs in the wagon; we'll have dinner later tonight. Why don't you take a nap and I'll see you when I get done." He kissed her forehead before he went back downstairs and out to the barnyard.

He managed to get all but six logs into the wagon when he decided to call it a day, he could load them during the early morning hours. He went to the stream, washed off the sweat and grime from working, put some kindling in the fire pit and added two split logs. Next, he went up into the cache and got a venison roast and put it in the roasting pan. He went to the tack room and retrieved a couple of potatoes. He washed them in the stream and quartered them on the table before putting them in the pan with the venison roast before setting it on the rack above the flames.

Finally, he took the coffee pot to the stream, washed out the old grounds, filled it with fresh water and set it on the grill next to the pan. He decided that he'd pick three of the ripe tomatoes from his new garden and put them in a pan of cold water before he set the pan in the stream. He went into the barn and quietly went up the stairs to see if Priscilla was still sleeping. She was and the two puppies were nestled close to her. He went back down the stairs, found Mike and carried him to the stream, washed his cuts, put a moss poultice on them, wrapped the cuts in clean cloth, set him next to the fire and said, "You stay right there my friend and rest." He thought it would be a good time to round up the horses and get them in their stalls for the night. He put fresh hay and feed in each stall, refreshed the water in each trough and opened all the stall gates. He went out into the corral with a handful of carrots and whistled for them to come. When they did, he fed a carrot to each and walked each one to a stall, shut the gate and continued until he had all twelve settled in for the night. At that point he felt he had done all he could do. He walked over to a chair by the fire pit next to the stream and took a nap, dreaming of Priscilla and a life for both of them.

-57-

She kissed his forehead and whispered in his ear, "I'm starved. What's for dinner?"

Todd, though still groggy, said with a smile, "You are, I thought I would start with dessert first." He got out of the chair and chased her until she collapsed in his arms out of breath.

"First, we'll eat dinner and then if you're a good boy, you can have me for dessert later."

"If that's the way you want it, then sit yourself down me lady and let your prince charming serve you a feast." Todd had gone into the cabin before he sat down and brought out tin plates, cups, and eating utensils for the two of them; he took the roast and sliced it. He put two slices on each of their plates along with the roasted potatoes, and sliced thin cold tomatoes. Next he put the small coffee pot on the table and put a gauze sack of chamomile tea into the hot water and poured the hot tea into cups for both of them. Priscilla said grace, like she did at her dining room table. They ate and made small talk. After they finished eating, he took a thicker slice of meat, cut it into chunks and fed it to the dog; the best he could do for the puppies was to give them a bowl of water to drink, there was no milk available.

They left around eleven the following morning after a very pleasant and passionate night. She said, "I have never felt so free; these last few days have made me feel young again and have renewed my spirit. Can't we just stay here forever?"

"I'd like nothing better than to have you and Megan live up here with me. You have only seen a very small part of what it takes to live here. I work seven days a week with very little time off for myself. If I had you and Megan to worry about, keep you fed, clothed, and protected, then I would have to work twice as hard as I do now. Course, if I died from exhaustion you'd be a rich widow and Johan could become an excellent suitor once again. I don't want that to happen. I am working on a plan so that in a couple of years, maybe sooner, I won't have to work so hard. Then we can plan our future together. I know that's not what you wanted to hear, but if everything works out like I plan on, we will be set."

"Does any of it have to do with the bags that were tied to your saddle horn the other day?"

"The bags contained rocks with what I think are gold seams running through them. I left them at the assayers and by Thursday of this week, I'll have my answer one way or another. You'll have to be patient with me just a little while longer. In the meantime, however, I plan on making the rest of my time spent with you and Megan memorable and enjoyable. Why, we might even take a walk into town, arm in arm, with Megan to tag along with us."

"But Johan might see us, then what?"

"Part of my plan is to see how jealous I can make him. I even plan to drop some hints that we are more than just friends. It should make it quite interesting at his expense."

"He's a powerful man in Lander; I wouldn't push him too far.

He might just have you eliminated permanently and where would that leave me?"

"Well, with me out of the way, he could pick up where I left off." She turned and looked at him and gave him a punch in the arm.

"What did you do that for?"

"Maybe I'll just start up with him when we get back at the boarding house just to make you jealous."

"Hmm, I'll have to think about that just in case that happens," as he reined up the teams in a stream so they could all drink; he got down, helped her down and carried her to the edge of the stream near a willow tree; he then picked Mike off the top of the wagon so he could cavort with the puppies for a few minutes. He took Priscilla in his arms, squeezed her till she thought she was going to pop and said, "I don't take jealously well, you saw that last week. I want all of you and I am not sharing you with anyone from here on out. Do I make myself perfectly clear on that subject?"

"Absolutely; now, can we take a little time before we get back to town to pick up where we left off last night?"

"Only if you promise you won't tease me anymore."

"I won't."

"And you won't punch me either?"

"I will if you tease me."

They found a nice patch of wild flowers and while she got ready for him, he got the teams up on dry land and unhitched them where they could graze while still in their harnesses; he said to Mike, "Guard." The puppies were exhausted and just stayed by the edge of the stream panting as they watched Todd and Priscilla make love on top of the wild flowers. While they were lying there, he held her close as they watched puffy white clouds roll by in the deep blue sky.

Later, they dropped the puppies off at Joe's who said, "Weaning them won't be a problem and I will find good homes for them, too." They arrived at the lumber mill around 8 pm; there was only a caretaker there. Todd pulled the wagon up to where they usually unloaded wagons; he took the horses and put them in their stalls. He borrowed two horses, saddled them and told the caretaker, "I'll be back in the morning to settle up with the owner."

Epilogue

The metallurgist told Todd that the rocks were of high quality. Not having seen the actual site where they came from, he guessed they would yield at least several hundred thousand dollars worth of gold from the site. His recommendation was to hire someone who knew what they were doing in the construction of a mine shaft.

The gold in the rocks was weighed and a bank draft for $3,054.00 was given to him.

This was more than Todd expected and he was elated with the prospects of having found such a find. He decided that two years was too long to wait to marry Priscilla. He had already told August to prepare a will where everything would go to her and Megan should anything happen to him. He would also have to have legal work done to protect him regarding a mining operation and his ranch.

He went to Henderson's and bought a garnet ring; next he went to the vegetable, fruit and flower stand for a dozen white and red roses and finally, he went to the boarding house.

He found Priscilla in the kitchen making supper for her boarders and he whispered in her ear, "Would you come into the sitting room for a few minutes."

When she did, he gave her the flowers, kissed her and said,

"Pretty soon you won't have to work anymore. Will you...," but before he could finish his question, Megan came bounding in the back door.

"Mom, where are you?"

Todd Morgan can't wait to tell everyone how this plays out in
his next book

- Hearts -

About the Author

Born, raised, and educated in Rochester, New York. My intent was to study Agribusiness after high school. The Vietnam Conflict was just ramping up and the local draft board had other ideas for my future, which in turn changed my long-term outlook. I was given a five-day window of opportunity, either accept the draft board's decision and go in the Army or enlist in one of the other services. I chose the US Air Force and that turned out to be the best decision I ever made.

I served a total of 34+ years in the US Air Force, including Active duty, NH Air National Guard and US Air Force Reserve, which included Iraq I. I retired at the rank of E7 (Master Sergeant).

Using the GI Bill, I got an Associate's and a Bachelor's Degree in Business Administration. In my later years, I earned a Master's Degree in Educational Media. Using my business background and my education, I have taught business courses in For Profit Schools, Community Colleges, and at Virginia State University.

I have owned my own business four times over and worked for many years with the Department of Employment Security in Massachusetts and the Virginia Community College System, retiring from John Tyler Community College, Chester, Virginia in 2006.

I began my writing career a couple of years before I retired.

I was enamored with the west and used my initial passion for wanting to be a farmer to help write my stories (though I never did follow that passion).

I write my stories to entertain and to educate about US History.

I am a member of Western Writers of America and Citrus Writers.

I share my time between Florida and North Carolina.